Coming Home

Amy Iketani

Published by Amy Iketani, 2023.

This is a work of fiction. Similarities to real people, places, or events are entirely coincidental.

COMING HOME

First edition. September 22, 2023.

Copyright © 2023 Amy Iketani.

ISBN: 979-8223230717

Written by Amy Iketani.

To Alisa and Leo.

May you always have the courage to follow your dreams.

Chapter 1

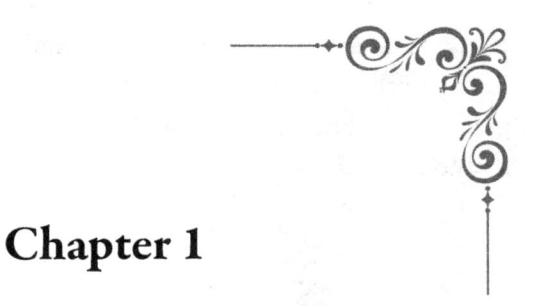

The relief Louise felt when she walked through her apartment door was instant. It had been a very long day, as usual. Her headache throbbed in the background as she locked the door, kicked off her shoes and made her way to the kitchen. It was dark, only the city lights coming in through the windows illuminated the room. She stumbled to the light switch on the wall, careful not to stub another toe. Louise always felt instantly calm when walking around her apartment. She had great taste in furnishings and would be a home body if doctors could work from home.

Louise took a glass out of the kitchen cupboard and filled it with water. She took a couple capsules of the headache medicine and drank the water eagerly. She didn't even mind the train ride home tonight, even dozing off a few minutes. The train was nearly empty, just the usual mix of drunks and professionals. It was already past eleven at night. Normally she would go right to bed but she was off tomorrow. She felt like she wanted something stronger than water. She poured herself a glass of Pinot Grigio and headed towards to the shower.

She turned on lights as she moved from room to room. Louise began stripping off her scrubs as soon as she walked into her bedroom, her sanctuary. She had heard once that the color blue was calming so she painted her walls a light sky blue, her comforter was a deep ocean blue and her room darkening curtains were a sapphire blue, the blue that matched her lake back home. She did not often think of home. She wasn't sentimental like that. Louise, or Lou, as they called her back home in Erie, left right after high school graduation. She did not want to stay in Erie, she had loftier ambitions and wanted more than Erie could provide. If that meant saying goodbye to the city, and certain people, then it would be worth it to her.

Louise sipped her wine and then stepped into the warm shower. The feeling of exhaustion from the day being washed away was very exhilarating. She had an extra hard day at work. As a pediatrician, she was used to getting called on cases of bumps, bruises and broken limbs, but today a little boy was sick and his parents couldn't get a proper diagnosis. After Louise had multiple tests done on the boy, they found out it was leukemia. It was difficult to say as a doctor, even worse for the parents to hear, but now that they knew what they were dealing with, they could fight it with medicine. Her thoughts were still on the little boy when she came into the living room and turned on the tv. She relaxed on her leather couch and wanted to watch something that would take her mind off of things. The wine had helped and she allowed herself to get interested in a movie and fell asleep.

The next morning, Louise woke up with a renewed energy. Her best days off were the ones that allowed her to stay home. No plans. Just cooking, reading, relaxing, going for a walk or watching a movie. She opened her curtains to let the sunshine in. Louise had started making her breakfast of scrambled eggs and toast when her phone rang.

"Hi Ben."

"Hello babe. Don't forget about tonight! We can't be late."

"I know and I won't," said Louise.

"Okay, I'll call you later. Gotta go."

Benjamin Brock was a neurosurgeon at the hospital. He was also Louise's boyfriend of nearly two years. He was a few years older and handsome. He fell for Louise as soon as he saw her that first day she entered the hospital. He made no secret of the fact that he wanted to ask her out, so when Ben finally did, she accepted.

His phone call left Louise anxious. She had hours before she had to start getting ready for his event, but already she felt the pressure of looking perfect on his arm. Ben could be a bit demanding, but she supposed when everyone caters to your every want, you can't help but develop the ego along with it. Louise did love Ben, otherwise she would not still be in a relationship with him.

She tried to relax and enjoy a quiet day at home. She picked up a novel from her coffee table. A Kristin Hannah she had been trying to finish for weeks, when her phone rang again.

"Hi Ben."

"Hey babe. I have reservations for dinner after my awards ceremony tonight," Ben said. "So try not to eat before the ceremony."

"Sounds great."

"Okay, see you later!"

The anxiety started to feel like butterflies in her stomach. No longer able to concentrate on the words on the page, Louise returned the book to the coffee table and turned on the television. At least anything on tv would calm her nerves about walking into a room full of surgeons ready to give awards to each other about how wonderful they all are. She had been to events like this with Ben before and always felt out of place. Yes, they were both doctors and it should be easy for her to mix and mingle with other doctors, but as soon as she said she was a pediatrician, they didn't really know how to respond to that.

Ben would be outside her apartment building in thirty minutes. He always used the same car service because they were so prompt. This gave Louise enough time for one last look in the mirror. She decided to leave her long brown hair down, just putting curls in it. Her black dress was off the shoulders but came down to her knees.

She chose this dress so that she could wear the diamond necklace Ben had given her for Christmas. Her make up was flawless and she sprayed herself with perfume before grabbing a shawl and purse and catching the elevator to the lobby.

The car was waiting right out front as promised. Ben got out to open the door and commented on how beautiful she looked.

"Thank you," Louise replied. "You look very handsome yourself."

"Well, I thought a tuxedo would be best," Ben said, bringing his fingers up to adjust his bow tie. "I just hope it doesn't run too long. Our reservations are for nine."

The event was just as Louise expected. A ballroom full of every type of surgeon you could imagine. There were cardiac surgeons laughing at jokes told by the plastic surgeons. The orthopedic surgeons were planning golf tee times with the vascular surgeons. Louise always got asked at these types of events if she will become a pediatric surgeon. She wanted to say 'Not if I can help it,' but usually just answered, 'Yes'. This made them light up and take over the conversation leaving Louse free to just smile and nod.

To Louise, the night seemed to drag on endlessly. She was hungry and already had two glasses of wine. She asked the bartender for a glass of water just as they called Ben to the stage for his award. It was something to do with his latest publication in the medical journals about his work with Parkinson's patients. She really was proud of him, but when he started talking about the details of his findings, she just zoned out for a while. She didn't want to tell him this, so she always acted interested. For Louise, this confirmed the fact that she couldn't really be a surgeon. She loved the interaction with her patients, even when the kids cried while getting a shot. She liked her patients to be awake when she saw then, not under anesthesia in an operating room.

Louise was beyond relieved when Ben grabbed her arm and said it was time for dinner. The driver took them to the best French restaurant in New York City, Le Jardin. She had never been here before, but was sure Ben had, since the hostess seemed to recognize him and led them to a table by the window. He held the chair for Louise and they both sat down to look at the menu. When the waiter came, Ben asked for champagne. The restaurant had chandeliers, white linen tablecloths and candles lit at every table.

"We are celebrating tonight!" Ben explained to the waiter. "Dom Pérignon, please."

"But of course, sir!" The waiter replied. "Congratulations!"

"Thank you. Hopefully the start of many more celebrations tonight," Ben said, looking at Louise. His expression was smug.

She didn't know what Ben meant but continued studying the menu for something she understood. She didn't speak French, only took Spanish in high school, so she decided to rely on him to help her choose.

"I really don't know what anything is, Ben."

"It's okay, babe, I'll order for you. What are you in the mood for?"

"Fish maybe, not snails. Baked fish sounds good," Louise answered.

"Oh yes, their fish is wonderful here. Also, their steak just melts in your mouth." Ben paused, "I think I'll get the steak."

They ordered when the champagne arrived. When the waiter popped the cork, everyone around looked at them and then smiled, sensing a celebration. With their glasses filled and bubbles dripping down the sides, Ben raised his glass to hers.

"To our future!" Ben said. They clinked glasses and took a sip of the bubbly champagne. Ben and Louise enjoyed the sparkling wine and didn't set their glasses down until the food arrived. She was famished and tipsy. Her baked fish with rice and vegetables looked and smelled delicious. Ben's steak, baked potato and carrots looked equally appealing. Louise could not wait to dig in and picked up her fork immediately. It was so flaky, buttery and soft that she barely said a word during dinner. Ben ate and talked the entire time.

When their plates and glasses were cleared, the waiter asked if they wanted dessert. Louise yawned and Ben declined dessert. When they were finally alone, he reached his hand over to take one of her hands.

"This has been such a wonderful evening. I know these events can be boring for you and I appreciate the effort you make for me."

"Oh Ben," Louise started.

"Wait, let me finish," Ben interrupted. "I enjoy being with you and I really want you to move in with me. I want to be with you all the time. I love you." Ben paused, reached into his jacket pocket and pulled out a black velvet box. "Louise, will you marry me?"

Stunned and completely taken by surprise, Louise felt like everything that happened from the moment she saw the black velvet box was in slow motion. She brought her hands to her mouth, unable to hide her utter surprise at the question, and just stared at the box that she knew contained a ring. She also knew that whatever answer she gave at that moment would change the course of her life for good. Did she want it to change? Did she want to marry him? Louise liked Ben, even loved him, but was she ready to be married? She liked having her own place, her sanctuary. She started thinking of the things she would be giving up. Time had stopped, she felt as if she had days to answer his question. The ringing of her phone brought her back to reality.

She looked from Ben, to the box, to her phone. It was on the table next to her and face up. Dad. In the midst of the chaos in her mind, she couldn't understand why her father was calling. It did not make any sense, so maybe that was why it was so easy for her to put up a finger to Ben and push out her chair.

"Just a minute, I have to take this."

Leaving Ben holding the velvet box, she grabbed her phone and walked towards the lobby. When she found a quiet corner, she answered.

"Hello?"

"Hello Lou," her father replied. "I, uh, hate to call so late, but something happened tonight, with your mother."

"Is she okay?" Louise asked anxiously.

"Well, she's in a coma. Hit and run. They don't really know much more than that. I guess we have to just wait and see."

Louise could hear him choke up at the end of his sentence. "Do they have a prognosis?"

"The doctors say she's lucky. Her air bags saved her from any further injuries, but she has some broken ribs and hit her head, so..."

"Dad," Louise started, "I'm coming home. I'll get a flight as soon as possible."

"Okay, Lou." Then the line went dead.

Louise stood holding her phone. She looked at the time. Ten twenty. If she left now, packed a quick bag and headed to the airport, she may be able to get the last flight out, or at least far enough to rent a car the rest of the way. She knew flights into Erie International Airport were limited, but something deep inside her told her to go. Louise almost walked out of the restaurant door when she suddenly remembered Ben. Ben! She didn't even give him an answer.

She returned to the table. "Ben I have to go. I'm so sorry. Something terrible has happened and I have to go home. I'll get a taxi."

Ben stood up. Louise didn't see the black box, he must have put it away.

"Okay, babe."

"I knew you would understand. I have to go home." Louise said as she grabbed her shawl and left the restaurant.

Chapter 2

Louise walked through the front door of her childhood home at nearly six in the morning. She was able to get the last flight of the night out of New York City, after some very fast packing, and fly as far as Buffalo. Louise knew Buffalo well, it was where she went to college and medical school. She was able to rent a car, drink copious amounts of coffee and drive to Erie. The green highway signs that counted down the miles to her hometown gave her a twinge of comfort. It had been over ten years since she had lived here, having only returned a handful of times since then for various holidays, but only for a few days at a time. This was different, this felt like she was driving into the unknown.

Louise had called her supervisor and explained the situation. She was given a leave of absence from the hospital. She knew she needed to explain everything to Ben. He had called again while she was at the airport.

"Babe, where are you? I am at your apartment but you're not home."

"I am at the airport," Louise replied.

"Airport? What the heck are you doing there?" Ben asked in a harsh tone. "You said you were going home."

Louise, realizing the misunderstanding, explained to Ben about the phone call from her father. She relayed the information her father had given her about her mother's coma and hoped he understood her need to be by her side. Of course Ben would understand, he was a doctor. The only wild card was how long she would be gone. She did not know and could not give him an answer. She promised to call him everyday with updates.

"Dad," Louise said, walking through the quiet house. She saw him lying on the couch. She knelt beside him and took his hand. At this moment he looked so frail, so old. He wasn't though, only in his sixties, Louise always pictured her father tall, muscular and strong. It was starting to feel like she had been away a lot longer than ten years. His hair was almost completely gray, his cheeks a bit sunken and more wrinkles.

"Dad," she said again.

Thomas Jensen opened his eyes and smiled. "Lou, you came. Or am I dreaming?" He smirked and sat up.

"Hi Dad," Lou replied. "I'm home." She smiled and gave her dad a hug. "How's mom?"

"She's the same. They kick me out of the hospital at nine each night, so I guess as long as I don't get a phone call, she's the same."

"Can I make us some breakfast? I'm starving."

"Sure," Tom said. "I don't think I have eaten since lunchtime yesterday."

Lou gave her dad a quick look and thought he looked a lot thinner, now that he was standing. It was early August and the last of the warm days. Her dad wore shorts and a polo shirt, most likely still his clothes from yesterday. Lou looked around the house. Newspapers were piling up on the kitchen table. The trash needed to be taken out and there were dirty dishes in the sink. The house needed a good cleaning.

"Why don't you go take a shower and change clothes. I'll make us a breakfast feast," she said.

Her father did as he was told. Tom was thankful to have someone else in the house. He walked around the boxes that were stacked in the living room. He would have to explain those to Lou later.

Instead, he went upstairs to freshen up. Since Louise and Anthony had both moved out and gone on with their lives, it was just Thomas and Laura at home. It was a gorgeous home. One of the older homes on the lake. Four bedrooms, three baths, but most of their time was spent in the back patio and porch. You could walk right from the porch, onto the sand and into Lake Erie. The boat dock was empty. Tom had given the boat to Tony when he got married, figured he would have more use for it. Now that Tony had a daughter of his own, they will make their own fishing memories with it.

Lou had put plates out for them when her father walked into the kitchen.

"Smells good," Tom said with excitement. "I could eat a horse!"

"Well, I had to make do with what was in your refrigerator, which is not much by the way. How did mom not have this fully stocked? I thought she went shopping a couple of times a week."

"Your mom has been, uh, busy lately," Tom looked down at this plate and started eating. He hoped to avoid any more talk about life at home. There were things Lou did not know, yet.

"Speaking of mom, what time do visiting hours start?"

"Eight," he replied. They both looked at their watches and saw that they had ten minutes.

"Eat up and we'll head out."

"Ok, Lou, but maybe we should drive separately. I can't sit there for long periods of time. It is just too much."

"That's fine, Dad," Lou replied. "I have other errands to run anyway."

Tom smiled, happy to avoid too much explanation, he put the dishes in the sink. "I'll get to these when I come home."

Louise and her father each drove separately to the hospital. Tom showed her the way to Laura's room on the fourth floor. The nurse had taken her blood pressure when they walked in.

"This is my daughter, Louise, from New York City. She's a doctor," her father explained.

"Well, nice to meet you Louise. I'm your mother's day nurse, Kelli," she replied. Nurse Kelli looked from father to daughter and frowned. "I'm sorry I can't give you any better news, but there is still no change." Nurse Kelli finished her testing and left the room.

Lou pulled up a chair and took her mom's hand opposite her father. They both talked to her and to each other. It was surreal to Lou how different two days could possibly be. Yesterday she was relaxed, at home reading, getting dressed up to go out and all of a sudden Ben had a black velvet box. Ben. Lou hadn't talked to him since the airport. He can wait.

Lou noticed that when her father talked to her mom about coming home, he got very emotional. Like he was pleading with her to do more than just wake up and walk in the door. It was deeper than that. Her father said he was going to get some coffee. For some reason, she even questioned whether he meant in the hospital or at home. Well, he did say he couldn't stay here long. Lou changed seats and took the one her father vacated. It was padded and reclined. She had grabbed a book from home and started reading amidst the silence of the room. Silence except for the beeping of the machines.

She had begun chapter three when a man walked into the room. He was dressed in street clothes, so most likely not a doctor or nurse. The man was startled to see Lou sitting on the chair and she could see he almost turned and walked back out. Like a deer caught in headlights, he slowly entered the room and cleared his throat.

"Hello, I'm Stanley. Stanley Frey, a friend of Laura's," the mystery man said. Clearly uncomfortable with the situation.

"Hello, I'm Louise, her daughter," Lou replied, eyeing this strange man up and down. "How do you know my mother?"

"Oh, well, we work together. Or worked together. She may want to retire after this," Stanley took one more hesitant step inside the room. "She's talked about you. You are the doctor, right?"

"Yes, that's right," Lou answered. "But she's never mentioned you."

Stanley shifted his weight from one foot to the other. "Well, she's only been working part time. We worked for Lake Erie Realty together. I don't suppose my name would come up." Stanley took a step backwards toward the door. "I'll just go and leave you alone with your mother. I can come back another time, to check on her recovery."

Stanley turned around and left the room. Lou was left with a strange feeling. What was he not telling her? Does her father know about Stanley? She decided that it could wait. It was past noon and she was hungry. She packed up her things and kissed her mother goodbye. She squeezed her hand and said she would be back later.

In the car, Lou called her brother. "Hi Tony, are you home?"

"Yes, where are you?"

"I'm here, in Erie," Lou answered. "Can I come over? I'll bring lunch."

"Sure, but you don't need to bring any food, there is plenty here. The game is on."

Lou looked at her phone again. It was Sunday, of course there was a game. Was it football season already? No, August was baseball, right? It didn't matter, she was never really interested in sports like her dad and brother. "Okay, I'll see you in ten."

Tony had bought a house near their parent's, but a little smaller. Lou always called it a cabin, which made him mad. It was the perfect size for him and his small family. Tony married Suni, his Japanese wife, after college. He became an EMT and Suni became a nurse. They had an adorable daughter, Hannah, who was five. Their cabin on the lake was peaceful and as long as they did not have any more kids, it was just the right size. It sometimes surprised Lou that they all went into the medical field in some way. Perhaps, subconsciously, they just wanted to help people.

Lou parked her rental beside a pick up truck that she didn't recognize. Well, it was a game day, his friends were probably here, too. She grabbed the bag from Topps that contained the popsicles she couldn't resist buying at the grocery store, since it had warmed up today. She walked in the front door and was immediately greeted by Hannah. Her arms spread out and ready to be picked up, which Lou was happy to oblige.

"Hey big girl, do you remember your Aunt Lou?"

"Yes!" Hannah shouted, "Hi Aunt Lou!"

Lou kissed Hannah's cheek and carried her into the kitchen. She released Hannah and gave Suni a hug. "How are you doing?"

"Hi Lou, I'm good," Suni replied. "I didn't know you were in town."

"Me, either," said Tony, coming up behind her. They hugged and Lou handed him the bag of popsicles.

"These better go in the freezer, unless you want them now," Lou said. "And, yes, I came as soon as I found out about mom." Suni took the popsicles and Tony led her to the living room.

"We can talk about mom later, there is someone you should say 'Hi' to first." Lou followed Tony into the living room, not knowing which of his friends were here for the game.

Jude stood in the middle of the living room when Lou approached the couch. Their eyes never wavered from each other. She felt her palms go sweaty, her heart begin to race, and her breathing grow faster. Jude felt all of the same feelings as Lou, she could tell. He even gave it away when he physically wiped his palms on his jeans.

"Hi Lou."

"Hello Jude."

Silence. It was Jude. Jude who grew up with her, who became high school sweethearts with her, who took her to prom, and was her first kiss. Jude, who she dumped and broke his heart when she left Erie to go to college. She had said she couldn't do a long distance relationship because she wasn't coming back to Erie, and now she was standing in front of him in her brother's house. Jude. So many feelings and emotions came back for both of them. Did she not expect to run into him while she was here?

Speak, someone speak. "It's good to see you, Lou."

Lou walked over to give him a hug. "It's good to see you, too."

Jude looked at Tony, "I'm gonna go. I'll give you time to talk and catch up." Then Jude looked at her, "I'll see you around."

"Sure," was all Lou could say. She watched him as he walked out the door.

Tony was unaware of the hurricane of emotions that swirled inside of his sister and it took Lou a minute to remember why she had come in the first place.

"Hey, who is Stanley Frey?"

Tony looked from Lou to Suni and took a deep breath. "A lot has changed since you left," Tony started. "Mom and Dad have been having a rough time lately, not getting along." Tony saw that Lou was hearing all of this for the first time. It was easier for him to say because he has had a year to process things. She was hearing it for the first time ever. "They were getting ready to separate and Dad was going to move out. I am sure you've seen the boxes at the house." She nodded but remained quiet, listening. "Stanley is mom's boyfriend."

It was too much for Lou. Not only did she learn that her mother was in a coma, she found out that they were separating. On top of that, she ran into Jude. Her emotions were frazzled and she needed to sit down. Tony knew this was only going to be the beginning for her.

Jude sat in his truck for a few minutes, unable to leave. The girl who left him ten years ago was back. He knew their mother was in the hospital, but he never dared to think she would come back. He wasn't naive enough to think she would stay for him. But meeting her tonight definitely shook him. He hoped that they would meet again before she left.

Chapter 3

After spending the next afternoon on the back porch watching the waves, Louise decided to rip off the figurative bandage and call her friends. She knew she damaged these relationships as well when she just left ten years ago, but she didn't want another blind meeting like she had earlier with Jude. Lou had three best friends in high school, besides Jude. She decided to call all three and make plans, since she figured she was going to be here for awhile. She pulled out her phone and saw a missed call. Actually several missed calls, all from Ben.

Lou took a deep breath and called him back first. "Hi Ben."

"Louise, I've been trying to call you all day. How is everything?"

"I saw mom and there's still no change," Lou answered, deciding to leave the other surprises out of this conversation.

"Do you want me to come there?" Ben asked.

"No, Ben, there's nothing you can do. Plus, there are some things I have to deal with here first. I'll call you later."

"Wait, what things?"

"Nothing important, I'll call you later tonight." Lou hung up.

She took another deep breath, then another. Lou wasn't sure how her other friends would react to seeing her here again. All she could do was try to make amends for leaving and not keeping in touch.

"Hi, Rose?" Asked Lou.

"Yes, who is this?"

"It's Lou. I'm in town for a little while and would love to meet up. How does that sound?" She was half expecting her to hang up.

A long pause, "Okay, I'm free today. Actually we all hang out at Leon's bar Sunday afternoons. If you want to see everyone, that is."

"Well, sure. Who is everyone?"

"Me and Danny, Avery and Leon."

"Okay, I was going to call them next anyway. What time?"

"Four, Pilgrim's Bar on State Street."

"Okay, I'll see you there."

After checking on her father, Lou went upstairs to change. She remembered when the six of them were inseparable. She always knew Rose and Danny would marry. She supposed people thought that of her and Jude, too. Avery was the wild one, dating everyone and anyone. Leon was the stable friend to go to with our problems. No wonder he ended up a bartender, now he hears everyone's problems. Lou didn't know how this was going to go, they may be happy to see her, but she left so abruptly and she didn't come home much. There may be a lot of hard feelings still.

When she walked into Pilgrim's Bar, it was a strange feeling for her. She was obviously over twenty one, but she was never over twenty one when she lived here, so it still felt a bit illegal. Leon saw her first and waved for her to the bar. Everyone was already there. This really was their regular routine. Everyone exchanged hugs and kisses on the cheek and they made room for Lou to sit between Rose and Avery. Leon had some bruises on his face and arms.

"Leon what happened? Are you okay?" Asked Lou.

"Yea, sure. Just had a bit of an accident. I'll be fine," replied Leon.

Leon was African American, but even with his dark complexion, she could tell those were bruises from more than just a little accident. Rose was pretty, with her auburn hair and big green eyes. Danny was Italian. He had thick, dark hair and wore a gold cross necklace, probably to show off his chest hair. Avery was the beauty queen, drama queen and cheerleader. Even now, she just needed to sweep her blond hair over her shoulder and bat her long eyelashes to get any guy to do her a favor.

They started with shots of whiskey, then beers. To look at them from a distance anyone would think they were the best of friends, such a tight knit group of people. Each friend took a turn giving the highlights from the last ten years. They fell into a rhythm that was comfortable and familiar. It was civil, cordial and a little cautious to begin with. The shots and beers helped loosen everyone up and it slowly turned to laughs, memories and toasts to whatever they happened to think of. Avery had been giving off some hostile vibes and after a couple hours of camaraderie, let Lou know what she really thought of her when Jude's name came up.

"You crushed him when you left! He was so broken and hurt by what you did!" Avery yelled. "He cried, you know! Cried in my arms. That's what you did to him!"

"Let's just calm down, Avery," Lou said, trying to defuse the situation.

"Avery, that was a long time ago," Rose said.

"We are not here to bring up bad things from the past, Avery. Leave if you're going to do that in this bar," said Leon with authority.

"You all can sit here and pretend that everything is back to normal and forgotten, but I can't forgive what you did to my Jude!" Avery yelled.

There was a stunned silence before Lou spoke. "You and Jude?" Lou looked from Leon to Rose to Danny. Their silence confirmed that it was true. Lou put money on the bar. She wanted to pay her tab and get out quick.

"We've been together ever since. You are hurting him just by being here. Leaving was the best thing you did for him." Avery added. She was standing now, almost in a defensive position. She was someone who was always ready to throw a punch.

Lou started to walk away. "Well, it was good to see you guys again. Thanks."

Rose ran after her as she headed for the door. "Lou, that's not how we all feel. We are glad to see you and catch up. Everyone had a little too much to drink, Avery isn't thinking straight."

"Did you know Avery was with Jude?"

Rose looked down at the floor, "Yes, but it's not like she says. They are on again off again at best."

Lou simply hugged Rose and left the bar. Her mind was spinning on the ride home. She had no right to be mad, she knew that. It was irrational. She left him, of course he would find someone else, even be married with kids by now. But not her. Not Avery.

Lou knew there wasn't any food at home, and now understanding why, she stopped at Topps to get some groceries. On edge, she scanned the other customers in case anyone recognized her. She knew that their reactions wouldn't be all rainbows and sunshine. She just wasn't prepared for it. Too many things were happening at once. Her brain was in overload and she now just longed to go home and sit on the beach. The lake would help her. Driving across town is starting to get emotional. Their first date, the first time she drove a car, her favorite restaurant and the mall. Comparing memories to how things look now can also be depressing. She prayed her mom would come out of the coma fast, for more reasons than one. She had to get out of here, again.

Lou pulled up to the house and saw the lights on. Her father was still awake. She brought her bags of groceries in, set them on the counter and starting putting things away. She saw her father sitting in the living room watching the news. After the counters were clear, she went in to see her father.

"Hi Dad, are you hungry?"

"No, I had a bowl of cereal. That's all I need tonight," Tom replied. "Tony said you went to see them today."

"Yes, Hannah is getting so big!"

Tom laughed. "Yes, I can't keep up with her anymore. She's definitely a handful."

"Dad, how come you didn't tell me about you and mom?'

Tom wasn't expecting this question, not yet. He wanted to bring it up in his own time. He turned to look at her. "How am I supposed to tell my baby girl that her parents aren't getting along. It was hard enough to tell Tony and he's older and married with a child. I was going to move in with him. I know they don't even have the room, but I could have slept on the couch. I would give your mother the house." He paused, remembering the plans they must have made over these last several months.

"Who's Stanley?"

"How do you know about Stanley?" Her father asked.

"He came to the hospital this morning."

"Oh, I forgot. That's usually why I don't stay long. I try to avoid him."

"How did they meet? He said they work together."

"Yes. Your mother started staying late and working more. It was only a part time job, so I knew this wasn't right. I simply asked her one day and she admitted she was seeing someone else. We agreed on a separation to see if that changed anything." Her father paused and looked up at her, "I don't like going to the hospital and seeing her like that. They don't even know who hit her."

Lou sat back in her chair and looked at her father. "Well, for now, those plans are on hold. Until she wakes up and tells me herself, I want you to relax and eat a normal dinner. I am starving and I'm making spaghetti." Lou stood up and went over to her father. "I'll bring you a plate when it's done." She kissed him on the cheek before heading to the kitchen to prepare dinner.

It was hard for Lou to see her father so unhappy. Was it all her mother's fault? Was it Stanley's? She would try to refrain from judgement at least until her mother woke up. Oh please wake up! Her phone let her know there was another text and another voicemail from Ben. He was another loose end for her, but because he was so far away, he could wait. There were more immediate people to deal with here. She needed to talk to Jude. As much as she tried to avoid him, they needed to talk. Tomorrow. She could deal with Jude tomorrow.

Chapter 4

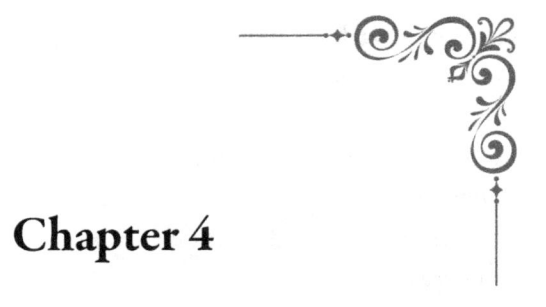

Each day slowly turned into the next. No good news but no bad news. A routine had developed. Lou cooked for her father and they visited Laura in the hospital. They both avoided talking of Stanley. Tony came over, sometimes alone and sometimes with the family. It was so good to feel somewhat normal around here when possible. Lou was avoiding a lot of things in her personal life that if not dealt with soon, would come crashing down on her. First was Jude. She was too scared to invite him for dinner, so instead suggested he come for dessert and a drink on the beach.

"I'd be happy to," Jude replied.

Lou made a chocolate cake, the round kind with two layers. She slapped Tom's hand when he tried reaching for a finger full of icing. He just laughed and did it anyway. She loved her dad. He was always the one to go to for support and advice. Mom was the disciplinarian. She was quick to set the kids straight, but fair and firm. Lou loved them both and prayed they would work it out when she woke up. If she woke up.

There was a knock on the door. Seven o'clock. That would be Jude.

"Hi, come on in," Lou said.

"Thank you for inviting me. I wasn't sure you would want to see me while you were in town," Jude replied.

"Well, after feeling the wrath of Avery, I wasn't sure it was such a good idea, but I had to see you, Jude."

"Wait, what do you mean the wrath of Avery?"

"I'm surprised she didn't fill you in right away. The other day, I met her, Rose, Danny and Leon at Pilgrim's and she just went off on me, about you. How I hurt you." Lou felt uneasy under his gaze, so she turned and got three plates and a knife.

"I don't see Avery very often," Jude replied. "Not much anymore. I will admit we dated, but nothing serious."

Lou didn't look up, it was none of her business. She cut the cake and took a piece into her father, who was watching the news. When Lou came back into the kitchen she handed Jude a beer and said, "Let's go outside. It's almost sunset." They took their cake and beer to the beach.

The sky and water were glowing orange and red. Erie was known for having beautiful sunsets, but tonight was the most vibrant she had seen in a very long time. "This is my happy place," said Lou.

"I know what you mean. I don't think I could ever leave," replied Jude. Then, realizing what he had just said, "I'm sorry, Lou, I didn't mean anything against your leaving. I'm proud of you for becoming a doctor. You did it."

"It's okay, I deserve it." They both ate their cake and sipped their beers. "I'm sorry."

"For what? Following your dreams? Just stop it, Lou. I understand why you did it."

"But I'm sorry for how I did it. I was young and stupid." Lou heard her phone ring and looked at the screen, Ben. Jude saw it, too.

"Who's Ben?" Asked Jude.

"My boyfriend." She looked over at Jude. They were sharing a log on the sand and she sensed him straighten at the word.

"Is he nice?"

"Yes, but he's a surgeon, so he's got an ego, too." Wanting to change the subject, "What do you do, Jude?"

"I'm a painter."

"Oh, like houses and stuff?" Lou asked.

"Something like that."

There was a silence that fell as they watched the sun disappear into the lake. The lake, itself, brought back memories for them that they haven't talked about since they were kids. But tonight, it was like the elephant in the room. As it got darker, they could hear the waves on the shore.

"You know, after graduation, I became a lifeguard on the beach," Jude said.

Lou knew where this conversation was going and wanted nothing more than to avoid it.

"Brad works for the marine rescue team," Jude continued.

Lou felt tears fill her eyes. Jude looked at her.

"Do you ever think about that night?" Jude finally asked. The question he had been aching to ask everyday since she left. The night that changed the lives of Lou and Tony Jensen, but most importantly, the lives of Brad, Jude and Jackson Weber.

"Yes," replied Lou, wiping at the tears that were now running down her cheeks.

"I don't want to ever forget," started Jude. "Mostly to remind myself how stupid I was so that nothing like that ever happened again. I guess that's why my brother and I went into jobs that help people in the water."

"And my brother and I became health care workers. I became a doctor and he is an EMT," Lou said. "We were just kids, we didn't know the consequences. We were just trying to have fun and we will spend the rest of our lives making up for it."

"Fun," repeated Jude. "That night changed our lives forever."

"I've never talked about it after that night," said Lou.

"Maybe you should. I know it has helped me. My therapist said that carrying around that guilt is only hurting me, it will never change anything or bring Jackson back." Jude paused and looked at

Lou. He took her hand. "She said that we feel the guilt so strongly because as adults, we look back and know what we did was stupid and reckless, but that's the adult in us talking and laying judgment. It's the seven year old in us, who didn't know any better, who must be forgiven."

Jude heard her sniffling. He reached into his pocket and pulled out a napkin, the only thing he had. Her hand reached out and accepted it.

"I've tried talking about it with my brother," said Jude, "but Brad never went to counseling and is still carrying the guilt. He was the oldest and it hits him differently. I think that's why he works to make the lake safer. The guilt is going to eat him from the inside out. I even think part of him is still searching for Jack. His water rescue team has helped lots of people, but he will never be able to help the one person who needs it the most."

Lou looked up at him, "Jackson?"

"No, himself," answered Jude.

After they sat in silence for a few minutes, thinking about that night over twenty years ago, Lou asked if he wanted another beer.

"Sure," he said.

It was also an excuse to give them some space. It was a heady experience for her to be sitting next to the one person she thought she would be spending her life with, but also the person she shared a traumatic event with as kids. Jude had been holding her hand. What was she thinking? She should not have invited him over here, but how could she not. Jude was part of her life for so long. They played in the sand together even before they could walk. The four of them were together every day, Tony and Brad with her and Jude. Jackson was too little to hang out with them. But he still loved to tag along. Poor Jackson, who will forever be five years old.

Lou returned to the beach with more beers. Jude was no longer sitting on the log, he had walked towards the water, shoes next to the log. She walked in her bare feet near the water's edge.

"It's going to get colder soon, can you feel it?" Jude asked.

"Yes, the chill is in the air."

"Another summer winding down. I like summer the best. You can do more things, wear less clothes and eat ice cream all day long," Jude said.

Lou laughed but watched Jude, really looked at him. He was tall, lean, muscular and tan. His summers on the lifeguard tower were paying off. His dirty blond curly hair was longer than he usually wore it, maybe another rebellion against the end of summer. But his blue eyes sparkled from the sunset after saying the last thing about eating all the ice cream. Jude was still attractive. Maybe more so. He aged well, had stubble that added to a ruggedness he didn't have at eighteen. How did she look, she wondered? How did she look to him?

"You don't look like you eat ice cream all day," she said. What did she just say? Did she say that out loud?

Jude took a sip of beer, looked back at Lou and laughed. "Well, thank you. You don't look so bad yourself."

"Now I know you are drunk. Your vision is impaired," joked Lou.

Jude turned his whole body to face her. "Okay, it's on. Tomorrow I'm going out on my boat and so are you. We'll see how bad you look in a bathing suit." He winked and raised his bottle of beer.

"Fine, but it's not going to be pretty," Lou replied. She was half joking. Her bathing suit was old, not much need for one in New York, but she did take pride in her physical health and appearance. She was a doctor for goodness sake, she took care of herself. "I'll bring the beer."

"Sounds good to me," Jude said. "Do you remember how to fish?"

"Remember how to fish? What kind of question is that? Of course I remember. I remember that I'm better than you," she teased.

"Maybe when we were ten. You've been in the big city too long.'

He was right, she hadn't fished in ten years or more. She had better stop the trash talk before she couldn't get herself out.

"Okay, what time?" She asked.

"How's eight sound? Come to my place, the boat is hitched to my truck."

"I will. Thanks, Jude." They hugged on the beach then went back into the house.

"Good night, Mr. Jensen," Jude said to Tom.

"Good to see you, Jude. Good night to you," Tom answered.

They walked towards the front door and then Jude turned. "Thank you for inviting me tonight. I'm glad we had a chance to talk and clear the air. I have to admit I was a bit nervous. After seeing you at Tony's that first night, I have been anxious ever since."

"But why would you be anxious? I'm the one that was scared for everyone's reactions coming back to town after how fast I left. I've taken my hits on the chin because I deserve it, you don't."

"I guess I was just afraid of finding out you left because of me or something I did," said Jude.

"No it was never you. I don't know how to explain it, I just had to get out, to leave, and I'm sorry I hurt so many people in the process. I'm sorry I hurt you."

Jude gave her another hug before turning towards the door. She waved good bye as he drove off in his truck. She closed the door and leaned back on it. She felt like a teenager going over their conversations. Lou felt like a weight had been lifted off of her shoulders. They covered a lot of topics and pulled some skeletons out of the closet. She hoped it was all for the good, not to come back and haunt them. Even though a weight was lifted, she still felt like she had only gone through round one.

Her father came into the kitchen to say good night to her.

"Did you have a nice talk with Jude?" He asked.

"Yes, dad, we had a very nice talk. We talked about the night I left, about Jackson and Ben, my boyfriend."

"Well, that was a lot of heavy topics for a piece of chocolate cake."

They hugged good night and he went up to bed. Lou decided to stay up a bit longer. She turned off the television and grabbed the book she had started earlier. She could always rely on her mother to have some Jane Austin in the house. Her thoughts kept going back to Jude. Eventually, giving up on the book, she pulled out her phone.

"Hi babe, how are things going over there?" Asked Ben.

"Still good, no changes."

"So you don't know when you're coming home, yet? No pressure, but people are asking. You also owe me an answer of your own," Ben reminded her.

She did not need reminded, in fact, she was trying to forget all about it. "Not now, Ben. I've got too many things going on here. Between mom in a coma, Dad wanting to separate, my friends ripping my head off and then memories of childhood trauma, it's a lot to deal with."

"Sure, you take your time and work it all out. I'm here for you, babe."

"Thanks, Ben. I'm tired, but I just wanted to hear your voice. Good night."

"Good night, I love you," Ben said.

Lou went upstairs after turning off the lights. She would deal with the dishes tomorrow. It was a good day, but she was ready for today to end. Tonight she would dream about boat rides.

Chapter 5

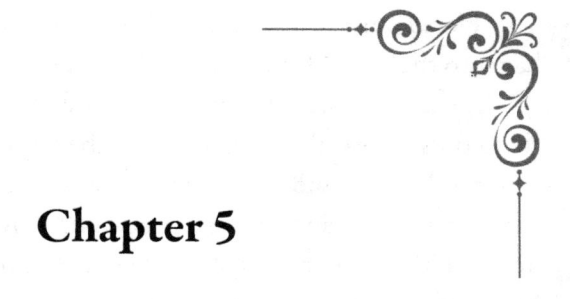

Lou and her father had breakfast together as usual, but she explained that she was going out on Jude's boat. She made a sandwich for his lunch and wrapped it up in the fridge. She said to tell mom she hoped she woke up and would see her later. She hugged her father and went out to her car with the cooler of beer. She had been second guessing her decision to be alone on Jude's boat with him since she agreed last night. Was this a bad decision? They were just old friends hanging out, but old friends with a history.

The moment she pulled up to Jude's house she knew this wasn't going to feel like a romantic date, that was for sure. Jude's older brother, Brad, was carrying fishing rods and gear to the truck. She could feel Brad's eyes on her as she parked in the street and carried the cooler to the truck. Brad was five years older than Jude. He was taller than Jude and had brown hair that he kept cut short.

"Hi Brad," Lou said.

"Hey, I heard you were coming along. Long time no see," Brad replied.

"I brought the beer," Lou offered.

"Great. I can see now why he invited you," Brad said.

"Hey, play nice boys and girls. We have got some fish to catch," said Jude as he came around the boat. "Good morning, Lou. How are you today?"

"I'm good, thanks."

"Here let me help you with those." Jude took her cooler and tote bag into the back of the truck and they all climbed in.

It was a tight fit with Lou in between the brothers, but thankfully, it wasn't a long drive to the boat ramp. Soon they were loading the boat and pushing off. It was a beautiful August day, the sun was shining and it wasn't too hot. When Jude found a place he liked, they cut the engine and settled in for the fishing to begin. Mostly the boys talked about personal things, jobs, cars and the lake.

"So what is Lisa and Brian doing today?" Jude asked Brad.

"She was taking him back-to-school shopping and then meeting us on the boat ramp. Brian wants to see what we catch, so we'd better catch a lot," said Brad. He smiled, then looked at Lou. "You never met Lisa and Brian did you?"

"No, Brad, I haven't," she replied, not sure where this was going.

"Of course, there's a lot of people you haven't seen since you left ten years ago," said Brad quietly.

"You're right, again, Brad. I'm sorry."

"Lisa is my wife of nine years. Brian is eight." Brad was getting quiet and Lou wasn't sure if he was ready to start yelling. She knew there was some anger in him, she just didn't know how much. He was clenching his jaw, preparing to say something.

"Brad, we are here to have fun. Don't ruin it," pleaded Jude.

"Have fun like we are one big happy family?" Brad turned to Lou and pointed his finger. "She is the reason we aren't anymore."

"Brad, stop! Don't say something you're going to regret," yelled Jude.

"Listen, I know what I did hurt a lot of people. I left, it was selfish and sudden. I'm sorry," replied Lou.

"Well, that was just the beginning," Brad started. "When you left Jude, it tore him up." His voice softened. "When our mother saw how hurt Jude was, it reminded her of losing little Jack. She had barely gotten over that after ten years, now another son hurt that she couldn't fix. Our dad drank himself to sleep everyday. He wasn't as affected by Jude's pain, he lost touch with reality after Jack. But they stuck together until Jude turned eighteen. That's when they both took off. Dad first, he just never came home. Mom went out to Ohio to stay with our Grandma. We don't see any of them anymore. It's just been me and Jude, until I met Lisa."

There was silence. Brad had talked so calmly and matter-of-factly that it was like he was reading the sports scores. Lou had no idea about any of this. When she left town, she never really looked back. She was surprised to see that she was tearing up. She didn't even know it until Jude was handing her another napkin.

"Thank you for telling me. I had no idea," said Lou.

"I really wasn't sure if you did or not. Part of me believed that if you knew, you would have done or said something. No one is that much of a monster," replied Brad.

"I didn't, I promise," Lou said through tears that came easily. She wept for the two boys who not only lost their little brother, but lost their mother and father in the process. They all remained silent, watching the water and their lines. She sat with her guilt.

It was Brad who yelled out first. "I've got one! And he's big!" They continued fishing in companionable silence. Enough had been said, so they were each left to their own thoughts. Another punch to Lou's chin, but she took it like a champ. An attack she didn't even know she had to prepare for, but it was done. Brad's feelings for her were out in the open and they could only move forward. That was okay, she liked forward. They all ate the sandwiches Lou packed and drank all the beer. If this awkward threesome could have a good ending, she thought they found one. Brad let Lisa know they were heading in and they would be waiting for him. He built a family from the ashes, she hoped the same would happen for Jude. He deserved someone who loved him completely.

Lou could spot Brian a mile away. He was running, jumping and bouncing off all the rocks along the shoreline. He certainly was happy to see his daddy. Even without any make up, Lisa was very pretty as she chased after Brian. Jude and Brad hitched up the boat and were unloading the coolers, buckets and equipment when Brian grabbed one of the buckets of fish.

"Careful, son, they're heavy," Brad called out.

"They're not heavy for me, dad," Brian said proudly. Brian still wanted to jump from rock to rock along the shoreline. However, with the bucket in one hand, he was more off balance than earlier. The rocks were slippery from the algae and the bucket made him lean to the right. When Brian jumped to another rock, he lost his balance, fell and screamed.

"OUCH!" Yelled Brian.

They all ran to Brian, who was laying on the rocks. The bucket and its contents strewn along the shoreline. Lisa got to him first, but when she tried to pull him up, he screamed even more. Lou kicked into doctor mode and ran to his side.

"Brian, where is the pain?" Asked Lou.

"My arm!" Cried Brian.

Lou could tell by looking at it that it was broken. "Lisa, call 911. Brad, find me several sticks about ten inches long. Jude, get me my tote bag, there's a first aid kit in there. Brian, look at me, I have to fix your arm."

Jude came with her first aid kit and Brad, with the sticks.

"Hey buddy, you're going to be ok. Lou here is a doctor," Brad said to him.

A quick look at Brad told her to keep going. She took the flannel shirt she had tied around her waist and ripped it into strips.

"Now Brian, this might hurt a little, so I need you to be brave and strong, okay?"

"Okay," replied Brian.

"I need to wrap your hurt arm and I'm going to use these sticks. Your mom, dad and uncle are all here to help you," said Lou as she looked around the little circle of people balancing precariously on the slippery rocks. She took hold of Brian's hand and tried to straighten his arm. Brian cried out, but Lou kept going. When she felt it was straight, she had Lisa hold the sticks in place as she wrapped the flannel around the arm and sticks. She made it as tight as possible.

"Good job, Brian, I'm so proud of you," said Lou and was repeated by his parents and uncle. Promises of ice cream and favorite movies were made. They heard the ambulance getting closer and they all lifted Brian from the rocks and onto the stretcher when the EMTs had it ready. Lou could tell everyone was scared and nervous, she has seen it a million times. Parents try to put on a brave face for their child, but she knew better. The parents were really just as scared as the child. It was natural.

Brad and Lisa rode in the ambulance with Brian. They both mouthed a quick 'thank you' before the doors closed. That left Jude and Lou. They looked at each other and then the mess around them. Lou started picking up the trash and debris from all the excitement. Jude just kept looking at her.

"You were pretty great today," He said.

"So were you, you take direction like a pro," she replied.

"No, I'm serious. You are great at your job. We are lucky you were here today. Thank you."

Lou stopped and looked at Jude, "You're welcome. Now let's get out of here."

Back at Jude's house, Lou helped unload the truck. She grabbed her empty cooler and tote bag. Jude said he would get the rest later.

"There's plenty of fish if you want to stay for dinner," Jude said,

Lou thought of her father at home and her mom at the hospital, she needed to see both today. Plus, she felt like she was spending too much time with Jude. What was she doing? "I'll take a rain check. I need to see my mom today."

Jude waved as she drove off. It was quite an adrenaline rush today. She thought she had made peace with Brad, not just with their conversation on the boat, but now he saw her doctor skills in action. He couldn't keep up the argument that her leaving Erie was only a bad thing. It had its good points, too. She hoped she had made some progress today, at least.

At home, Lou checked to make sure her father ate his sandwich. He did and a piece of cake. She asked if he was ready to go see mom and he nodded his head. Tom asked how her day was. She skimmed over most of the conversation with Brad, but when she got to the part about Brian falling and breaking his arm, he got very concerned.

"It was a good thing you were there, Lou," her father said.

"Well, I was just glad to help. I hope mom is going to get better soon."

They got out of the car, entered the hospital and rode the elevator to the fourth floor. The same thing they had been doing for almost two weeks. Lou never ran into Stanley again, but she knew he still came because she asked the nurses. Nurse Kelli was more than happy to give her the scoop. She also let them know that mom was stable, no changes. Lou and her father both sat on opposite sides of her bed, holding her hand and reading a book in companionable silence.

Chapter 6

Today was cloudy, but there wasn't any rain in the forecast. This was important because it was Emily's first birthday party. Rose had called Lou the night before and invited her. It was last minute because they weren't sure if the weather was going to cooperate or not. More likely, Rose and Danny didn't know if they wanted the drama that followed Lou to infect their daughter's first birthday party. In the end, they decided to invite her and give it another try. She was glad to have another opportunity to smooth things over with her friends.

The party wasn't until the afternoon, so Lou had time to cook for her father and take him to see mom at the hospital. They were both getting used to the routine. Even Nurse Kelli was happy to see them and gave them any updates there might be.

"She's doing great," Nurse Kelli would say. "Just waiting for her to wake up is all."

It was always encouraging to hear, but day after day, it could also be discouraging. Nurse Kelli had a wonderful bedside manner. She would hum or sing while doing her blood pressure checks or even changing the linens. Nurse Kelli even admitted to turning on the television from time to time,

"I've read that sometimes, when the sounds are familiar to the patient, they are more comfortable and wake up, so I thought I would try it. I put on a game show or two, then a soap opera, a talk show and the news. Anything I think she might watch while at home and had just dozed off for a few minutes." Nurse Kelli went about tidying up the room and after bringing Laura a fresh pitcher of water for just in case, she was gone.

Tom and Lou were left with the silence of the room, aside from the beeping of the machines. They each held a hand of Laura's and prayed to themselves. It was Lou who spoke aloud first. "Mom, my birthday is coming up. You can't miss that! I want you to make your special lasagna. Nobody makes it like you do." Her father nodded his head in agreement.

Lou told her father, and her mother, about her plans for this afternoon. She first needed to buy a toy. What do you get for a one year old girl? Her father suggested a stuffed animal. She remembered Tony saying, when Hannah was young, nothing with batteries that made loud noises. Lou laughed to herself, she will stay out of the electronic toy isle. Father and daughter spent most of the morning in comfortable conversation while Laura laid in the bed like Sleeping Beauty. They each kissed and hugged her before heading out to the car. At home, Lou made them lunch and cleaned up the dishes.

When Lou felt comfortable with leaving her father alone, she went shopping. She was faced with a multitude of choices for a one year old. There were so many options that didn't involve batteries, but, in the end, opted for a doll. She was soft, cuddly and had red hair like Emily and her mother. Perfect. After purchasing a gift bag and card, she felt armed and ready to face the party drama.

Rose and Danny Cross lived a little bit out of the city, more towards Edinboro. There was more land, more trees and definitely more cows and horses. Lou pulled into their long gravel driveway and knew instantly that this was the kind of situation that would be difficult to get out of later. She wouldn't worry about that now, she grabbed her gift and walked towards the noise.

It was evident that the party festivities were in the backyard. The sky was still fairly cloudy with just a touch of wind, but Danny had insisted on having a tent to cover the party, just in case it decided to rain. As Lou came around the house and into the backyard, she realized there were a lot more people invited than she thought. She had never been to a one year old's party before and didn't realize it would be so grand. There were more people here than there was at her last birthday party in New York City.

Rose saw Lou walk in and waved at her. Lou waved back and gestured towards the gift bag. Rose pointed to a large table, already laden with gifts, that was near the back door. She added her gift to the pile and went to find something to drink. Rose had made her way to her by then and gestured to the area under the tent where all the food and drinks were served.

"Help yourself and mingle," said Rose.

"I didn't know there would be so many people here," Lou replied.

"Well, you know, grandparents, siblings, friends, coworkers and neighbors. They all expect an invite," Rose explained. "But you'll know some people here today, Avery, Jude, Leon and even Tony and his family. Just act cool and avoid Avery if you have to."

Lou explained to Rose that she had no intention of ruining her party. If Avery tried to start anything again, she would leave. It sounded so simple and she hoped it would be. Rose went to mingle with the other guests while Lou went to find a drink. Under the large white tent she found Leon.

"Hey Leon, how are you doing?" Lou asked.

"Hi Lou, I'm good. Just staying near the bar to make sure they do it right," replied Leon.

The Crosses had an open bar and it seemed that Leon was taking full advantage. His bruises weren't as visible, but he was losing his balance and could easily get a few more bruises if he wasn't careful.

"Maybe you've had enough, Leon," Lou suggested.

"Oh this is just juice," Leon explained, but his stumble as he came to pat Lou's arm suggested otherwise. She led him to a chair to sit. She asked the bartender for water and handed the bottle to Leon.

"Drink this," Lou said as she took the glass of juice away. She sat down next to him.

"You know, I didn't drink anything since the accident. It scared me, you know. I hit something and don't even remember it. I just remembered waking up in my car in front of my house. The car was pretty beat up, probably hit a mailbox or two, but I only got a few bumps and bruises." Leon took a long drink of the water. "Until today. I had a drink today because my girlfriend broke up with me." He started tearing up. "She said she didn't want to be with a drunk anymore. I tried to tell her that I have changed, that I never had a drink since the accident, but she left anyway."

Lou touched his shoulder and sat with him. Just then she heard Avery's voice and saw that she and Jude arrived together. Leon repeated his story to Jude while Lou went to get him something to eat. She gave Jude a smile as she handed the plate to Leon.

"Thanks, Lou," Leon said.

"You're welcome, Leon," she replied.

"Hey man," Jude said. "Maybe this weekend we can go fishing together, how does that sound?"

Leon simply nodded his head. Jude knew the heartache he was feeling, but also knew that drinking wasn't the answer. When Leon looked like he could be left alone, Avery put her arm through Jude's and headed towards the crowd. Lou spotted Tony, Suni and Hannah and just as she stood up to greet them, Hannah jumped into her arms.

"Aunt Lou!" Hannah yelled.

"Hey there, my sweet girl! How are you?" Lou asked.

"I'm good. We got Emily a pink blanket with butterflies all over it! I hope she likes it," Hannah said.

"She'll love it!" Lou exclaimed.

Lou released Hannah, who was already wiggling to get down, so she could join in all the games. Rose had two bouncy houses, bubbles, a bunch of balls to throw and kick and a balloon artist. It was like a small circus in the backyard, what kid wouldn't love it here? Lou and Tony talked about their mom and dad. Lou expressed concern about whether their father could really live alone in the house. She figured that was why she was there. Tony couldn't get away to the hospital as freely as her and their father, so Lou gave him updates when necessary. So far, there really hasn't been any updates other than 'no changes'.

"Brad thought he might come today," said Tony.

"Oh really? Is Brian's arm doing okay?" Lou asked.

Tony laughed, "Oh yes, he's still horsing around like any other eight year old boy."

"I'm glad you guys are all still close. That's nice," Lou replied. "I was afraid that they would act differently towards you when I left."

"Well, things were, um, awkward for a while, but we're guys. All we need is an invite on the boat and some beers and we are best friends again. Brad, Jude and I are like the three musketeers. Well, at least when our wives allow us to be." Tony smiled and asked the bartender for a bottle of water. "You want a pop, Lou?"

Lou had to think a minute about what Tony meant. But seeing the Coke in his hand reminded her that soda is called pop here. "Sure." It really was turning into a lovely day. Cooler than it had been because of the cloud cover, but no rain. Avery kept Jude away from her, or was it Jude keeping Avery away. Either way, she was glad. She was spending too much time with Jude anyway. Ben had called again this morning and she gave him a run down of all that had been happening. He wanted her to come back, but she was not ready. She knew what she was going back to and she was not ready to face any of it, yet.

Ben told her about the surgeries he had been performing. The award he received had sparked interest in him from other hospitals, even other areas of the country. "We could move, babe, if you want to," Ben had said. She just didn't know. Her head wasn't clear. The old desire of getting out of Erie as fast as possible was long gone now. But did that mean she wanted to move again? No, it didn't. She didn't know what it meant.

Rose's announcement that it was time for cake brought Lou out of her moment of melancholy. Everyone gathered, as best as they could, around Emily sitting in a high chair. She wore a paper hat and bib and had a small cake in front of her. Lou had never witnessed this scene before and had no idea what to expect. Were they just going to let the child eat that whole cake? She observed from the side as Emily reached into the cake with both hands and smeared it all over her face. Apparently this was the objective because Rose and Danny were smiling and taking pictures.

Lou's eyes scanned the crowd. Was everyone else enjoying this spectacle as much as Rose and Danny? Her eyes stopped on Avery and Jude. Avery kept reaching for Jude's hand, but he kept them in his pockets. When she couldn't get ahold of his hands, she wrapped her arms around his. Jude just shook this off. Avery, getting more and more visibly upset at his lack of affection, simply put her arm around his waist. They didn't see Lou watching them and they certainly wouldn't know she saw the way Jude rolled his eyes at this latest attempt at possessiveness.

Lou smiled, but it was short lived. She could see how uncomfortable he was and knew it was for her. Jude was taking his punch on the chin for her. It wasn't until this moment that she knew what Avery had said about their relationship was a lie and that Jude was telling the truth. Jude put up with her for companionship, not love. The realization instantly made her sad and guilty. What had she done to Jude all those years ago? She started to feel like their friendship was salvageable, but the hurt was still there. The hurt that made him turn to Avery.

Chapter 7

Lou had stayed to help Rose and Danny clean up after the party. They gave her a plate of food to take home. 'For your dad' they said. Lou thanked them and backed out of the Crosses driveway. She didn't really have any further plans that day, which is partly why she offered to stay and clean up. She decided, last minute, to swing by the hospital. Usually she always came with her father, but she didn't mind coming back later with him if he wanted her to.

She didn't worry about the food in the car, it was still relatively cool today with the overcast sky. She was walking down the fourth floor hallway when Nurse Kelli gave her a half smile and a nod. Not her usual bubbly greeting. It was when she entered her mother's room that she understood why this would be uncomfortable.

Stanley Frey was sitting on the padded lounge chair holding Laura's hand. It was so loving and sweet that Lou felt frozen in the doorway. Stanley immediately released Laura's hand and stood up.

"Hello, Ms. Louise," Stanley said.

"Hello, Stanley," Lou replied. "Please sit, it's okay."

Unsure if he should sit or run, Stanley slowly sat back down in the chair as she asked. He did not, however, take Laura's hand again. Lou sat on the opposite chair and took her mother's hand. Before she started telling her mother all about Emily's birthday party, she turned to Stanley.

"Do you come everyday, Stanley?" Lou asked.

Stanley hesitated, not sure if he should be honest. "Yes."

"Are, I mean, were you and my mother serious?"

"Yes."

"But you knew she was still married?"

Again, a slight hesitation, "yes." Stanley looked down at this hands, unsure what to do next or what the next question might be.

Lou remained calm. "I don't like you, Stanley," she said matter-of-factly.

"I understand," Stanley replied. Then added, "I'm sorry." This was more than Stanley could bear. He stood up, excused himself and left the room.

The air in the room seemed to lighten a bit. Lou took a deep breath and relaxed. She began to tell her mother all about the birthday party. She mentioned how Avery behaved, that Leon was drinking again and doesn't even remember his accident, and how a one year old ate a cake by herself. Lou laughed and enjoyed the time alone with her mother. She missed spending time with her.

Laura loved to cook and because they had such a large house, everyone came to the Jensen's house. Being on the beach was a plus, too. Lou and Tony would run around all hours of the day and night. Even the three Weber boys would come and go as they pleased. They didn't live too far down the road. They mostly rode their bikes or a parent would happily drop them off for a few hours of peace. Until the drowning, of course, that changed everything. Jude and Brad would still come over, but it was no longer the carefree giggles of innocent children. It was the somber movements of kids who didn't know what to do next.

The Jensens' home always felt like a safe place. The kids would slide a chair up to the kitchen island and see what Laura was cooking that day. It would either be pasta, chocolate chip cookies, banana bread, meatloaf, pigs in the blanket or even carrot cake. It didn't matter, Laura was happy to oblige when samples were requested or tiny hands demanded.

Lou felt a tear escape as the memories of her childhood flooded out. She had a good childhood on Lake Erie, that was for sure. She just hoped her mother would recover so she could get back to what she loved, cooking. Or was it Stanley? Lou was unsure of so many things in her life, could she even trust her own memories? How long were her parents unhappy? Her father admitted to a year, could it have been longer? She told herself it didn't matter, she just wanted her mother to wake up, but it did matter. Deep down, it mattered.

Nurse Kelli came in the room. This time she was her normal, talkative self.

"It's time for Wheel of Fortune," Nurse Kelli announced. "Your mother never misses it."

She took the remote from the bedside table and clicked through the channels until she heard the familiar jingle. Nurse Kelli went on to check Laura's blood pressure and other vitals.

Lou stood up and smoothed out her skirt. "I didn't realize how late it was. I'd better be going." She thanked Nurse Kelli and went down to her car.

The whole way home, Lou debated whether to bring up Stanley to her father. Would she be opening a can of worms she didn't really want to deal with? In the end, she decided she would bring him up. It was the elephant in the room and they had to deal with it. She brought the plate of food into the kitchen, heated it up and called for her father to eat.

Lou told her father about the birthday party and that Tony and his family were there. She mentioned the games and gifts, but eventually said she stopped at the hospital.

"Dad, how long were you and mom unhappy?"

Tom set his fork down, "Now Lou, it wasn't like that. We weren't unhappy, just drifting apart. You probably can't understand that, since you aren't married, but after more than thirty five years, it's bound to happen."

She did know, though. After only two years with Ben, was she still happy? Coming home put such a spin on her perspective, she didn't even know which end was up anymore.

"When did you feel the drifting?" Lou asked.

"It wasn't one particular moment. It was just over time, we did our own things and suddenly you realize we aren't doing anything together anymore." Tom picked his fork back up and took another bite of chicken. They both thought about what the future might hold for their family. They each wanted Laura to wake up, but were they still headed down the same path as before the accident? That was the unknown piece of the puzzle.

There was a knock on the door that startled them both. It was already getting dark and they didn't know who it could be. Tony let himself in and joined them in the kitchen.

"Hey guys, just wanted to check on you both," Tony said. He looked down at the plate of food in front of them and knew instantly that it was from the party. "Aw, you managed to smuggle some food out I see."

"No, I helped Rose clean up, so she offered," Lou replied, stubbornly.

Tony pulled up a chair and he filled them in on how much fun Hannah had at the party. She bounced until her face was red, she ate until she couldn't eat anymore and requested so many animal balloons, the clown cut her off. They all laughed at what seemed like such a normal day for them. Tom excused himself to bed which left Lou and Tony alone.

"What else do you know about mom and dad's separation? Was it going to happen even before Stanley entered the picture?" Lou asked.

Lou could see that Tony was trying to think of what and how to say it. It was still new to her, but not to him. "It's really hard to know for sure," Tony finally answered. "Mom and dad just eventually stopped doing things together. Was it because she found someone else to do things with or was she just looking for something or someone to make her happy again? We may never really know the answer to that, except from mom."

"I guess that's true," said Lou. "I just can't help but think it was probably going on longer than we know, mom being unhappy. Could it have been all the way back to our childhood?" Lou got up to refill her glass with water, took a drink and sat back down. "It changes so much if it's true."

"No it doesn't. They stayed together all of these years, that has to mean something. If they were that unhappy, they could have separated, like now," Tony reasoned.

"Well, I for one, am getting tired of thinking about it and talking about it. It's just that seeing Stanley today and talking to him, well, it just brought up so many thoughts."

"You talked to him? What did you say?"

"Yes I did. I asked him if he loved mom and if he knew she was married. He said 'yes' to everything." Lou looked at Tony, "I thought you had met him before?"

"Yes, but I never really talked to him. There were a couple of times he came to the house, either he was dropping mom off or picking her up, but nothing more than 'hello.'"

Lou wanted to change the subject. "Do you want some chocolate cake? There is still some left from the other day."

"Chocolate cake, who made it?"

Lou tried to look offended, "I did, thank you very much, big brother!"

They both laughed as she cut a piece for him and one for herself. "You know, this reminds me, your birthday is coming up," Tony said.

Lou rolled her eyes as she put another piece of cake in her mouth. "It's not a big deal," she replied.

"How old are you turning, twenty nine? Oh yes, it is a big deal because it's all down hill from there!"

Lou pretended like she was going to fling chocolate cake at him using her fork. They laughed like old times. It felt good to be sitting in their family home, laughing in the kitchen. Tony hadn't heard that sound in years, it was good to have Lou back even if only for a few weeks. Tony never told Lou how he really felt about her leaving so suddenly after graduation. Even though he was in college at the time, he was still living at home. They were partners in crime and he lost his partner. It changed their relationship for him. Being here with her now feels good again.

"Bonfire!" Tony exclaimed, while holding his fork high in the air.

"What?"

"That's what we will do to celebrate your getting older, a bonfire. We will invite everyone, if that's okay with you?"

"Of course, why not go out with a bang?" Lou replied.

"Then it's settled. Leave all the details to me. Suni and I will get the pizzas, the beer, chips and the cake."

"Wow, don't ruin the surprise," Lou teased.

"Oh there will be plenty of time for surprises later," Tony teased back. With his plan all settled, Tony excused himself, hugged his sister and left.

Lou cleaned up the dishes and heard her phone ringing. She dried her hands and went into the living room to find her phone. It was Ben.

"Hey babe, I miss you."

"Hi Ben, I miss you, too."

"Well, let's fix that, come home."

"You know I can't do that while mom is still in a coma."

"Louise, you know as well as I do that comas can last months, even years. Is it really practical to be there the entire time?"

Lou did know that and she was starting to think it was time to return to her life. "I will compromise. I will give it a few more days and then come home, okay?"

"Oh babe, that sounds wonderful. I love you."

"Love you, too. Good night."

Lou didn't know if she could actually leave while her mother was still in a comatose state. She needed a miracle, a sign, or both.

Chapter 8

Tonight was the bonfire celebrating Lou's last year of being in her twenties. Tony had taken care of all the arrangements for this last minute party. It was a Saturday night, the middle of August and the weather was going to cooperate. Lou helped to collect some driftwood and started a pile on the beach. This bonfire would be epic. Lou didn't even care who came, she was going to celebrate her birthday.

Tom was sitting on the beach when Tony, Suni and Hannah arrived. Hannah immediately went to her grandpa and wanted to sit on his lap. Suni went into the kitchen to help Lou arrange the food. Suni unpacked bags of hot dogs, buns, chips, pop and cookies. Tony came up behind her with five pizzas, two cases of beer and a cake. It was enough food to feed the neighborhood. She helped arranged it all as best as she could and then walked away. She had a beach chair with her name on it calling to her.

The sun was low on the horizon, but wouldn't set for another hour or so. As soon as Lou walked outside, she saw Jude followed by Avery. They both came over to wish her a happy birthday, but Jude lingered.

"How are you doing? I haven't seen much of you since our chocolate cake date," Jude joked.

Lou smiled, "Well I see you have been busy. I've been busy, too."

"We didn't come together, for the record. I think she just waited until I got here," Jude said.

"It doesn't matter. Not tonight. Tonight is all about me!" Lou raised her beer as a private toast to herself.

"Oh, okay, I see how it's gonna be," Jude teased back. He grabbed Lou around the waist and tried to get the beer from her hand. They were twisting and laughing when Avery came to interrupt them.

"Jude, I need your help inside, please," Avery said, coldly.

Lou and Jude were still laughing as Jude followed Avery into the house, proudly holding the beer he had just taken out of Lou's hand. It was okay. Lou wasn't going to let anything bother her tonight. The sight of Brian in his cast let her know Brad and Lisa had made it. Lou was happy for another opportunity to make things right between them. Brad was wearing some loud swim trunks, he must be prepared to swim tonight. Lisa had on a bright yellow sundress that made her tan look even darker. They were a striking couple. They made their way to her and offered best wishes for a great birthday. Lou thanked them for coming and asked about Brian.

"He's great, thanks to you. Brian is tough as nails. The cast sure isn't slowing him down, except for wanting to go swimming," Lisa replied.

Lou's phone started ringing and she looked at it. It was Ben. She wasn't going to talk to him right now.

"Who's Ben?" Brad asked. Lisa had gone into the kitchen to see if she could help.

Lou looked out into the water, the sun was getting lower and the colors, darker. She didn't have to answer him and didn't owe him any explanation, except maybe she did.

"He's my boyfriend back in New York."

"Does Jude know?"

"Yes, he does."

Brad turned to face her, "You'd better not break Jude's heart, again. I see how you two are, it's like you are picking up right where you left things."

Lou turned to Brad, "It's not like that. We talked things out and we are friends again, just friends." She knew how protective he was of Jude, especially when it came to her. Jude was turning twenty nine soon, too. He can take care of himself. Just then Brian came up to Lou and gave her a hug.

"Happy birthday, Dr. Lou and thank you for helping to fix my arm," Brian said.

"You're so welcome, Brian," Lou answered. "I think you are the best patient I have ever had!" Brian smiled at the compliment. "I think there's some pizza and cookies inside if you want some."

All three of them went inside to get some food. Lou was just glad that the confrontation was over. She didn't like taking another punch to the chin, she actually hoped everyone was done with punching by now, but she didn't flinch. Lou saw Leon arrive, but not sure where he was now. The sun was dropping into the horizon and Tony came to light the bonfire. With cheers and fanfare, it was lit. Lou moved her chair next to her father and asked if he wanted something to eat.

"I've had plenty already," he replied. "Everyone has been bringing me plates of food. I'm now just enjoying the view." They sat without saying anything more. The kids were running around and playing in the sand. The guys were bringing over large logs to sit on with their significant others. It was nice to see everyone together again.

Lou went inside to get another beer. She saw Rose and Avery standing in the kitchen. They both turned when they heard Lou approach and held out a small blue box.

"Happy birthday, Lou," they said in unison.

"We wanted to get you something nice and we coordinated," said Rose.

Lou was genuinely touched and they seemed sincere. "Thank you, guys." Lou opened the square blue box and was surprised to see a matching set of earrings and a necklace.

"It's beach glass, from Lake Erie. We sell them in the store where I work," said Avery.

Rose took out the necklace and put it on her. Lou put the earrings on herself. She felt the colorful, shiny pieces of rounded glass. She was so touched by the gesture, she felt off balance looking at the two of them.

"Thank you both so much." Lou hugged her friends and said she hoped this was a new beginning for all of them. If nothing else, it was encouraging.

As Rose and Avery went back out to the bonfire, Lou stayed in the kitchen and grabbed a beer. It was more than she could hope, her best friends were accepting her again. With one hand still fingering the smooth stones on the necklace, Lou returned to the bonfire. She looked for an empty seat on one of the logs. She saw one, it was a log facing the lake. Lou sat down next to Tony and put her arm around him.

"Thank you for this," said Lou.

"Well, I can't take credit for the sunset, or the weather, or food, but I'll take that smile any day."

"You know what I mean, Tony."

"I do," Tony replied as he nudged her. "I am happy to see you smile. You came home amid trauma and drama and you carried yourself like the professional you are. I'm impressed."

"It hasn't been easy."

"Oh I know it hasn't. That's what makes me love you even more." Tony paused, "Are you happy in New York City?"

"Yes," answered Lou.

"Are you happy with Ben?"

Lou shifted a little on the log. "You know, I haven't told anyone this, but Ben proposed to me right before I came home. The same night I got the call about mom."

Tony was visibly surprised. "What did you say?"

Lou turned to her brother, "I never gave him an answer."

"But he's been calling ten times a day, you still never answered him?"

"No." Lou explained the night Ben took her out to dinner after receiving his award. It was a fancy restaurant, they were all dressed up and it felt nice. But when Ben took that little velvet box out of his pocket, she froze. Her life suddenly flashed before her eyes of dinner parties, award ceremonies, limos, high rise apartments and wedding bells. It was too much. She was quite literally saved by the bell on her phone. She had looked down and saw 'Dad'. It was her excuse to exit the situation and focus on something else. When she went back to the table, she told him she had to go home.

"How did he take it?"

"Well, he actually misunderstood, or rather, I didn't explain which home I meant. He called me while I was catching my flight because he was at my apartment. I explained about mom and that I would call him when I landed."

"But why haven't you told anyone else he proposed?" Just as Tony asked the question, Jude appeared behind them. Tony stood up, shook his hand and said something about needing to use the restroom. Lou remained on the log, looking out into the darkening lake.

"May I?" Jude asked before sitting down.

"Of course."

"Ben proposed?"

"Yes." Lou answered quietly.

"Why didn't you tell me?"

Lou glanced over at Jude, who was staring out into the dark water. "I didn't tell anyone. I didn't know how. Because I don't know what my answer is going to be."

"How do you not know the answer?" Jude wondered out loud. "Do you love him?"

Lou hesitated a beat too long, "yes."

"It sounds to me like you have a great life. Everything you dreamed of when you were in high school."

Lou took a sip of her beer. She felt comfortable with Jude. She watched the moonlight dance on the water, heard the laughter behind them and probably had one too many beers. "I don't know if it's what I want anymore."

"Which part?" Jude asked.

Lou looked at Jude who was now looking at her, "I'm honestly not sure."

Jude leaned over and rubbed shoulders with Lou, "everyone deserves the right to be happy in three areas: what they do, where they live and who they are with. If any of those don't make you happy, then you have the freedom to change any of them." Jude looked over at Lou. "Or all of them," he added.

Lou was starting to feel emotional. She didn't know if it was the alcohol, the raw honesty of the conversation, or the physical closeness of Jude. Lou looked over at Jude and he met her gaze. They held it for several seconds before she asked if he was happy.

"Sometimes," Jude answered. "I'm happy with two out of three." Jude winked at Lou.

Jude took a long drink from his beer. She wondered if it was the 'who he's with' that he was not happy with right now. She watched him.

"Of course, that's all just my opinion," Jude added.

Lou nudged him back with her shoulder, "how come you never left Erie?"

Jude let out a soft laugh, "I guess I'm just happy here. But seriously, I've traveled here and there for work, for pleasure, but there's no better feeling than coming home. It's where I'm the happiest."

"You know, it's so easy to come to the beach, look out at the lake and see nothing but water and sand. You can imagine it's just you in the world and believe that you can do anything." Lou took a sip of her beer. "I became a pediatrician because of what happened on that lake. I decided I would never again be put in a position of not knowing how to help a child, like your brother, Jackson. I wanted to make a difference and do something important."

Lou started tearing up. Jude took her hands in his and turned towards her. "I tried that route, too. I became a lifeguard and sat on top of that stand every summer to help stop drownings in the lake. Maybe I did when I blew my whistle or yelled at kids to come closer to the shore. Maybe I prevented parents and siblings from going through what my family went through." Jude squeezed her hands and Lou looked in his eyes, "But, I learned it's not up to us to save the world. That's not our guilt to bear. Jack's drowning was a tragic accident, one I will never forget, but we have to forgive ourselves, we were just kids. I've come to terms with it. I have forgiven myself and you should, too."

Jude gave Lou a hug. It was warm and friendly, just what she needed. "I'm here for you, no matter what you decide," Jude added. "Also, I never got to give you your birthday gift." He pulled out a small velvet bag and dumped the contents into Lou's hand. It was a bracelet made from beach glass. "I coordinated with the girls. I hope you like it." Jude attached the clasp as he put it on her wrist. They both stood up and hugged.

"I love it, thank you!" Looking around, she realize the crowd had dwindled.

"This was so much fun but it's late and I'm tired," Lou said. She took her beer into the kitchen and leaned on the counter. She exhaled slow and steady. When she turned around she saw Jude walking towards her. He was walking with an expression of determination.

Jude put his hands on her waist. "For the record, I've never stopped loving you and I never will. I just wanted you to know that." Jude leaned in to kiss her and Lou responded. It was slow and cautious. He had no right to kiss her, she had a boyfriend, maybe even a fiancé, but she was here, single and beautiful in her windblown hair and cheeks pink from the beer. The kiss might have started soft, but it became more like the kisses of their past, of lovers. It was Jude who pulled away. They both stood there looking at each other for a moment before he said 'goodnight' and simply turned and walked out.

Chapter 9

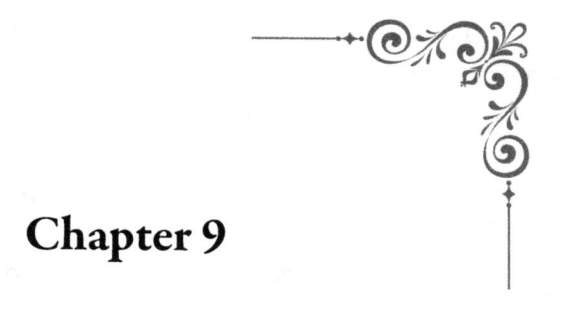

Lou was making breakfast when her father entered the kitchen.
"Did you enjoy your party, Lou?"
"I enjoyed every minute of it, thank you!"
"I see you've already cleaned up," her father said.
"Actually, everyone kept it up all evening, so there were only a few odds and ends this morning to contend with." Lou replied. "Tony called earlier. He wants to take the boat out. Are you up for a boat ride today?"
"Oh no, but you go. I'll stay around here or maybe go sit with your mother. Don't worry about me."
"Okay, if you're sure." He was. Lou went upstairs to pack a bag for the boat.
Lou was excited to go out on the old boat. Their father gave it to Tony when he no longer wanted the hassle of the upkeep. That was fine with him. He had a dock in his backyard and got a lot of use out of it. When Lou pulled into Tony's driveway, her stomach dropped. Jude's truck was parked next to her brother's. Of course Tony would have no way of knowing what happened between her and Jude last night, but they did.
She tried to keep her mood cheerful when she walked in the house. Hannah ran right into her arms and showed her Aunt Lou the stuffed animal she was bringing on the boat.
"Her name is Bunny," Hannah proudly said while showing her stuffed pink bunny.

"Pleasure to meet you, Bunny," Lou replied. Hannah giggled and wanted to be put back down. Lou found the adults in the kitchen. She avoided eye contact with Jude and instead asked Suni what she could do.

"Everything's already loaded on the boat, so really it's just us," said Suni.

"Come on everyone, let's go!" Called Tony from out back.

Lou and Jude reached the doorway at the same time. He stepped aside and gestured that she should go first. She hoped things weren't going to be this awkward between them. Lou didn't want her brother or sister-in-law to pick up on it.

Unlike yesterday, there was some rain forecast for today, but it wasn't supposed to hit this area until evening. That is the main reason for Tony wanting to start the outing early. He was in the captain's chair, while Jude and Lou helped untie the boat from the dock.

"I see you never changed the name, Tony," Lou said.

"How can I change 'Lady Laura'? Mom and dad have had her forever. It's her name," Tony answered.

It was a fairly large boat, larger than Jude's fishing boat. This one was made for cruising around and sunbathing. Suni and Lou took their seats up front where the benches were. They didn't wear swimsuits, a bit too chilly for that today, but their shorts and t-shirts would still allow them to get a sun tan. The guys talked sports the entire time. Everyone kept a close eye on Hannah, who wasn't even allowed to step on the boat without her life jacket on. Bunny didn't need a life jacket, Bunny could swim.

When they found the perfect spot, Tony dropped anchor and brought out the coolers. There was plenty of food left from last night, so Suni made lunch, complete with chips, cookies and pop. Lou didn't mind eating the same food again, she just didn't want to be reminded of last night. After everything wonderful that happened on her birthday, the kiss was the only thing she remembered. She was sure it was the same for Jude.

Jude tried to keep his cool all afternoon. He didn't want to bring up the kiss with Lou, but knew the longer they didn't talk about it, the more awkward they would feel around each other. He did not regret kissing her, he just wished it wasn't so weird now. Maybe he should just apologize, he thought. He just wanted to get through this day. When Tony invited him to the boat ride, he didn't know Lou would be there. He was sure she didn't know about him, either. They were adults, they could act like nothing happened for a day.

The clap of the thunder made everyone jump. It also put everyone into motion. The ladies were collecting the food and trash so it wouldn't blow away, the guys were storing the coolers and pulling up the anchor. They began to drift. Another clap of thunder, only this time the dark clouds rolled in with it. It seemed to go from one o'clock in the afternoon to eight at night in seconds. Hannah was crying but safely in a seat in the back. Another thunder clap and Hannah was crying louder.

"Bunny! Bunny!" Hannah yelled.

"Honey, Bunny is okay. He's not afraid," Suni said to Hannah, trying to soothe her crying daughter.

"Bunny can't swim! Buuuuunny!" Hannah continued to wail.

With the anchor pulled up they started the engine. They couldn't go as fast as they wanted to because they were in a no wake zone. Rain was starting to fall and the ladies were still trying to secure anything that could fly away. The wind and rain were picking up. Suni put Hannah back on the chair and told her not to move. Hannah turned her head to see Bunny just as his head went under water. She had lost hold of Bunny when the last thunder clap made her jump. Hannah unbuckled her life jacket so she could give it to Bunny. With the quickness of a five year old, she was safely in her seat one second and gone the next.

Hannah had tried to give her life jacket to Bunny, but Bunny was barely visible. Hannah leaned over the edge of the boat but the rain made it slippery. She leaned too far and fell in the water. The adults were keeping and eye on her, but also concerned about getting out of there. They were almost out of the no wake zone when Suni turned and saw an empty seat where Hannah was a second ago.

"Hannah! Hannah! HANNAH!" Suni's screams were all they could hear over the rain and thunder.

All heads turned to the back of the boat. Hannah was gone. Tony shut down the boat. Tony, Jude and Lou all shared a look of 'not again'. Jude was the first one in the water, his lifeguard instinct taking over without hesitation. Tony thought to turn the boat around but without knowing when she fell in, he didn't want to risk hitting her. Suni was still crying and screaming for her daughter when Lou was next to jump in, followed by Tony. Suni scanned the water for any sign of Hannah, but the wind and rain weren't helping.

Jude was further out and heard splashing up ahead. He took a chance and headed in that direction. Lou and Tony each went different directions to have a larger search radius. But Jude stayed straight, towards the splashing sound. Everyone was yelling her name. Jude heard a response. He was a strong swimmer, stronger than the rest, he knew. He was not going to let another child drown on his watch, not if he had another breath in his body. The cry became louder as Jude got closer. He knew Hannah could swim, something he made sure every child in his life learned, but in these conditions, even a strong swimmer could drown.

On the boat, Suni tried scanning the water in every direction. Tony was swimming off the port side and Lou was swimming off starboard. Jude had headed off the stern, his instinct was that we passed her and she was behind them. He wasn't completely sure he was right until he spotted her little face coming up for air. Jude swooped one arm under the little girl's chest and turned back towards the boat.

"I've got her! I've got her!" Jude yelled as loud as he could.

Suni noticed his change in direction and yelled back, "Did you find her?"

"Yes, I've got her!" Jude continued to yell and swim.

Suni put her hands to her mouth and yelled to Tony and Lou. "He found her!" Upon hearing this, they also started swimming back to the boat. Tony climbed in and started the motor. Lou climbed in and reached down to help lift Hannah into the boat. She was conscious and breathing, but took in a lot of water. Lou took over medical treatment of Hannah as Jude slowly climbed into the boat and lowered himself onto the floor. Jude was exhausted and Lou knew he never would have stopped until he found her or drowned while trying. She was glad it was the former and not the latter.

Lou turned Hannah on her side and let her cough the water out. She was responding well and becoming alert. Suni sat down and held her. Everyone was emotional and crying. Lou never expected to be in a boat with Tony and Jude reliving Jack's drowning. At least this one had a happy ending.

"Take us home, Tony," Lou yelled. "This storm is getting worse. None of us should be out here."

Tony hit the gas and got them home as fast as possible. Everyone remained huddled under the roof that covered the captain's chair. Tony was navigating through the rain and waves, Suni was holding Hannah tight, muffling her sobs, and Jude had his arms around Lou because she was shivering. Lou thought of their kiss, as she stood wrapped in Jude's arms. When the family's dock came into view, everyone breathed a sigh of relief. Tony kept saying how sorry he was, he thought they would beat the storm.

"It's okay, everyone is home safe," Lou told her brother after giving him a hug.

Jude gave Tony a slap on the shoulder, "It's all good."

Now that the adrenaline rush was over, Tony realized how badly this could have ended. He hugged his daughter and looked at Jude and Lou. "I don't know what we would have done if you both weren't here today." Jude looked at Lou and gave her a side hug.

"Well, this dynamic duo had better leave you guys alone," Jude said.

"Give her plenty of fluids and lots of rest," Lou instructed to Suni.

Tony checked his phone, "You guys better get back to your homes. There's more rain coming soon." Lou and Jude nodded in agreement and left the Jensen family to rest for the night.

Chapter 10

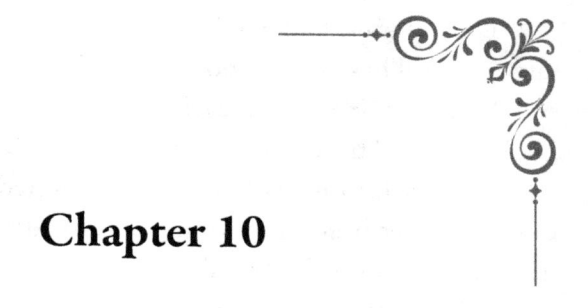

Jude and Lou stood on Tony's front porch waiting for the right time to make a run for each of their cars. They waited between lightning and claps of thunder to run into the rain. They both said a countdown together and then ran. Lou sat for a minute before starting the engine. She was freezing and shaking and took a sip of the water she left in the car. Jude was still sitting in his truck, but then got out. Lou was startled when he started knocking on her window. Lou unlocked the doors and Jude sat down next to her.

"My truck won't start."

"Well, leave it here. I can drop you off and you can get it tomorrow," Lou said.

"Thanks," Jude answered.

Lou started the car and backed out of the driveway. She headed towards Jude's house and knew it wouldn't take long to get there. Neither one of them wanted to talk about what had just happened. Not what happened today or last night. Lou felt like the sparks and electricity she felt inside the car were far more dangerous than anything happening outside. Jude was trying with every fiber of his being to keep looking straight ahead. They were almost to his house. A couple more minutes and she was pulling into his driveway. She put her car into park and took her foot off the gas. Jude finally broke the silence.

"Do you want to come inside? I need a drink after today," Jude said. Lou still hesitated. "Look, I can offer a change of clothes and a stiff drink, maybe even some leftovers if we are lucky."

Lou turned the car off. "Okay, just until the storm passes."

They ran into Jude's house and he turned on the light switch. Lou had never been in his house. Brad had kept the family home, Jude bought this little bungalow with an equally sized building out back. His work shed, he called it. Jude excused himself and ran upstairs to get some dry clothes. He returned with a pair of gray sweatpants and a Steelers t-shirt for Lou. He was wearing blue sweatpants and a Bills t-shirt. "Bills?" She asked.

"Hey, they're doing really good right now," Jude joked back.

Lou went upstairs to change. She wasn't sure which door led to where, so she wasn't surprised when the first door she opened wasn't the bathroom. It was Jude's room. She didn't dare turn any lights on so she could only get a general sense of his presence here. He made his bed and picked up his clothes, that was a good sign. She went further down the hall and found the bathroom. Here she turned on the light and stared at her reflection. What was she doing here? She was playing with fire. She would have one drink, maybe something to eat and leave. She would return his clothes when she saw him next or leave them with Tony.

Jude was well aware that Lou had never been inside his home. He actually had no intention of her ever seeing it. He quickly scanned the rooms downstairs and felt they were adequately tidy. Jude had lived alone for ten years, he was not messy or dirty. Dishes were always clean and carpets were always vacuumed. Clothes were washed and his bed was made. Jude could hear footsteps upstairs. Why didn't he leave the bathroom light on for her? She wouldn't know which room was which. He found whiskey and two glasses. In the fridge, he found yesterday's roast and mashed potatoes. He made two plates and heated them up.

When Lou entered the kitchen her stomach started grumbling. She was hungrier than she thought. "Mmm, what's that smell?"

"It's just my leftover roast from yesterday," Jude answered.

"You cook?"

"Yes. You?"

Lou looked around the room, "I love to cook. It's relaxing."

"I feel the same way." Jude handed her one of the whiskey glasses. "To you," he announced.

"To us," she corrected.

Jude winked at her and they both took a sip. He pulled one of the kitchen chairs out for her and she sat down in front of the steaming plate of roast, mashed potatoes and carrots. "It smells delicious."

"I hope you like it." Jude said.

Lou thought it was the most delicious roast she had ever eaten. They ate in comfortable silence, taking turns sipping whiskey and eating roast. Outside, the weather continued to get worse with threatening thunder, lightning and rain. Jude and Lou were unconcerned for now. They were enjoying this quiet time, just the two of them. Lou's phone rang. It was Ben.

"I'd better go," Lou said. She made no move to get up. "What are we doing here? I can't just sit here and pretend to play house. I have a life in New York. I'm going to be leaving soon."

It was Jude who stood up first, "You don't think I know that? That I'm not reminded every time I see you that you belong to someone else? I'm sorry that I was never good enough, not a good enough reason for you to stay here."

Lou walked over to Jude, "that was never the reason I left, you were never the reason. I just had big, stupid dreams. Bigger than this city could provide. At least that's what I believed then." Her phone rang again.

"I know in my head that it was the right decision for you. It just took me ten years to realize that," Jude said.

Lou heard the notification of another voicemail. Ben would have to wait. "I'd better go. Thank you for dinner, the drink and the clothes." Just as Lou was gathering her wet clothes, the whole house went dark. Jude went to the front door and saw the whole neighborhood was without power.

"I'm sorry, but it's just not safe for you to drive. A power line is probably down and it could be in the street," Jude said. "Call your dad, make sure he's okay. Tell him to sleep on the couch if he's not already upstairs."

Lou did what Jude said. She knew what he said was true, it wasn't safe to drive. There could be multiple power lines down and with the wind and rain, it was just too dangerous to chance it in the dark. After making sure her father was safe, Lou called Tony. They were fine.

While she was making her calls, Jude gathered an assortment of candles and flashlights. He even slid a gun in the kitchen drawer when he thought she wasn't looking.

"Well we didn't have dinner by candlelight, but we can have dessert. I have ice cream that is probably going to melt if we don't eat it," he announced.

"Well then, I suppose we had better eat it," she agreed. If she wasn't leaving, she would make the most of the situation.

Jude returned with two bowls of ice cream and two spoons. They sat together on the couch surrounded by candles. Playing with fire. There couldn't be a stronger warning for her than open flames. They settled onto the couch eating the melting chocolate ice cream.

"Do you remember the first time I took you to Sara's for ice cream?" Jude asked.

"Yes, I was so excited to have the orange and vanilla swirl cone, but when I grabbed it and turned around it landed on the concrete."

"And you looked so sad the waitress felt so sorry for you, she gave you another one for free!"

"That was the day we spent all day on Presque Isle, just laying on the beach, renting bikes, walking the trails and then ice cream at Sara's. It was a great day."

They finished their ice cream and Jude reached for her bowl. "I'll wash them."

Lou followed him into the kitchen, "I'll dry." As he handed her each item to dry, their hands touched and it was like touching a hot stove. Neither one of them spoke. With the chore done, they stood silent in the kitchen.

Lou finally broke the silence, "You never did give me a tour of your house."

Jude stepped closer to her, "It's not very big, just a few rooms upstairs and downstairs."

"Well, I've seen the downstairs," she whispered.

Jude closed the distance between them in one step. They kissed with a passion that they had been denying. This was not the cautious kiss from inside her kitchen, this was the desire that they thought they quenched a decade ago. Their hands were searching each other, backs, necks, arms and chests. Lou tried taking Jude's shirt off, but instead Jude picked her up and carried her up the stairs. They entered the room she walked into earlier that evening. He sat her on his bed while he removed his shirt. Lou removed hers and Jude joined her on the bed.

Jude stopped when Lou let out a moan. "What is it?"

"Nothing, I just had a muscle spasm," Lou answered. Jude stood up. "What's wrong?" Lou asked.

"This. Us. Are you sure about this?" Jude asked. "I can't deny that I want this to happen, but I also don't want to cause any problems for you."

Lou didn't reply. Instead she stood up and took his hand and placed it on her hip. She took the other one and kissed all the way up to his shoulder. She kissed across his slightly hairy chest and over to his other shoulder. Jude dropped the hand that was on her hip as Lou continued to kiss his back. He leaned his head back and waited for her to come back to his front. She didn't. Instead, she slowly slid his sweatpants down to his ankles from behind. When she finally stood in front of him, she could see he was aroused. She loosened the tie on her sweatpants and let them fall.

Jude couldn't take it anymore and wrapped his arms around her and laid her on the bed. His kissing started on her mouth, then quickly turned into searching. Searching her body for the familiar feel of a decade ago. His hands slid over her body. Her hands reached for his firm bottom. The first time they made love that night was fast and urgent. They were both satisfying a hunger they had been denying since they first saw each other at Tony's house a couple of weeks earlier. The second time was slower. They took the time to learn each other's bodies. Kissing, touching, caressing, remembering. There was no room for guilt or remorse. Tonight was all about pleasure. If she left again, like she said she would, could he handle it? Lou never made him any promises, she was always truthful about having a boyfriend back home. This was selfish, but wasn't he allowed to be selfish for once?

They slept together in his bed. The bed in which he also slept with Avery. This was different. He had never felt so whole when he slept with Avery. Lou was different. Secretly he wished she would stay, but he could never say that to her. Her life was in New York. This was her goodbye to him. He watched the sun slowly creep through the window. He didn't want to wake her. Jude enjoyed the feel of her next to him and the smell of her body. He knew this dream would end as soon as she woke up.

Lou slowly stirred in the bed next to Jude. The memories of last night were coming back into her head. She wanted to stay here forever. She was laying naked next to the boy that took every ounce of discipline to leave ten years ago. That was the hardest thing she ever had to do. Last night was perfect. It confirmed what she knew all along, that she would always be Jude's. She didn't feel any guilt, she was taking back control of her life.

Lou turned to put her arm across Jude's chest. "Good morning."

"Good morning," he answered. "Are you hungry?"

Lou looked at the digital clock on the table. It was blinking, so she knew the power was back, but still didn't know the time.

"It's seven," Jude said, raising his arm with the watch.

"Starving."

"Okay, I'll start breakfast if you throw the wet clothes in the dryer," Jude replied.

They both picked up their discarded clothes from the floor. It wasn't awkward. Jude felt happy. He knew it wouldn't last, but for now it was enough. As they followed each other down stairs, they both knew that it was also symbolic of returning to their normal lives. Back to reality.

Chapter 11

Jude and Lou ate their eggs, bacon and toast in silence. It didn't seem this awkward an hour ago. Perhaps the longer they process what they just did, the worse it would become. Only the sound of the dryer kept their thoughts on track. They glanced secretly at each other as they ate, not really wanting to know what the other was thinking. Since they had lost power, they weren't able to charge their phones until this morning. They were both startled when Lou's started ringing, she knew exactly who it was.

"Hello Ben."

"Hi babe, are you okay?" Ben asked, anxiously.

"Yes, why wouldn't I be?"

"Well, I called your father last night. I looked up his number and he said he hasn't seen you since that morning. All night your phone went right to voicemail. I got worried, babe."

"Ben, I'm fine. We had a terrible storm and it took out power lines. I stayed with a friend, power is back on and I'm heading home. I'm sorry you were so worried," she answered. They talked a bit more, mostly it was Lou just trying to relieve Ben's anxiety that something terrible had happened to her.

When she hung up, the drier beeped. She went to get all of their clothes out and change when Jude came in from the side door. "Tree is down."

Jude went to get his chain saw while Lou assessed the area. It wasn't a big tree, but it was blocking his driveway. Luckily it missed

Lou's car. She heard the buzz of the saw and went to help him remove the debris. They worked together for nearly an hour before he felt it was safe enough to drive through. Jude and Lou went back inside to change. She changed into her clothes and he put on jeans and a sweatshirt.

"I'll take you back to your car, but first let me swing by the house and check on dad."

"Sounds good."

When Lou pulled into her driveway, she saw Tony's truck. She immediately felt uneasy. Was her father okay? Lou and Jude each jumped out of the car and ran up the steps. As they both burst through the kitchen door they were looking into the surprised faces of Tom and Tony.

"Where have you been, Lou?" Tony asked. "We've been trying to call you." Then the realization hit that she had been with Jude.

"Is everything okay? You both got your power back on?" She asked Tony and her father.

"Yes, dear, we are fine. Nothing a good night's sleep didn't help," her father said, eyeing her and Jude. Tensions were starting to ease in the room when Lou asked about Hannah.

"She's doing great, no side effects. Thank you, both, again," Tony said.

Jude walked over and shook Tony's hand. "Anytime, brother." Lou walked over and gave him a hug and kissed his cheek.

"What are you doing here, anyway, Tony," asked Lou.

"Well, I was looking at Jude's truck and I think it's just a dead battery. I can jump it, but I was checking to see if dad still had that battery tester."

"Yes, I think I know where it is," Jude offered and headed towards the garage. Tony followed.

Lou took a sip of the coffee her father offered then excused herself to go upstairs. Did they suspect anything? Lou didn't care, they were adults after all. She went to her room and curled up on the bed. Why couldn't her mother just wake up already, so she could go back to her real life? She was making bad decisions and this was not like her. Her life was organized, safe and secure. Home was her past.

Tony followed Jude out into the garage. Jude went to the work table Tom had along the wall and started going through drawers. Tony's presence made him nervous, like when he and Lou were teens and got caught kissing on the porch. Tony was his best friend, but first and foremost, he was her big brother.

"So you got through the storm okay last night?" Tony asked.

"Oh yea, I just lit some candles. Luckily there wasn't any more damage than a tree down in the driveway," Jude answered.

"And Lou was with you?" It wasn't really a question.

"Yes, she was."

There was an awkward silence as Jude continued to fumble around in drawers. It was exacerbated by the fact that Jude couldn't concentrate with Tony nearby which made him search the same drawer multiple times. He opened the first drawer that he searched five minutes ago and there it was. "Found it."

The two friends returned to Tony's house to work on Jude's truck. The ride didn't take long, but felt like hours. Tony needed to say something to Jude. He wasn't even sure what he needed to say. Lou was a grown woman who could make her own decisions and mistakes. He was no longer the big brother who needed to look out for her. But she had a life in New York. He just needed to make sure Jude understood that fact.

Jude lifted the hood of his truck and used the battery tester. "According to this, it's not the battery." Jude ran his hands through his unkempt blond curls and grabbed the bag of tools he kept in the back of his truck, for just in case. They both pushed their sleeves up and got to work. It was a process of elimination when it came to his truck. It was practically older than he was and required a little finesse when it came to fixing what ailed it. Tony knew this truck all too well, also. He tried convincing Jude to buy a new one every time it broke down.

"You've got the money, painter, why not splurge?" Tony would say.

"Have you seen my house?" Jude would joke back. "I'm prioritizing. I need to fix up the house first."

"Oh sure you do," Tony would say. "For who?"

"When I find her, I will let you know!"

Tony had a soft spot for Jude. He always felt that Jude got the short end of the stick most times in life. He prayed that he would find a nice girl to spend his life with, preferably not Avery. They both kept busy tightening nuts and securing screws. They had grease all over their hands and up their arms from reaching down into the engine.

Suni came out with some lemonade which gave them an excuse to stop and take a break. They had been working steadily for an hour and Jude was actually surprised it was taking this long.

"Maybe it's time for a new truck," Suni said.

The two friends looked at each and laughed. "What's so funny?" She asked.

"I've been telling Jude that same thing for years!" Tony said.

Jude sat on the front stoop. "It was my dad's. I guess it's a reminder of him, what he used to be, what we used to be."

Suni walked over to Jude and sat next to him. She put her arm around his shoulders. "I'm sorry, Jude, I didn't know your father, but I don't think he would want his son to settle for an old truck that he left behind. You deserve better. I feel like you are punishing yourself for things that were not your fault and out of your control. The truck is a symbol of all the broken things in your life. Sometimes you can't fix them. Sometimes we just need to move on."

Jude's eyes were tearing up. He had never thought of the truck that way. "Damn Suni, you need to charge people for that kind of therapy!" Jude said. "I never made that comparison before, but I think I know what you mean." He looked at Suni then back at Tony, "You'd better hold on to his one, Tony."

"Oh, I plan to," Tony answered.

"Uncle Jude!" Yelled Hannah as she came bursting through the front door.

"Hey sweetheart, how are you doing?" Jude asked the bouncing girl who just jumped in his lap.

"I'm sad."

"Why on earth is my sunshine sad?"

"Bunny never came back." Hannah said.

Jude looked up at Suni and she just shrugged. "Well, maybe Uncle Jude can help find Bunny. Maybe you're looking in the wrong places." Jude made a mental note to grab another bunny at the store.

Suni made Hannah get back inside so the boys could continue working on the old truck. Hannah smiled and listened to her mother. Tony and Jude picked up more tools and returned to the engine.

"You know, I did want to talk to you about Lou," Tony started.

"I know."

"You seem to be spending a lot of time together lately."

"I know."

"She has a boyfriend. Well, really a fiancé."

"I know!" Jude stopped working and turned to face Tony. "Listen, I understand she's only here for a short time and will be leaving soon. I can handle it. I'm not eighteen anymore."

"I just don't want you to complicate her life any more than it already is," Tony said.

Jude's reply was nearly a whisper, "I know."

Jude was nearly ready to set the piece of junk on fire when he finally found a hose that had become disconnected. "Got it!" He announced.

"Great! Start her up." Tony said.

The puttering start soon revved to a loud roar. Jude packed up his tools and threw them in the back of the truck. "Thanks for your help, buddy." The friends shook hands and Jude drove off. Tony wanted nothing but the best for Jude, but mostly wanted him to get a new truck.

Tony heard his phone ringing, but with his hands all greasy, he didn't want to touch it. He would let it go to voicemail. He picked up his bag of tools and his father's battery tester and headed inside. Suni came running up to him holding her phone.

"It was Lou. Apparently she tried to call you but you didn't answer." Suni was jumping with excitement. "She's awake! Your mom is awake!" Suni came over to hug her husband, but Tony showed her his hands and went to wash up at the sink first.

"Wow! That's wonderful news! We should go over there." Tony said after his hands were clean. They hugged and thanked God for this miracle. Tony called Lou to see what they should do. She said they were going to the hospital. Tony could meet them there if they wanted, but their mother would not be coming home today. They still wanted her for observation one more night. Tony said they would come, but wouldn't stay long. He didn't want to overwhelm her with everyone standing around her bed.

"Okay, we'll meet you there," Lou said. "She's awake!"

Chapter 12

Lou and her father arrived at the hospital first. When they entered Laura's room on the fourth floor, Lou got emotional. The sight of her mother sitting up and awake was the most wonderful thing she had ever seen. They took their usual seats, Tom on one side and Lou on the other, only this time they could talk to her mother and she could respond. Laura smiled when they walked in and held out her hands. They each took one and smiled through the tears.

"Mom, you're awake!" Lou said.

Laura nodded her head, "They tell me I was asleep a long time."

"Eighteen days," Lou answered.

"Oh Laura, it's so good to see you," Tom said. His eyes were filled with tears as he looked at his wife. "I'm so sorry about everything."

"It's okay, Tom, there is nothing to apologize for. I'm back now," Laura replied.

Nurse Kelli entered even more cheerful than in the past two weeks. "Good afternoon, Mrs. Laura, how are you feeling today?" Nurse Kelli directed the question to her patient, but her joy was felt by everyone in the room. "I finally get to ask you that question and actually get an answer!"

"I feel great," Laura announced. "When can I go home?"

"Well, we want you to stay with us one more night, just to be sure there aren't any complications. How does that sound?" Nurse Kelli asked.

"I supposed I can keep you company one more day," Laura answered. She like Nurse Kelli.

"Tom, are we still going on that cruise? We aren't too late to book it are we? I was so looking forward to going on our first cruise. We've never been to Mexico."

Lou and her father looked at each other with confused looks. "What cruise, sweetheart?"

"The one the Bakers were talking about at their party the other night. It sounded wonderful and you promised you would call your travel agent." Laura looked at both of their faces and frowned. "We're too late, aren't we?"

"Mom, what's the last thing you remember? Do you know why you are in the hospital?" Lou asked.

Laura tried to smooth out her graying hair. "Well, the doctor told me I was in an accident and asleep for a couple of weeks." She paused to concentrate. "The last thing I remember was dinner at the Baker's over the holidays." Laura looked at Tom for confirmation.

Tom wasn't sure what to say. "Laura, dear, that was over two years ago. The Baker's moved to Florida after the new year two years ago."

Just then Tony, Suni and Hannah entered the room. Hannah jumped up on the bed to give her grandmother a hug. "I missed you, grandma!"

Laura, after just finding out she didn't remember anything from the last two years, tried to smile at the five year old. "I've missed you more, my sweet Hannah."

Lou stood up and gestured for Tony to meet her out in the hallway. "She has short term memory loss. I don't know if it's temporary or not, but the last thing she remembers is a dinner party that happened over two years ago!" Lou started pacing the hallway.

"Wait, so her and dad.."

"Exactly!" Lou said, running her hands over her face. "They are still in love and planning a cruise together!"

"And Stanley?"

Lou stopped pacing and looked at Tony, "Who knows?"

Tony turned to look at their mother awake and talking to Hannah. "What if her memory comes back?"

"But what if they make better memories in the meantime?" Lou's head was spinning.

"The doctors say she's fine, though, otherwise?" Tony asked Lou.

"Yes."

"Okay, then we play along. Let's encourage them to go on a cruise and hope for the best. She may never get her short term memory back," Tony said.

"Okay." Lou and Tony nodded in agreement and went back into the room.

Laura commented on the balloons Suni was holding that said 'Get Well Soon' and all the flowers that filled the room. "You had a lot of people praying for you to get better," Suni replied.

Nurse Kelli came in followed by a staff member with a dinner tray. "I know this is a wonderful and joyous occasion, but we don't want to overwhelm our patient. Let's let her eat some dinner, okay?"

Everyone moved to give them room as they brought the dinner tray to her bedside. One by one they kissed Laura and said they would be back later. Laura waved and blew kisses as they walked out the door.

Everyone met back at the family home. Lou's head was hurting from thinking about everything. Lou, Tony and their father sat in the kitchen around the island. Suni took Hannah into the living room to watch television. No one was expecting this turn of events. It was such a shock.

Tom had been packing boxes for months in order to move out. He wasn't even sure where he was going to go, but Laura had wanted him out. She had wanted to be with Stanley. How was Stanley going to take it when she says she doesn't know who he is? Laura still felt enough love for Tom that she was excited about going on a cruise with him. That was extremely encouraging. Only time would tell. Lou took out her phone to order pizza. She saw missed calls from Ben and Jude. First pizza.

While waiting for the pizza to be delivered, Lou took her phone outside and sat on one of the logs still on the beach. She sat in silence for a moment enjoying the orange hues of a sun ready to set. This was her favorite moment. Lake Erie sunsets. If she could have this as a painting on her wall, she would be in heaven. She closed her eyes and breathed deep, feeling the tension ease in her body. Then she remembered why she was out here. Her first call was to Ben.

"Hi babe, how are things going?"

"Actually, things are great! Mom woke up about two hours ago and we just came from the hospital."

"That's wonderful! Now you can come home."

Lou was annoyed that his first thought was so selfish. He just wanted her there. But shouldn't she be happy to go back, too? "I guess. They are keeping her for observation tonight."

"You don't sound excited, babe. This really is great news!"

"I know. It's just that she also has some short term memory loss and it's a concern."

"Maybe I should come, then? I can talk to her doctors. I am a neurosurgeon, babe, it's my specialty," Ben offered.

"No, Ben. I'll be home before you know it. There isn't any other reason for me to stay," Lou confirmed.

"Okay, I love you! See you soon."

"Love you, too."

Lou stayed on the log looking out to the dark water. The sun had set and now it was time for the moon. She thought about what Ben said, maybe it was a good idea to have him come or at least talk to the doctors. Coming was out of the question, she concluded. Too many explanations and introductions. She was not ready to get into all of that with Ben. Lou heard someone approaching from behind.

"Is this seat taken?"

"No, dad. Have a seat." Her father sat down beside Lou on the log. "A lot of great memories out here."

"Yes, and hopefully many more to come. I feel like I've been given a second chance with your mother. I could never have hoped or prayed for this kind of outcome. It's a miracle."

"It really does seem like it. You know this means I have to go back to New York, right? Now that mom is awake, she will be coming home and I can get back to my life in the city."

"I know, Lou," her father said as he patted her knee. "You remember I used to call you Lulu when you were a child. You would run to the water and bring me shells or beach glass."

The mention of beach glass made her instinctively touch her bracelet. The bracelet Jude gave her at her birthday party. She had taken the necklace and earrings off when she came home to change this morning, but not the bracelet. Absently, Lou played with the beach glass bracelet. Her father noticed.

"That's a pretty bracelet," Tom said.

"Thank you, I got it for my birthday."

"From?"

"Jude."

Her father took a deep breath. "Erie has always been my home. My parents lived here all their lives and I will, too. I'm happy here. I couldn't imagine myself living anywhere else. Your mom and Tony, too. I don't see them wanting to live anywhere but here on this lake. But you're different, Lou. You liked it here, but you could see yourself living somewhere else. It was that wonder and yearning that took you away." Tom looked at his daughter, "as long as you are happy."

"When I graduated, I felt like the whole world opened. Yes, I like it here, but I wanted more. Maybe that was stupid and selfish, because I hurt a lot of people," Lou admitted.

"You are only twenty nine, you still have plenty of time to conquer the world."

"It's not that I wanted to conquer the world, I wasn't that ambitious," Lou said. She laughed at the idea. "I think I was just searching."

"Did you find it, yet?" Her father asked.

"You know, it was Jude who said we must be happy in three areas: where we live, what we do and who we are with. I had all three, dad. I did. Now I'm not so sure anymore."

"Well, Jude sounds like a smart man."

"Yes, he is." Lou admitted.

"Well, it's been a long day. What do you say we go get some sleep?"

"Sounds perfect."

THE NEXT MORNING, AS Lou was coming down to prepare breakfast, she was surprised to see her father already at the kitchen table drinking coffee.

"Good morning, sweetheart, how did you sleep?"

"Like a log," Lou answered. She poured herself a cup of coffee and sat opposite her father. "What are you doing up so early?"

"I just called the hospital. They will be releasing your mother around eleven this morning."

"That's great news!" Lou replied. "I'll change all the bed linens and do the laundry. Maybe even make mom's famous lasagna." Her phone started ringing and she looked at the screen. "It's Ben."

Tom got up to refill his coffee while she answered Ben's call.

"Good morning, babe, I'm at the airport. Can you pick me up or should I take a taxi? I don't have your parent's address, though." Ben said.

"Wait, back up a minute. You are where?" Lou asked, sure that she had heard him wrong.

"Erie Airport, well Erie International Airport, but I've seen larger houses than this airport. I got the earliest fight I could. Can you come, babe?"

"Hold on." Lou muted the call and spoke to her father. "Ben is here! In Erie, at the airport."

"Wow. Well, I guess we'd better get him, right?" Her father asked, half jokingly.

"Yes, but I've got to get this laundry done before we need to get mom. Can you go?" Lou asked.

"Me? I suppose. I don't even know what he looks like," Tom said.

"Just look for a well dressed man, who looks out of place with no luggage. That will be Ben," Lou said. Her father rolled his eyes. "Okay, seriously I will give you a photo." Tom nodded.

"Hello, Ben? I'm in the middle of laundry and house cleaning before we bring mom home, so my dad is going to come get you, okay?"

"Your dad?"

"Yes, just look for a grumpy old man, that will be dad," Lou replied. She had to dodge the sponge her father threw towards her head. She laughed. "He'll be there in fifteen minutes."

Tom grabbed his keys and went out to his car. Lou's heart was beating out of her chest. She thought she was having a panic attack. She had never had one before, so she wasn't completely sure. She went through a mental checklist in her head and was pretty sure she ticked all the boxes. Fifteen minutes there and fifteen minutes back, she had thirty minutes to prepare for Ben to arrive at her house. This was going to be a long day.

Chapter 13

Ben came through the front door and walked into the living room. He was overdressed, wearing a suit and tie. It looked out of place, but that was Ben. She was sure he owned a pair of jeans, but she was also sure they were designer. Lou had been peeking from the upstairs window so she had seen the car pull in. Tom came in behind Ben and gestured at the couch.

"Make yourself comfortable, Ben. I'm sure Lou will show you later where you will be sleeping. Would you like something to drink or eat?" Tom asked.

"No thank you, Mr. Jensen, I'm fine." Ben replied. He walked over to Lou and gave her a big hug and kiss. "Hi babe, it's so good to see you."

"You, too. How was your flight?" Lou asked.

"Like I was telling your father, I've never been in such a small airplane or such a small airport. It was a new experience for me." Ben replied.

"Well, let's get you settled upstairs. We are going to the hospital to pick up mom soon." Lou showed Ben to her room. It was her childhood room with a double bed. "I'm going to leave you to change if you want, into something more casual. I have to make some more phone calls before we leave." Lou left him in her room. She returned downstairs and went into the kitchen.

Her father was holding up a shot glass in the sink, "What's this?" He asked Lou.

"Never mind," Lou walked over and took it from him. "It has already been a long day and it's only ten in the morning. I called Tony while you were out picking up Ben. I just need to call Jude. He needs to know."

Lou walked outside to the beach to call Jude. She looked back towards the house and saw her bedroom window. She wondered what Ben was doing right now in her room. Would he be going through her drawers, her closet, her bedside table to find hidden secrets? She didn't think he would find anything.

"Hello, Jude?"

"Hi, Lou. How is everything?"

"Things are good. We are still on track to bring mom home this morning. We are going to the hospital at eleven and should be home shortly after."

"Maybe I can meet you back at the house. You'll have enough family and commotion at the hospital without my adding any more." Jude said.

"You have no idea." Lou enunciated each and every word.

"What's wrong, Lou? What happened?" He was getting anxious. "Did somebody say something to you?"

"No, it's nothing like that."

"Lou, you're worrying me. What is it?"

"Ben. He's here. In Erie. At my house," Lou said.

There was silence on the other end, except for what Lou thought sounded like some swear words. "Okay. It'll be fine. I just never thought I would have to see the man face to face."

"Neither did I." Lou admitted. "But he's here and I wanted to give you a heads up with plenty of warning before you just walked into the house."

"Thanks."

"I'll see you later at the house." Lou said.

After hanging up, she checked the time. It was nearly time to leave. She returned back into the house and saw that Ben did not change, only removed his tie. Well, that was Ben. Lou grabbed the keys and they headed towards the hospital. Ben made snide comments about the hospital and staff the whole way up to the fourth floor. Tom and Lou entered Laura's room, but Ben walked down the hallway, seemingly to track down some doctors. That was Ben.

Laura was dressed with two bags of things to bring home with her. She had paperwork, instructions and medications. She just needed the official discharge papers. Tony and his family came into the room and everyone gave Laura a hug and kiss. She was happy to be coming home. It was going to take Tom some time to get used to her saying that. He sat on the bed beside her and took her hand.

"I'm glad you are coming home, too," said Tom.

Ben burst into the room followed by two doctors who looked like they had other places to be. "This is Dr. Malcolm and Dr. Patel. They know your mother's case and agree that her amnesia, or short term memory loss, will most likely be permanent due to where the injuries occurred." Both doctors nodded and it was Dr. Patel who handed Tom his wife's discharge papers.

"Good luck, Mr. and Mrs. Jensen. If you have any questions or concerns, please give the hospital a call," Dr. Patel said.

Ben stepped aside as both doctors exited the room. Tony was the first to step up and hold out his hand. "Hello, I'm Tony, Lou's brother."

"I'm so sorry," said Lou. "Ben, this is my brother, Tony, his wife, Suni and their daughter, Hannah. Everyone, this is Ben, my boyfriend."

Ben looked at her when she said that last word, but she did not look over at him. They weren't engaged, yet, although she would not be surprised if that little black velvet box wasn't in his pocket right now. There was some talking and mingling as Ben made some small talk with Tony. Lou, for one, was ready to get the hell out of this room. "Let's go home!" She announced.

More talking and moving as everyone grabbed vases of flowers, potted plants, balloon bouquets, mom's belongings and mom. They agreed to put Laura in one car and her things in the other. Lou helped her mother in the front seat of the car, which meant her father and Ben were in the backseat. They would survive, it wasn't that far.

When they all arrived home, Laura asked to be taken to the backyard. With Tony on one arm and Lou on the other, Tom follow them out. They sat her on a rocking chair on the porch. They were afraid she was still too unbalanced to walk in the sand. She hasn't walked in eighteen days, so it would take time. Tom sat in the rocking chair beside her. Lou and Tony left them alone to talk. They had some catching up to do, two years' worth.

"You know, a funny thing happened yesterday after you all left," Laura said.

"What's that, dear."

"A strange man came into my room and sat down next to me. He took my hand and said he was so happy I was awake. I pulled my hand away from his and rang the nurse. The nurse came and asked him to leave. I think he had the wrong room." Laura explained.

Tom never knew when he should bring up Stanley, but it seemed now was the time.

"So you didn't know that man?"

"No," Laura replied.

"Does the name Stanley Frey mean anything to you?" Tom asked.

"No, should it?"

"No," Tom said and looked out towards the water.

While Tom and Laura were outside getting reacquainted, Lou and Suni were preparing lunch. They weren't really expecting anyone else, except Jude. He will probably be coming around one. Lou had one hour to figure out how she was going to stay calm sitting with Ben and Jude in the same room.

Hannah went out to sit with her grandparents. Laura didn't remember how she had gotten so big. Laura found that certain things were making her sad, that she had lost precious time. It was an unsettling thought. She knew she might never remember everything, but she was worried about the things she was forgetting. Tom told her not to be too hard on herself. Tom held her hand. Her memory may come back, but if it didn't, that was okay, too.

Tony went into the living room to sit with Ben. He was enjoying looking at all the photos, bookshelves, and music collection. "It's like a time capsule in here," Ben said. "Louise, are these pictures of you?" Ben yelled from the other room.

"If it's a picture of a girl, then yes," Lou joked.

"Well, I'm not sure, that's why I asked. It looks like two little boys playing in the sand."

"Oh, it's probably me. I did have my tomboy phase growing up," Lou answered.

Lou came into the living room to see what Ben was getting into. "I thought you would keep him out of trouble," Lou said to Tony.

"I never made any promises. It's not my fault if he finds every embarrassing photo of you in this house," Tony joked.

Ben laughed. "I'm having fun. Can't I have a little fun, Louise?"

"Sure, but not at my expense," Lou answered.

Ben kissed her. "Have I told you how much I've missed you?"

"Not in the last ten minutes, no." Lou answered.

"You know, I'm still waiting for an answer," Ben reminded Lou. "Did she tell you I proposed right before she came here?"

"Ben, not here. Not now," Lou said harshly.

"Okay, okay, not now." Ben moved around the room. "Here you are all dressed up."

Without even looking, Lou knew exactly which picture he found. Senior prom.

"Who's the boy?" Ben asked.

Tony gave Lou a quick look, realizing for the first time that Lou never mentioned Jude to Ben. "That is Jude."

"Was he your boyfriend?"

"Yes."

"Was it serious?"

"At the time, yes," Lou admitted.

There was a knock on the side door. Lou knew immediately who it was. She was starting to feel lightheaded. Lou stumbled on her own feet as she turned towards the kitchen just as Jude caught her arm and held her. Lou pulled away and went to get some water. Jude, looking past her shoulder saw a man in a suit holding their senior prom picture. Ben looked from the picture to the man who was exactly ten years older than the version in the photo.

"Hi, I'm Jude. You must be Ben."

"Yes," answered Ben. "I see you've heard of me, but I have never heard of you." Ben put the prom picture back on the table where he found it. "Tell me why an ex-boyfriend is still hanging around the house?"

Jude, who had arrived in a red polo shirt and blue jeans was now having to defend himself to a man wearing a suit in the middle of the living room. It was such an odd picture. Jude's six foot frame was slightly taller than Ben, but when Jude put his hands on his hips and straightened up, he looked feet taller rather than inches. Jude was clenching his jaw and remained silent. Why did he have to defend himself to anyone?

"Jude is my best friend, Ben," Tony interrupted. It was like watching a stand off at high noon. "He is here to check on my mother." Tony looked over at Jude and motioned to the backyard. "Mom and dad are sitting out back, Jude. Why don't you go say 'hi.'"

"Nice meeting you," Jude said as he turned and went out the back door.

"What the hell was that all about?" Tony asked Ben.

"Well what am I supposed to think? The one person Louise never mentioned is an ex boyfriend who just happens to walk through the door. It's a little suspicious. Especially since she doesn't take my calls, doesn't text back and still hasn't answered my proposal."

Tony saw that Ben was getting frustrated and upset. "Let's go into the kitchen and get a drink. I know where they keep the whiskey." The two men entered the kitchen just as the lasagna was coming out of the oven. There was also salad, rolls and brownies.

"Dinner is ready," Lou announced.

"Drinks first," Tony said. He took two shot glasses out of the cupboard and poured them each a shot of whiskey. "To mom!" They said.

"Where's mine?" Lou asked.

"And mine," asked Suni.

Ben gave his glass to Lou and Tony gave his to his wife. After refilling the glasses, they made their toast and drank. Everyone made a plate of food and spread out around the house and beach. Tony didn't tell Lou there were sparks flying earlier, instead he tried to keep the men in separate rooms. This was easier said than done, since Jude was friends with everyone.

Jude came into the kitchen where Ben and Lou were eating.

"Hey Lou, is there anything else I can help with?" Jude asked.

"Yes, you can help me by answering why my girlfriend hasn't been answering my calls?" Ben asked Jude.

"Maybe that's something you should be asking your girlfriend," Jude answered.

"I would, but she hasn't exactly been telling me everything that has been happening around here lately." Ben glared at Jude. Jude took a step closer to him and Ben stood up.

"If there is something you are insinuating, then just come right out and say it," Jude said to Ben. They each took another step closer to each other.

"STOP!" Lou yelled. "Both of you! Enough. He is an ex, you are my boyfriend. Why is that so hard for you to understand." This time Lou spoke directly to Ben.

They both took steps backward and seemed to calm down. Jude left the kitchen and found Hannah. Lou turned to Ben and took his hands. Ben's dark hair was messed up from the confrontation. Lou used her fingers to put it back into place. His brown eyes looked sad. "I have known Jude since we were kids, he is Tony's best friend. He comes around a lot. I didn't know that until I came home. It was awkward at first, but we talked and now we are friends again."

"Who broke up with whom?" Ben asked.

"What? Why does it matter? We broke up."

"Who, Louise?" Ben asked, again.

"I broke up with him. It's over," Lou said softly.

Ben replied even softer, "Not for him."

Chapter 14

Last night was exhausting. After everyone finally went home, Lou's parents went to bed. She and Ben didn't talk much more after their conversation in the kitchen. They both had a lot to think about and it was better not to say anything else out loud. Lou felt bad for Jude, he didn't deserve to be treated that way. Why didn't she tell Ben about him? Deep down she knew why she never told Ben. It was like keeping a part of her home all to herself.

Ben did not sleep well. The bed was too small and uncomfortable. He was already sitting in the corner chair when she woke up. "Good morning, babe."

"Good morning," Lou replied.

"I already booked tickets for us to go home this evening," Ben said.

Lou sat up, "You did, so soon?"

"Soon? It's been three weeks, babe. You can't keep putting the hospital off. Pretty soon they will find someone else for your position."

"But it has only been a day since my mother woke up," Lou replied. Ben just looked at her. "Okay, we will leave tonight. That means I need to say goodbye to my friends."

"Like Jude?"

"Don't be a jerk. I have other friends." Lou got up and got dressed. She thought about packing. She didn't bring much with her three weeks ago, so packing wouldn't take long. That could wait. They went downstairs together and greeted her parents.

"We really didn't get a chance to talk," Laura said to Ben. "Lou says you are a neurosurgeon. That's wonderful. I sure wish you could help with my memory."

"Yes, ma'am. I wish I could too, but the regimen your doctor prescribed of vitamins, liquids and plenty of rest is exactly what I would suggest as well," Ben answered.

They sat around the table and enjoyed coffee, toast and eggs. The men read the paper and Lou excused herself to make some phone calls. She knew Ben would have already set everything up for her to return to work, no need to call her supervisor. Lou was sure he was already expecting her at work tomorrow morning. She did, though, want to see her friends here before she left. She didn't know when she would be back. Lou called Rose and Rose said she would set it all up. They agreed to meet at Pilgrim's Bar, she would text her the time when everyone could make it. Lou went back into the kitchen.

"I've decided that I am going to call our travel agent tomorrow and book that cruise in December," Tom announced.

"Oh Tom, that sounds wonderful. I can't wait to tell the Baker's," Laura said.

"Now you remember I told you that they moved?" Tom asked.

"Yes, dear, I remember. I meant I wanted to call them. They can tell me all about it before we go on ours," Laura replied.

Lou loved listening to their interaction. She had been so worried about their separation and here it all had worked out. She hoped everything would all work out. She also wished she could stay longer. She had three weeks with her father, Tony and Jude but only one day with her mother. It was not fair.

While Lou was waiting for the text to tell her when to meet her friends, she went upstairs to pack. She put on the beach glass necklace and earrings that Rose and Avery bought her. When Ben saw them, he offered to help her. He took the necklace while she held up her hair. He secured the necklace around her neck and asked about them.

"What is that stone? I've never seen anything like it before."

"It's beach glass," Lou explained. "My friends Rose and Avery got me the matching set of necklace and earrings. You will meet them later today."

"Who is the bracelet from," Ben asked. Ben could see her forming the name Jude. It was unmistakable. "Jude?"

"Yes."

Ben stood up, his bag already packed and walked down the stairs. Lou didn't want to keep hurting him. She just didn't realize how much Jude was still a part of her life. She supposed he always was. It would be so hard to leave him, again. There was no way Ben would let her meet him face to face, it would have to be over the phone. That was one phone call she was dreading the most.

Lou was able to pack everything she needed for New York in one carry on. It was sad to leave her childhood room, but promised herself she wouldn't stay away like she had in the past. Downstairs, Ben sat in the living room. He was not drawn to the lake like she was. Lou went to sit on the beach. This was another sad goodbye. She would miss the lake most of all. Finally, Rose's text came through. Everyone would meet at the bar in thirty minutes. Lou returned to the house to get Ben.

The Pilgrim's Bar was a fun atmosphere. Lou could understand why it was her friends' favorite choice for a hang out. She had told Rose specifically not to call Jude, she didn't explain, but Rose said that she would not. Lou walked through the dining tables, pool tables and dart boards to reach the bar in the back. Rose, Avery and Leon all turned to look at the man approaching with Lou.

"Hello everyone, this is Ben. We are leaving to go back to New York tonight and I wanted to introduce you all before we left." She moved so that Ben could see all three of them. "This is Rose, Avery and Leon."

Ben shook each of their hands and Leon poured them all a shot. Lou welcomed the burning liquid because she didn't know what Ben was going to talk about with her friends. She sure hoped Jude's name would not be brought up. Ben ordered a martini, the rest of them had beer. Rose talked about her family. Lou explained about the lavish first birthday party. Ben said that sounded perfectly normal to him. He and Rose clinked glasses. Avery flirted with Ben and she could see him flirting right back. Lou knew that if she wasn't standing right there, Avery would have her claws in him already.

"Well, Mr. Tall Dark and Handsome, will you be coming back to Erie more often?" Avery said the words so seductively, even Leon was blushing.

"Enough, Avery. Go find someone who is available," Lou said.

"Oh you mean like Jude? Is he still available?" Avery asked.

Rose grabbed Avery by the arm and pushed her past Lou, "Let's go to the ladies room, Avery."

Ben simply sipped his martini and glanced around the bar, half expecting Jude to show up. Lou asked if Ben wanted to play pool, she didn't even know if he played.

"I'm not exactly dressed for pool, babe." Ben had worn another suit and tie.

Rose and Avery returned from the ladies room. Lou could only imagine what Rose had said to her. Avery was on her best behavior after that, although her scowl spoke volumes. They ordered some fries and sliders and more drinks. Ben actually enjoyed talking to Leon about running the bar. Everyone asked Lou about her mother and she was happy to report that things were going well. So well, in fact, her parents were going on a cruise after Thanksgiving. They were happy that it worked out so well. Everyone hoped that the memory loss would be permanent.

Ben checked his watch for the twentieth time and said they had to leave in order to catch their flight. Lou said goodbye to all her friends and promised to come home more often. There were tears and well wishes as they left the bar.

They still had to stop at the house to get their bags. Lou called Tony to let him know they were leaving and would be at the house in ten minutes. They were just getting out of their car when Tony pulled up. Lou hugged everyone and couldn't stop crying. They had been through a lot the last few weeks and she would not change a thing. Hannah reached up to Lou and wanted to be held. She was still carrying Hannah when they went into the house. She put Hannah down so she could hug her parents one more time.

Ben grabbed their bags and put them in the car. She would finally return her rental, so no one needed to take them to the airport. Lou promised to come home again soon. Ben promised to take care of her. Ben shook everyone's hands and went to stand by the car. Lou knew he wanted to leave, she still wasn't ready. It was funny how, over the last ten years, home rarely crossed her mind. Now she will never be able to get it out of her head.

It was very difficult and dangerous for her to drive while crying, so Ben said he would. She waved out the window until she could no longer see the figures on the front yard. Lou felt in her pockets for tissues but only found a napkin. She looked at the napkin before wiping at her eyes. It was just a napkin, she thought, but then her thoughts went to Jude. She never properly said goodbye to Jude, Ben would never allow it. It wouldn't feel right for Ben to witness their parting. Lou didn't think she could pretend they were just friends, not in front of Ben. It would have been too much. It was for the best.

They were sitting at the gate waiting to board. Ben was talking on the phone to another surgeon about a procedure he needed to do tomorrow. He was deep in conversation when Lou's phone rang. Ben gestured with his hand that she should move away from him to take the call. Lou stood up, walked to the adjacent gate and saw who was calling.

"Hello, Jude,"

"Hi, Lou. Where are you now? Can I see you?"

"No, I'm at the airport now. I'm sorry I did not come to see you. It happened so fast." Lou hoped he was buying the excuse.

"Lou," Jude paused. "I wanted to see you before you left, again. I wanted to tell you I love you and that it's okay. I love you enough to let you go, again. I will never forget you."

"Oh Jude, I didn't want to leave like this," Lou said.

"Just promise me you will be happy, Lou. You deserve three out of three," said Jude.

Lou continued to hold the phone to her ear, even though the line went dead. She cried and held a napkin to her eyes. She slowly put her phone back in her pocket and dried her eyes. She was not going to let Ben see her like this. He would know immediately why she was crying and get mad, again. She took deep breaths before turning around and returning to Ben. She would never let him see her cry over Jude again.

Chapter 15

Getting back into the rhythm of the hospital had been harder than Louise thought it would be. Staying busy had helped her get through her depression. In fact, each day that went by was better and better. Today she had a consultation for chicken pox. The parents were adamant that it was the measles. Louise had to request the little girl's immunization record from their own pediatrician to confirm she already had the measles vaccine. It could not be the measles. She showed this confirmation to the girl's parents and she almost had them convinced until someone else mentioned small pox. It took a while, but after promising them that small pox was eradicated throughout the world decades ago, they conceded and took the girl home.

Louise was finally home by herself. Her apartment was her safe haven. Ben had called earlier and said that he wanted to stop by later. Ben was becoming very clingy since they returned from Erie. He called and texted her more often. It was as if he was afraid that if he turned his back, she might fly away again. Since she had been back in New York, Louise tried seeing what she had done from Ben's perspective. One moment he was pouring out his love to her, proposing marriage, and the next moment she is in her hometown and not returning his texts and calls. Then, to top it all off, finds her hanging out with an ex boyfriend the whole time.

Louise told herself to cut Ben some slack. He was handsome, kind and loved her dearly. She was a lucky lady to have Ben as a boyfriend. She would make more of an effort to show Ben how she felt about him. She loved Ben, he deserved an answer. She poured herself a glass of white wine and waited for him to come. Louise was flipping through channels on the television when she heard the knock on the door and the turn of the key.

Ben walked in and came to sit beside her, "Hi babe, how are you tonight?" He put his arm around her and kissed her.

"Better now," Louise replied. They kissed on the couch until he remembered his surprise. Ben got up and picked up the dozen roses and the box of chocolates he left by the entrance table and brought them to Louise.

"Oh my goodness! They are beautiful," Louise smelled the roses and gave Ben a hug. She got up to find a vase. He followed her into the kitchen and watched as she filled the vase with water and added the roses.

"You know this would be a whole lot easier if you just moved in with me. Instead of my driving all the way over here to see you or your having to come to my place to see me. We could just be in the same place at the same time."

Louise was very familiar with Ben's argument, but he was wearing her down. It did make sense, especially if they did decide to get married, it would probably happen eventually. "Maybe," Louise conceded.

Ben was not expecting that answer. He nearly lost his balance while leaning on the counter when she said it. "What? Did I hear something other than 'no'?"

Louise smiled and continued arranging the roses in the vase. "I do see the benefits of it, especially if we want to build a life together, eventually."

Ben came to her side and kissed her. This time the kisses were more passionate. She had just given him more hope for their future than he has had in months. Ben was never sure where Louise's mind was at. Was it here with him or back there with someone else? He just had to have faith that the fact that she returned to their life in New York City was because this was where she wanted to build her future.

It was getting late and Ben was tired. He invited Louise to his apartment tomorrow night, he had a surprise for her. He kissed her good night and let himself out. She had to admit, sharing an apartment would be easier.

The following night Louise went to Ben's apartment straight from work. His apartment was on the twenty eighth floor, a much better view than hers on the sixth. She knocked and then let herself in. She hung her coat on the coat rack and took off her boots. It was November and cold, bundling up was necessary.

"Hello?" Louise called out. She headed towards the kitchen where she could hear some noise.

"In here, babe," Ben called back. "I'm just finishing up. Come get a glass of wine."

Louise poured herself some wine and watched Ben work. He was adding grated cheese to the salad and pronounced it done. Ben carried the plates of garlic steak and red potatoes to the table. He placed the bowl of salad to the side and brought the wine to the table. He pulled out Louise's chair and placed the napkin in her lap.

Ben was a great cook. He just didn't cook very often. The steak and potatoes were delicious and he even had cheesecake for dessert. This, he confessed, he bought at the bakery across the street. The dinner and evening was wonderful. It reminded Louise why she loved him. He reached across the table and took Louise's hands.

"So the first time I did this, it did not go as planned. I'm hoping tonight is different. Louise, I love you very much. I want you in my life, I want you by my side. Please say you will marry me." Ben pulled out the same little black velvet box and opened it.

Louise's face was red, she was tearing up and could hardly see the ring when Ben opened the box. "Yes," she said. She didn't even recognize her own voice. "Yes!"

Ben had steady hands as he took the ring from the box and placed it on Louise's ring finger. He came over and kissed her. Louise stood up and they hugged. Even Ben allowed himself to get emotional. After months of uncertainty, she finally said 'yes'.

"Wait, I have a surprise!" Ben remembered.

"There's more? I thought this was the surprise."

"No, follow me." He led her into his bedroom. Louise didn't see anything different until he opened his closet. It was completely empty.

"What happened? Where are all of your things?" She asked.

"I'm giving you my closet. I moved my things to another closet. There's plenty of room in this big place." Ben made a sweeping gesture with his arm, "this is all yours, babe."

"Thank you," was all Louise could say. Ben was making such an effort to show her how much he loves her. She knew they would be happy together. She couldn't wait to call her family back home with her good news. She looked at the clock. It was already past ten, too late to call. It could wait until morning.

He grabbed her and they landed on the bed. They were both excited for the future. He started to remove Louise's shirt and she was removing Ben's. This would be a night to remember for a number of reasons. She would be moving in with Ben, her fiancé. She liked the sound of that. They made love that night with a renewed passion. It was better and sweeter. From this night on, this would be their bed, their apartment and their life.

The next day they both had off. This did not happen very often, but when it did Ben was grateful. It was the reason he had planned the dinner for last night. It would give them the entire day together. He didn't make any plans, they would do what ever they wanted today. Ben woke up first, not ready to leave the bed beside Louise, but went into the kitchen. Last night was memorable.

He was drinking coffee and reading the paper when Louise woke up. "Good morning, babe."

"Good morning," she said. She walked over to him and they kissed. It seemed normal and natural. She poured herself coffee and sat down next to him. "I thought I could start having movers bring some things over. I don't have a lot, the furniture is not mine, it came with the apartment."

Ben smiled at the thought, "Whenever you're ready."

Louise took another look around his place. "Is all this furniture yours or was it here?" She asked.

Ben stopped reading to look at his furniture. "You don't like it? It's mine, but if you want to change it, that is okay, too."

"It's not so much that I don't like it, it's just not enough. You have a couch, but no coffee table. You have one chair where there should be two. You have three bedrooms, but two do not have beds. What if my family want to come visit?"

"Okay, okay, go shopping. Spend my money, I don't care," Ben replied.

"You have no art on your walls. This side is all windows," Louise said as she gestured to the side with the floor to ceiling wall of windows. "But this side is empty."

Ben came up behind her and wrapped his arms around her waist. "Please buy whatever you want, just don't spend it all in one place," he teased. "What do you want to do today?"

"Nothing."

"We can do nothing all day long," Ben said with a wink.

"But first, is there any of that cheesecake left?"

"Actually, I don't think we even got to it last night."

"Perfect, we will have it for breakfast," Louise announced. She pulled the cheesecake from the fridge and cut a slice for her and one for Ben. They ate it with their morning coffee, feeling so decadent and indulgent.

"You can have cheesecake for breakfast every morning if you want to, babe," said Ben.

Ben and Louise spent the whole day inside. She knew this day would have to end eventually, but until that time, she was enjoying every second. They stayed in their pajamas and watched a movie. This was how she remembered the beginning of their relationship, the casual feel of going from eating a meal to making love. It felt right.

They both had to work in the morning and Louise did not have any clothes at Ben's place, yet, so she had to go home. "I may see you around the hospital, doctor," Louise said with a kiss.

"Yes, doctor, our paths may cross," said Ben.

Louise let herself out and braced for the cold weather outside. She took a taxi home and walked into her apartment with a new perspective. Tonight it felt lonely. She decided to start the process of having her things moved to Ben's place right away. She looked around her place and agreed that she didn't have much, just some clothes and personal items. She would create a new home with Ben.

When Louise crawled into her bed that night, she finally felt confident in her decision to stay with Ben. She had to admit that she had doubts back in August, but now she was sure. She was happy where she was, with what she was doing and who she was with. She was still three out of three. This made her think of Jude and looked down at the beach glass bracelet on her wrist before drifting off to sleep.

Chapter 16

Winter brought multi-car pile ups, skiing accidents and hypothermia to the hospital. It was a never ending stream of broken bones, frostbite and concussions. Louise was called whenever children were involved and followed up with their care. Today, one of her patients was a child who was involved in a car accident. He was not properly restrained in his car seat and he had a concussion. She was being paged all over the hospital and going from an infant with a rash to a teenager with a nail in his hand. Normally, Louise loved the adrenaline rush that came with never knowing what was behind each door or in each ambulance.

Today was different. Today she was questioning her work in a hospital setting. Ben always knew he wanted to be a surgeon, so he saw his life in a hospital. Louise enjoyed the job here because Ben was here. She liked it, but she also knew that being a pediatrician gave her options, more options than being a neurosurgeon. Pediatricians could have their own practice. She could have returning patients, colds and fevers, and immunizations. Louise had considered this in the past, but figured that in a city the size of New York, competition and cost would be high. So, she stayed where she was comfortable.

Louise finally had time to sneak away for lunch. She usually enjoyed the green space that was right outside of the hospital and she would sit on a bench under the large maple tree. Since it was winter, and cold, she sat in the corner of the cafeteria. She pulled out her phone and saw that Ben had called. Instead of calling him back right away, she decided to call her parents to share the good news. Even now she was holding out her left hand and admiring the large diamond on her finger.

"Hi mom, it's Lou."

"Hello sweetheart. How are you doing?"

"I'm doing well. How are you guys doing?"

"Well, right now I'm planning our Thanksgiving menu. I sure wish you and Ben could come. It would be so nice to see you again," Laura said.

"I know, but I just can't get away right now," Lou said and paused. "I do have some news, though."

"Oh Lou, what is it?" Her mother asked.

"Ben proposed and I accepted. We're engaged!" Lou announced.

"That's wonderful! Congratulations!"

"Thanks, I'm happy. I'm in the process of moving into his place. We have not set a date, yet, but I will sure let you know when we do!" Lou promised.

"I'm happy for you, Lou. You deserve it."

"Ok, well, I have some more calls to make before my break is over. Say 'hi' to dad!"

"I will. Love you, sweetheart," said her mother.

"Love you, too."

Louise's next call was to Tony. She wasn't very good at keeping in touch with him. It was easier with her parents. She decided he should hear about her engagement from her, no one else.

"Hey Lou," Tony said when he answered.

"Hi Tony, how are things?"

"Things are good, how about you?" Tony asked.

"Things are good, too," Lou answered. She didn't expect it to feel this awkward calling her own brother. "So, I have some news to share."

"Okay, what is it?" Tony asked. He was feeling a little anxious and wasn't sure what Lou was trying to say or why she had called. It was the first phone call since she left in August with Ben. Tony wasn't exactly happy with how things played out when Ben came to Erie, then ended up taking her away the next day. It left Tony with some bad feelings.

"Ben proposed and I accepted. We are engaged," Lou said. It wasn't with the same enthusiasm as when she used that line on her mother. It kind of lost some of the joy because of how Tony was responding.

"Oh okay," Tony said, with a pause. "When is the date?"

"Well, we haven't set one yet, but I will let you know," Lou offered.

"Sure."

"So how is your family?" She asked, trying to change the subject.

"They are good. Hannah just turned six and growing like a weed. Suni is pregnant, so she's taking things easy,"

"Wait, what? That's wonderful news! Congratulations!" Lou said.

"Thanks. Just wait until you and Ben start having kids. It's the best."

Lou hesitated before asking her next question. She hated that she wanted to ask, but she did, "How is Jude?"

There was a long pause before Tony finally said, "I haven't seen him since you left."

Lou wasn't expecting that answer. Jude and Tony were best friends, why would they not keep hanging out. Well, the insinuation was there, Tony was blaming her. Was she the reason Jude was hiding or moving? "Oh, you haven't heard from him at all?"

"No," Tony answered. "I see Brad once in a while. He says Jude is staying busy with work."

Louise knew her leaving would be hard, but now the guilt was eating at her. They should have never slept together, that was for sure. They should never have crossed the line of their friendship. Things had been going so well, they were hanging out and being nice to each other.

"Okay, well, I will let you go. I'll let you know when we set a date." Lou said.

"Did you tell mom?" Tony asked.

"Yes, I just called her before you. She said she's planning her Thanksgiving menu. They seem happy, back to normal."

"It seems so. They are still planning to go on the cruise, so that's good." Tony said.

"I'm so glad it worked out for them."

"Well, it seems to be working out for you, too. Congrats, again. I gotta go," Tony replied.

After they hung up, Tony felt bad for lying to his sister. He hadn't seen Jude since August, but he had spoken to him. Jude made it clear he didn't want to talk about Lou, so they didn't. Tony just assumed that meant not discussing Jude with Lou as well. He thinks Jude is doing fine, probably hurt, but he was throwing himself into his work and painting. He told him he was fixing up his house, too, and that it was coming along great. Jude always did like fixing things, and people, so Tony was sure the house was even better than he let on. The news of Ben and Lou getting engaged was probably the best thing Tony could hope for right now, for Jude's sake.

Lou wasn't sure how to feel after her conversation with Tony. She was happy for Tony and his family, also for her parents, but she was sad for Jude. That little bit of sad news overshadowed all the happy news she heard and shared. She ate her sandwich and drank her water in silence for the rest of her lunch break. She shouldn't have asked about Jude. Not knowing was better than this.

The rest of Louise's day went fast as she checked on all of her patients and continually met new ones. She even managed to get a quick call to Ben squeezed in and that brightened her mood a bit. He said he wanted to plan an engagement party at his apartment next week. He was going to send out invites tomorrow, so she was to let him know who she wanted to invite. She told him Valerie. She was Louise's good friend at the hospital. Valerie Ortiz was a pediatric surgeon and they often worked together on consultations. They also love hanging out together after work. Ben said he would send her the invite tomorrow.

It was starting to feel real. She loved looking at her ring, it was big and beautiful, but it wasn't the size of the diamond that mattered, it was that she finally made the decision to make the commitment. Lou was always afraid that she would never want to commit to anything or anyone. That she was destined to always be searching for something better and more exciting. This ring symbolized a big step for her. She just prayed she would have the strength to follow through.

Lou went home that night, to her apartment, and made arrangements for movers to come to her house tomorrow and pack everything and take it to Ben's place. She had a day off tomorrow and would make the most of it. If Ben was going to have a fancy engagement party, she had better prove her commitment and be living there, too. She would be sad to let go of her little sanctuary of an apartment, but now that she knew what it meant to share your space with someone you loved, she was ready to try. Lou poured herself a glass of wine and sat on the couch. She decided to give Valerie a call.

"Hey Louise, how are you doing? Congratulations by the way!" Valerie said.

"Thank you, Val. I'm good. I have movers coming early tomorrow morning, but once they leave, I need to go shopping.

Ben is having this big party and he desperately needs some more furniture. Actually, he needs art, curtains and bedding, too, but we'll focus on furniture tomorrow. Are you in?" Lou asked.

"Yes, you know I love to shop!" Val replies. "I have connections all over the city. You just tell me what you are looking for and I will take you there."

Valerie grew up in the city. She really did know everyone and everyone knew Valerie. She was a beautiful Latina woman with short cropped black hair and long eyelashes. She loved being single, but as she says, she is always on the lookout. She was older than Lou, but only by a few years. She lived in the apartment building next to the one Ben lived in, so it would be nice to be closer to Valerie, too.

"Tomorrow is dedicated to furniture. Our next outing will be art for his walls. They are so bare there is an echo in each room," Lou joked. The two women laughed and Lou took a sip of her wine.

"See you tomorrow!" Valerie said.

"Okay, it's a date." Lou replied and hung up.

Lou and Val had an easy friendship. Ben was not threatened by it, so she shared her days off with Ben and Valerie. Lou was watching the news when her phone rang.

"Hey babe, how was your day?" Ben asked.

"Hi Ben, it was good. I called my parents and told them the good news today," she said.

"Finally, I was wondering why you were waiting," he replied.

"No reason, just finding the right moment. I called Tony, too, they are expecting another baby," Lou announced. "He sounded so happy. Hannah is six already, so she will enjoy a little brother or sister."

"That's great news! We will have to invite them all over some day, to see the city," Ben suggested.

"Of course, that would be nice. I also talked to Valerie tonight and we are going to hang out tomorrow afternoon," Lou said.

"I thought you told me you were scheduling movers tomorrow. I told the concierge downstairs to let them in and someone was to stay with them the entire time they were here. I'll be at work." Ben insisted.

"No, they are still coming. But I really don't have a lot of stuff, so it'll be fast. I have most of it boxed up already," Lou replied.

"Ok babe, I can't wait. See you soon," Ben said.

Lou decided to call it a night. She would get up early and have everything ready for the movers to take. She was more excited to see Valerie. It seemed like ages since they were able to hang out together. She turned off lights and headed to bed. It was harder getting ready for bed when everything was packed up for the move. It was like living out of a suitcase. Well, it wouldn't be much longer. Lou brushed her teeth and crawled into bed. Things seemed to be moving forward pretty fast. Tonight she allowed her thoughts to drift to her family.

Chapter 17

Louise was in the middle of a crisis! Her curling iron was not getting hot and she could not find her other black high healed shoe. "Ben! I know it was here last week when the movers brought over all of my stuff," she yelled from the bedroom.

"Well then it must still be there, keep looking, babe," he yelled back from the kitchen.

The caterers had dropped off all the food and arranged it so professionally around the kitchen and island. He had the concierge order lots of roses and they were placed in vases all around the apartment. The place smelled like a funeral parlor, well maybe that was a bad comparison. It smelled like a wedding. Only it wasn't, it was their engagement party that Ben had sent out over fifty invitations to attend.

"I found my other shoe, but the curling iron still isn't getting hot," Louise yelled.

"Perhaps it's your curling iron's fault, babe."

Louise relented and decided to do something else with her hair. She would put it up. It looked better that way anyway. Guests were due to arrive in thirty minutes, but Valerie promised to come early. Valerie hadn't yet seen the furniture she helped pick out when it was all arranged in the apartment, so Lou wanted her to see the finished product first.

Valerie did a great job at recommending exactly where to go for what pieces. She picked out a red couch, two leather chairs and a glass coffee table for the living room. The dining room had a new round table that had the capability to extend out to seat ten people. Each bedroom had a new queen sized bed, their room had a king bed, a night stand, lamps, chair and dresser. It was chaos for a while because everything arrived within three days. Ben was pushed to his limits, but Louise promised the end result would be worth it. It was.

When everything was in place, Ben did agree that it looked beautiful. "Maybe you missed your calling, babe," he would say. The apartment did look fantastic and Louise was anxious for Valerie to see it.

"Is my phone in there?" Louise called from the bathroom.

"Yes, it's here on the kitchen counter, right next to the coffee maker," Ben answered.

"Okay, I'm almost ready, just need to find my hair spray."

Ben was only half listening at this point because when he went to look for Louise's phone, he picked it up and saw there was a missed call. Jude. "Um, okay, babe, maybe it's still packed up," he replied, still holding her phone. Why was Jude still calling Louise and how often have then been talking? Ben heard Louise coming down the hall and quickly returned the phone to the counter. He wished he didn't see it, but then again, he was glad he did. He waited for Louise to say something when she saw the missed call.

Ben observed Louise as she went to the coffee maker and picked up her phone. She hesitated when the lock screen lit up. She only froze for a minute then she laid it back down and made herself a coffee.

"Everything okay, babe?" Ben asked.

"Yes," she replied as she turned towards him. She came over and gave him a kiss. "I found my hair spray after all." Louise took her coffee back into the bedroom and left Ben leaning on the counter with his head spinning. She didn't say anything about the call from Jude.

The sound of the doorbell startled Ben and he walked over to open the door. It was Valerie. She made a grand entrance in her new designer dress, purchased just for this occasion. She took a tour of the entire apartment before searching for the guest of honor, "Louise, I'm here!" Valerie yelled down the hall towards the master bedroom.

Louise was glad to see her friend and they entered the living room together. She made sure to point out all the new purchases to Valerie as they made their way into the kitchen. "Is there any wine open?" Valerie asked Ben. Ben tried to hide his mood of growing suspicion, but perhaps he wasn't doing it so well. "Is everything okay, Ben?" Valerie asked. She looked around the kitchen as if there was something amiss.

Ben smiled unconvincingly. He turned to the wine cooler and pulled out a vintage red wine. "But of course, there is always an open bottle of wine around here," Ben replied.

Valerie smiled and held out a glass to be filled. Ben filled it as Valerie eyed her host. "Is something wrong, Ben?" Valerie asked again.

"No, no, I think I'm just nervous. I've never hosted a party this large before," Ben replied. "I just hope I thought of everything."

Valerie relaxed as she saw Ben relax, "Okay, but don't worry, everything will be fine. You have your beautiful fiancé by your side, plenty of food and even more importantly, lots of wine. What could go wrong?" Valerie turned to look for Louise, leaving Ben alone in the kitchen.

As the guests started to arrive and the evening went on, Ben seemed to have forgotten all about the missed phone call. Louise never brought it up and neither did he. When Louise had seen the notification of a missed call from Jude, her heart had stopped and her palms began to sweat. She hadn't heard from him since their last phone call from the Erie Airport in August. Neither of them had reached out to the other. In fact, the only news she had about Jude was the little bit Tony shared on their phone call a week ago. Why would he be calling now? What did he have to say after all this time? Apparently it wasn't important enough to leave a voicemail or a text. A random phone call that could have even been a mistake for all she knew. At least Ben didn't know and she would never tell him. It was nothing, Ben would just blow it out of proportion anyway.

Ben was playing the part of host well. Louise was playing the part of fiancé even better. She showed the ring to everyone who asked to see it. She received compliments on the apartment, knowing it was her touch that made it look stunning. "Ben had talent, but not for decorating," one person said. "I wouldn't have even suspected he had furniture," another one commented. Louise took a step back and watched him. There was an aura, an atmosphere, around Ben that drew people to him. He was handsome, charming and put together. She was still learning to fit into his world.

When they dated, it was different. She only had to enter his world when they went out on the town. They would have dinner or drinks and mingle with some friends or coworkers, but it was for a limited time and something Louise enjoyed every now and then. Now she was in his atmosphere twenty four seven and it wasn't always easy. He was a perfectionist that was learning to adapt to her carefree style. They were both adjusting and compromising. Ben smiled at Louise from across the room. She smiled back. She was the moon to his planet. Would that be enough?

Valerie came over to stand beside Louise. "I see you making eyes at your man," Valerie said.

Louise laughed, "Well, this is our engagement party. There had better be some spark there, right?" Louise replied.

"Okay, but right now I've got some news," Valerie started. "There is this big art gallery next to the hair salon I go to every week. I usually pop in to look around for anything new. Well, they are having this huge show in a few days and I thought of you. Maybe you can find something there that will catch your eye."

"Sure, that sounds perfect," Louise said. "I've been looking around but I haven't seen anything I liked. I want something big." She gestured to the far wall that was completely empty. "Something eye catching there and over there. Maybe two or three pieces."

"Okay, I'll get us all an invitation and we can shop some more!" Valerie said as she headed back towards the food. Louise followed Valerie.

"Hello ladies," said Ben. "Are you both having a good time?"

Louise looked at Valerie and smiled. "Yes, but I've been talking to so many doctors tonight, I feel like I should have some sort of illness," Louise joked.

"I hope it's not that bad," said Ben.

"No, not bad, I just haven't been in a room with this many doctors since graduating med school," Louise replied. She tried to be light hearted, but really she was feeling tired. She was tired of all these people in her house and looking at her. She looked at her phone.

"Are you tired, babe?" Ben asked. "Say the word and I will send everyone home." It was after nine. He was tired, too, but he was going to wait until people started leaving to make more of a gesture of cleaning up. Usually that was a sign for people to start leaving en masse.

"No, it's fine. Enjoy your party, but I am going to go in the bedroom and take some headache medicine," Louise said.

"It's our party, Louise. If you want to rest, go ahead. I'll get rid of everyone," Ben replied.

Secretly, that is exactly what she wanted him to do. She just nodded, walked to their bedroom and closed the door. Her feet were hurting so she kicked off her shoes. She did take a couple of Tylenol with a glass of water and sat on the edge of the bed. Louise felt bad for leaving the party, but she was exhausted. Valerie would help Ben get rid of everyone, she was sure. Guests did bring wine and cards for the occasion, which was very sweet, but Louise didn't know any of those people. She knew Ben liked to host parties but she hoped they were not all this grand.

Louise didn't realize she had fallen asleep until Ben came to her side and kissed her forehead. "Did you have fun?" He asked.

Louise opened her eyes and rubbed them. "Yes, thank you. It was a wonderful party. I'm so sorry I fell asleep. I had every intention of returning to the party," she insisted.

"It's fine. Everyone had food and alcohol in their bellies, so they were happy. They didn't even realize they were being pushed out the door. Valerie helped," Ben added. "The caterers cleaned up all the mess and left us some food for tomorrow. It's all finished."

She smiled at the description. "Well, in that case, I am glad they are gone," said Louise.

Ben leaned down and kissed her again, this time on her lips. "Me, too."

The party was a success. It was the talk of the entire hospital for days. Louise was starting to feel more included and knew more doctors by name. They had plans to meet a few couples for drink after work later that week. Ben was glad that she was feeling more comfortable around his friends. Sometimes he felt like she regretted moving in with him or even the engagement in general. Louise assured him that she was happy, although they have not set a date, yet. It was not such a big deal to her, they had plenty of time, but it was to Ben. He thought she would be happy to start planning a wedding, isn't that what little girls dreamed about? He must have very old fashioned thoughts about weddings. She would come around soon, he hoped. He already had the perfect venue in mind here in the city. It never occurred to him that she might not want to get married here.

Louise was riding the subway home. It wasn't nearly as long of a ride to Ben's place as it had been to her apartment. Well, she should start thinking of it as their place now. She loved the subway, the white noise of it and the feeling of the tracks. It was always fairly empty at night, it was a good place to think. She looked at the ring on her left hand and felt happy. Then why wasn't she excited at the prospect of planning a wedding. She knew Ben expected it to be in the city, but her family was in Erie. He wanted to invite a couple hundred of his closest friends, but her family and friends were hundreds of miles away. Money wasn't the issue, Ben wanted pay for everything. But money was not the issue for her either, she felt it should be in Erie, where she was from. It was just one more thing that delayed the planning. Who would it be to give in first?

Chapter 18

"Do I really need to go to this, babe?" Ben asked for the fifth time tonight.

"Yes, Valerie went through a lot of trouble to get us last minute invitations. We are both going and we are both going to enjoy it. Who knows, you might find something you like, too." Louise said. It was opening night of the big art show at the gallery Valerie recommended. She didn't look at the invitations well, she just knew they had to be there at seven. She hadn't heard of the artist, Henry something. She just hoped he was good. Louise was getting very tired of looking at these empty walls.

They were meeting Valerie and her date there. Ben arranged for a car to take them and would be here soon to pick them up. Louise was wearing a new gown that Valerie helped pick out for this occasion. It was a black strapless gown and she wore her hair up. She did not have any pops of color to wear with her dress, so she looked through her jewelry box. She spotted the beach glass necklace and earrings that Rose and Avery had given her on her last birthday. She decided those were perfect and put them on. They matched the bracelet that she still wore. Looking at herself in the mirror, she determined that she was ready to go to an art show at the gallery.

Louise grabbed the invitations from the kitchen counter and shoved them in her clutch purse. They went down the elevator and met the car out front. The ride to the gallery wasn't long. There was already a crowd out front waiting to get in. Louise and Ben had invitations so getting in was not a problem. They left their coats at the coat check and entered the main room. There were many rooms that led off from the main room. She assumed that these could easily be used for several art shows at once simply by closing off one or another. But tonight, this artist required the use of all of the smaller rooms along with the large main gallery.

There were so many people here. Some standing in the center of the room admiring the paintings from afar, others were up close examining each brush stroke. She noticed some people writing notes in the program they were all handed when coming in tonight. There were staff walking around with champagne and other beverages. Louise took a glass of champagne and decided to join the group of people in the center of the room to get a better perspective of the paintings on the wall and how they would look in their apartment.

Valerie and her date came up to Louise and squeezed her arm. "Aren't these paintings just gorgeous!"

Louise agreed that from what she has seen so far, they were perfect for their place. She just needed to look around some more. It looked like the paintings were endless. Each room that branched out from this main room contained even more. Valerie introduced her date and then they took off to look around as well. Louise was grateful for the time alone. She wanted to take her time and look at every painting in every room. She did not want to feel rushed. Ben would probably make her feel like she was taking too long. First she had to decide where to start.

Louise started on the left and chose to go clockwise around the room. These were more abstract, she noted. Lots of blues and greens. The brush strokes were horizontal on the canvas and she found herself being drawn into the calming effect of the colors. She always favored blues, she had them all over her apartment, to remind her of the lake. These abstract looking paintings weren't completely abstract. There was definition between sky, water and sand, they were just very well blended so that they seamlessly morphed into one. She could detect each nuance of color as if she has looked at this picture for years. It was almost as if she had.

Some paintings were predominately blue, others had more green. Paintings that depicted the sunset had a strong red center, while others had orange enveloping the canvas. Each one was better than the next. She did not know how she would ever be able to pick just a couple. She hoped Ben would allow her to purchase multiple paintings. Each wall was showing her a new way of looking at the water, the sunset, the waves and the clouds. They all worked together as one cohesive piece of art. One could stand on its own, but together you got the whole picture.

Louise moved along the wall and saw that these were coming more into focus. A kind of hybrid between abstract and realism. Just as one item was coming into focus, another was fading out. You could see definition on the rocks on the beach, but the sun became a blur. The waves of the water became the focal point as the sky blended into one color. It was magic on canvas. She could see on the other side of the room that Ben was bored, perhaps she should have let him stay home. Louise wished he would show more interest since this was something she was excited about. She pretended to be interested in his hobbies, why couldn't he enjoy hers?

Ben tried to look interested but all the paintings in this room were of water or sea scapes. It wasn't anything he was interested in. Ben would let Louise look around, go in all the rooms and pick out a few that she liked. He didn't want to be dragged to any more art shows, that was for sure. This was not his crowd. He had a couple glasses of champagne and whatever that was wrapped in a pastry crust.

As Louise moved to the far side of the room she saw more detail in the paintings. This was an artist who appreciated a water landscape. Some paintings were of birds or trees. Others of shells and stones. But these were of water with a slight ripple of a wave and as the sun was setting it reflected on the water. This artist knew his sunsets, too. It was like something so familiar. It was like someone had seen the sunsets that she had seen on Lake Erie and captured that moment. She felt like she was back at home, sitting on a log watching the lake she grew up with. Louise wanted to meet the artist tonight but couldn't remember his name. She knew it had to be on the brochure or the invitation. She pulled out the invitation and looked for the name. There is was, J. HENRY WEBER. Jude Henry Weber. Jude.

Just as Louise was putting the pieces of the puzzle together in her mind she heard her name. Heard it like she had heard it a thousand times growing up.

"Lou."

"Jude."

They both stood looking at each other for a moment. Louise felt as though her knees might buckle. Jude looked handsome. He was in a suit and tie. His hair was combed back and he was clean shaven. He looked as well put together as any of the surgeons that were at their engagement party. The thought of the party made Louise look for Ben. She did not see him.

"I didn't know this was your show," Lou said.

"Yes, my publicity team thought Jude sounded too quaint. They liked Henry better, so they went with my middle name. I insisted they keep the J, though." There was and awkward silence, "I tried to call you, but I wasn't sure you would want to come," Jude said. "So I did not even leave a message."

"Yes, it is really just luck that we did come," Lou replied. "My friend Valerie suggested it."

"We?" Jude asked. "Is Ben here?"

As if on cue, Ben came up beside Louise and offered a hand to Jude. Recognition showed on Ben's face as he realized who this was. He immediately withdrew his hand and put it around Louise's waist.

"Hello, Ben," Jude said.

"Jude. Nice show you have here. You are very talented. Congratulations," Ben replied.

"Thank you."

"Maybe you want to offer some congratulations to us, too" Ben said. He took Louise's left hand and brought it out for Jude to see. "We are engaged."

Jude looked from Ben, to the ring and then to Louise. Jude's expression never changed as he said 'Congratulations' to Lou. He kept his composure, even when Ben said his paintings were just pretty good.

"Ben, he has an art show in a major gallery in New York City that is invitation only and still brought a large crowd to stand outside in the cold knowing they had no chance of getting in. I would say that was better than pretty good." Louise stared at Jude the whole time.

"Fine," Ben started. "Pick out whatever you want and we'll get one. I am always willing to support the arts." Ben gave Jude a sideways glance and walked back towards refreshments.

"I had no idea you were an artist, Jude," Lou said. She could feel a tear fall from the corner of her eye.

Jude made a half smile, "I told you I was a painter."

Louise laughed. "But this," she said as she gestured around the room. "This is amazing. They are the most beautiful paintings I've ever seen. I see what you see. I see the sun how it dances on the water just before it hides behind the horizon every evening. How the clouds block the sun, yet rays of light still poke through. I can almost hear the waves as they crash on the rocks and the sea gulls sing when they think there is something to eat on the sand."

Lou looked back at Jude, his bottom lip and chin were starting to betray how he was melting inside listening to Lou describe his very soul. His strong exterior was being chipped away with each moment they were within inches of each other. Jude did not expect to see her tonight. He didn't expect to see her ever again. He had heard from Tony and Brad that Lou accepted Ben's proposal. It was over. The hope he dared to feel was shattered. He had thrown himself into his paintings. He knew many of the abstract works were done in anger. Too hurt to focus and too mad to care. Jude had thrown paint on canvas to cover the pain. His only love was gone forever and his only outlet was paint. His studio, the building behind his house, the one he wouldn't let Lou see, was filled with hundreds of paintings. Some were done with love, others were painted after she left in August. Then there were some that were so close to his heart, he almost didn't include them in the show this week. Those were in the other room. Each painting in the show had a price tag on it. He had sold many paintings already. He had sold hundreds, if not thousands, through the years. But the ones in the other room were priceless to him.

Jude reached out for Lou's hand. Again, he saw the ring, but now he saw something even more precious. He saw a single bracelet made of beach glass. Jude looked down at the bracelet and Lou took her hand away, embarrassed. She forgot about the bracelet. He looked up into Lou's eyes. "There is something I need to show you," said Jude.

Chapter 19

Jude took Lou's hand and led her into another room that branched off the main gallery. He took her to the middle of the room and watched her reaction. The wall she was facing showed more abstract paintings with browns and beiges. A few pops of colors here and there. You could almost make out a face if you looked at it long enough. Lou turned her head to the right and then the left. There were more paintings of a face and they were coming more and more into focus. The face was happy in some and sad in others. This face was familiar, not only because it was the same face in every painting, it was her face.

"I call this collection 'Louise,'" Jude announced. "Do you like it?"

Lou was speechless. Every painting in every corner of this room was like a reflection of herself in different states of emotion. She felt the emotion. She went up to one that was so lifelike she had to see for herself that it wasn't a photograph. There were portraits that focused on her eyes, other ones focused on her nose and still others on her lips. Some showed her hair down, then more had her hair blowing in the wind, and then others with her hair up like today. The girl in the portraits aged, too. Some captured the wide eyed expression of an eighteen year old. A few paintings showed a girl smiling who was in her twenties. Others looked like a woman who might be sitting on the beach for her twenty ninth birthday.

Lou couldn't pull her eyes away. She heard conversations behind her, "Oh Mr. Weber, your show is wonderful. Mr. Weber, why do you call this collection 'Louise'? Henry, could you sign my program, please?" None of that mattered to Lou.

"When did you paint all of these?" Lou asked.

"I had a lot of time the last ten years," Jude replied.

"I never knew."

"You never came home," Jude said. "I never intended for it to be a secret, I just don't really talk about it."

"So you have been selling paintings for ten years?" Lou asked.

"It started just as a hobby. Avery and Rose saw them at first and said they were good. They arranged to have some put in an actual store for sale and they sold. Then there was a demand for more. It just kind of grew."

"Is this your first show?"

Jude looked a little embarrassed, "No, I've actually had many shows. I have been to London, Paris, Amsterdam and Rome. I've seen many places around the world, but my paintings are always of the same things."

"The lake," said Lou.

"And you."

Lou was starting to feel a little overwhelmed. She had never been anyone's muse before and it was impossible to wrap her head around. But being in this room with dozens of versions of herself was too much. She had seen enough of the 'Louise' collection.

"I'm going to go find Ben. I hope you don't mind if I purchase a couple of your paintings. I am particularly drawn to the ones of the lake where the sunset is reflected on the rippling waves of the water. I remember that view. I miss it."

"I would be honored if you had any of my paintings," said Jude. He watched her walk out of the smaller room and into the large one. He knew each of these paintings by heart. Could remember when and where each one was finished. Jude didn't realize until Lou left the room how tense he was while she viewed the collection. His whole body was stiff as if one word of rebuke from her would just smash him to pieces. Jude needed a moment to compose himself.

Lou walked out of the small room as quickly as she could and walked straight into the ladies room. She stood at the sink, turned on the cold water and splashed it on her face. She looked at her reflection in the mirror and was reminded of the portraits hanging in the next room. As Lou stood there trying to collect her thoughts, she heard other women come into the restroom talking about the paintings and of Jude.

"He's so hot, right?" One lady asked her friend. "Oh my gosh, is he single? I didn't see a ring." The two women came and stood right next Lou while reapplying their lipstick. "Did you see the room of Louise? Wish I was her," the one woman said. "I know, right, I'd never let that one get away." The friend glanced over at Louise, then did a double take. "She looks like the girl in the painting," the friend said. They both took another look, shook their heads and left the restroom.

Louise had to get out of here. She went back into the main gallery room and searched for Ben. She spotted him over by the cashier. Ben must have also been looking for her because when she emerged from the restroom he started waving his hand to get her attention. Louise made her way to Ben's side.

"This nice lady is ready to take my money, babe. Please tell her which paintings you want delivered," Ben said. Louise saw that his credit card was already on the table. Ben looked impatient, he obviously wanted to get out of here fast.

Louise smiled at the lady behind the table. She pulled out her brochure and showed her the paintings she had marked. "Yes, ma'am, I would like number fourteen and number sixty three." Louise chose one large painting, almost as tall as her, that was a very realistic version of the lake she remembered. She knew exactly where she would hang it, in the living room. The other painting wasn't quite so big, but still a nice size for the bedroom. It was full of blues, greens and oranges. It represented the sunset just as it was ready to fall beyond the horizon.

The woman presented the receipt to Ben along with a form to fill out asking where the paintings were to be delivered. She casually looked around the room as Ben filled out the paperwork. Louise spotted Jude in the corner talking to an older couple about a painting of the lake with an overcast sky. The couple seemed very interested in what Jude was saying and perhaps that painting was going home with them tonight.

"Just leave it with the concierge, he will arrange to have them brought to our place," Ben was saying to the woman.

"Yes, sir. Thank you for your purchase," the woman added. "You are helping a great cause, the Jackson Weber Foundation."

Louise was struck by the name of the foundation. Another fact that Louise never knew about Jude, he had started a foundation in his brother's name. Ben took Louise's hand and started walking across the room. "Well, we ought to say good bye to the artist, himself, before we go. The man of the hour."

Louise did not like the tone Ben was using and didn't know what was about to happen. When they stood in front of Jude, Ben held out his hand. Jude shook it.

"Congratulations, again, Jude. We purchased a couple of your paintings. Why don't you come over to our place tomorrow night for dinner? You can see how they look hanging on our walls."

Louise knew Ben's invitation was also a challenge.

"Thank you, Ben. It would be my pleasure," answered Jude. Challenge accepted.

"Great. Well that young lady at the cashier's desk has all my info. How does seven o'clock sound?" Ben asked.

"Perfect. I will be there," answered Jude.

Ben released Louise's hand so that he could collect their coats from the cloak room.

"I'm so glad you came tonight, Lou," Jude said, taking Lou's hand. "I will see you tomorrow and congratulations, again."

Lou nodded and pulled away. She could see Ben waiting with her coat. Louise looked down at her hand and realized Jude had put a piece of paper in it. She quickly glanced back as Ben helped her with her coat but Jude had already moved to talk to a group of gentlemen. Lou just slipped it in her pocket to look at later. What else did he want to say?

Ben had the car take them home. "What a night! How do you feel?" He asked.

"I'm good. It was all just very overwhelming," Louise answered. "I didn't even know he was an artist." Louise said the last part almost to herself. She felt like she should have known. She thought she knew Jude, but she realized that she didn't. She turned her back on Jude ten years ago.

"Well, I enjoyed it. He did some pretty good work," Ben said.

"Thank you for buying me some paintings. They are going to look great on our walls."

"You're welcome, babe. Anything for you, you know that," said Ben.

Louise did know that. Ben didn't have to buy any of Jude paintings but he did. Even knowing he would have to look at them everyday, he still let her buy them.

Jude watched Lou's car as it drove away from the gallery. He tried to keep a smile on his face for the remainder of the night, but it was not easy. Jude had secretly hoped Lou would come to one of his showings, but he just couldn't believe she did. Showing her the 'Louise' collection was the hardest thing he ever had to do. A million people could look at those paintings, but the only opinion that mattered was one.

When the staff locked the doors for the night, they all turned to Jude and applauded. "Great night, Mr. Weber," said the gallery owner. "You sold sixty three paintings tonight. The crowd loved you. You should do equally as well your next two nights!"

Jude simply took a bow and thanked the staff for a job well done. He walked over to the cashier and asked to see Benjamin Brock's receipt.

"Yes, Mr. Weber. Here it is. They purchased number fourteen and sixty three," the woman replied.

Jude knew exactly which ones they were. Lou picked them out. "Thank you. Can you please add two more to their order? Numbers one forty nine and two fifty. They are a gift from me personally," Jude added.

"Number two fifty is a gift, Mr. Weber?" She asked.

"Yes, add number two fifty to their order, a gift."

Jude walked back into the room full of portraits of Lou. He stood in front of number two fifty. He had taken the most time with this painting, wanting to get everything perfect. Jude had to paint from memory, of course, but it wasn't hard. He had looked into those eyes enough times to know exactly the right shade of brown. He knew the angle of her nose and the curve of her lips. Everyone knew number two fifty but it really only belonged to one person, Lou.

Just then, two gentlemen came in to take it down and wrap it up. It felt right that Lou should have it. He gave Ben credit for buying his paintings, but he also knew he only did it to make Lou happy. As long as Lou was happy, that was all that mattered.

Tomorrow was another story. He had no idea why Ben really invited him to dinner. It was another curve ball he didn't see coming. Well, good or bad, it was another excuse to see Lou before he had to go home to Erie. If that meant putting up with Ben for one more night, even on his home turf, then so be it. Jude walked back to the beverage table and grabbed an unopened bottle of champagne. "I am going to need this tomorrow night," he said to himself and walked out the door.

Louise walked quietly back to the hall closet where Ben had hung her coat. He was in the shower, so she had a few minutes alone. She reached into the right pocket and pulled out the crumpled piece of paper Jude had slipped into her hand as she left. Lou had to bring it into the light to see it. "I will always love you." She quickly tore it up into a thousand pieces and threw it in the trash. Ben can never know.

Chapter 20

Ben and Louise rode home from work together in his car. Louise could feel the tension in the car as if it were a third passenger. They managed to leave early together which took a bit of sweet talking on Ben's part. He did not care, he had a guest coming tonight. They both showered and changed in time to let the caterers in to set up. Tonight's main course was pasta. Louise lit candles as Ben played some jazz music through the surround sound. She locked herself in the bathroom and was taking some deep breaths. Why didn't Ben let this go last night, why is he drawing this out another day?

Louise came into the kitchen just as the doorbell rang. It was seven o'clock. Ben and Louise were both surprised when it was the concierge carrying large items wrapped in brown paper.

"These were left for you, Mr. Brock," the concierge said.

"Yes, the paintings. Thank you. Do you need help?" Ben offered.

"Oh no, sir, I have help."

Jude walked in carrying two large paintings in brown wrappings. Ben took a step back as Jude brushed past him and leaned the paintings against the kitchen island. "Those two you ordered," Jude said pointing to the ones the concierge and Ben were carrying into the living room. "These two are a gift from me." Jude was speaking only to Lou.

Ben was busy unwrapping the two large paintings that were to hang in the living room and bedroom. Lou was unwrapping the two that Jude hand picked for her. She pulled back the corner of one and it was of a lake house. The water surrounding it was the deepest blue she had ever seen. And yet, it was so familiar. "That is my house!" Lou exclaimed. She looked up at Jude who nodded his confirmation. "I didn't see that one at your show." The other one was of her. It was the portrait that looked like a photograph. Lou dabbed at her eyes and said softly, "Thank you, Jude."

"You're welcome," he whispered back.

Jude and Louise turned to Ben who was tipping the concierge and thanking him for his help. "I'll ask tomorrow for someone to come hang the paintings," Ben said. "For now, let's eat before all this delicious food gets cold."

"Oh I almost forgot," Jude said as he pulled out the bottle of champagne he took last night. He had stuffed it in his coat pocket trying to carry the paintings into the apartment.

"Excellent," replied Ben who took the bottle and popped the cork. Ben filled three glasses with champagne and raised his to a toast. Jude and Louise followed his lead. "To Jude!" Ben announced, "And a successful art show!"

They all three clinked glasses and drank to Jude. "Well, isn't this nice," Ben said. "Come on everyone, let's eat." Ben tried to sound casual, but inside he was biding his time.

Again, Jude and Louise followed Ben's lead. They filled their plates with pasta and salad and sat down at the dinner table. At first they ate in awkward silence then Jude spoke.

"You have a beautiful apartment. It feels very inviting," Jude said.

"It's all because of Louise. She has an eye for beautiful things," Ben replied.

"Well, thank you. I can not take all the credit, my friend Valerie helped," Louise said. "She was at your art show, you may have seen her but she had to leave early."

"I may have, but I honestly don't remember," Jude confessed. "There were so many people that showed up. I was pleasantly surprised."

"So what's next for you, Jude? Another show somewhere?" Ben asked.

"Yes, probably. But after tomorrow I'm going home. I've been on the road for a couple of months and it's tiring. I just want to go home and see my family," Jude replied.

"What does your foundation do? The Jackson Weber Foundation," asked Louise.

"Oh my brother started that, Bradley. He created it years ago," answered Jude. Speaking now to Ben, "Brad works for the marine rescue team and he saw a need and wanted to fill it. It helps families who lost a loved one to drowning, provides free swim lessons to any age, even gives out life jackets to anyone who doesn't have one. His foundation provides a variety of services. He and Lisa are the founders. I help when I can, like with donations."

Louise was impressed, Ben was losing interest. "I guess what I really want to know, Jude, is why did you call my fiancé?" Ben put down his fork and looked directly at Jude.

"Ben, what are you talking about? Jude never called me!" Louise stood up and took her dish to the kitchen. "And how would you know who called me if you weren't snooping in my phone?"

"I was not snooping. It was right on the counter. Missed call from Jude," Ben said, speaking calmly and still looking directly at Jude.

Jude never flinched. He calmly placed his fork on the table and maintained direct eye contact with Ben. So this was why he was really invited him here tonight. The viper was ready to strike and just needed his prey. "I never talked to Lou, it was a missed call," replied Jude. "I was simply going to invite her to my art show."

"Well wasn't that convenient. If I wouldn't have gone, I would not have known anything about it," Ben said. Ben was fuming but remained calm.

"Do you really think your fiancé would not have told you once she found out it was me?" Asked Jude.

Ben was seething now. He was using every ounce of control to keep from punching Jude's smug face. "I never even knew you existed until the day I landed in Erie," Ben said.

Jude immediately turned to look at Lou who looked broken. She couldn't deny any of it. It was all true. She had kept Jude a secret from Ben. It was all coming clearer to Jude. He was starting to understand some of the anger that motivated Ben to plan this ambush. That was exactly what this was, an ambush. Ben knew that Jude had called Lou and apparently she never let Ben know. It was a test and a trap.

Jude pushed out his chair and stood up. He went to the closet and put on his coat. "Thank you for dinner. I'll see myself out," Jude said.

"No, wait! I'll ride down with you," Lou said. She glared at Ben as if to forbid her. He simply went about picking up the dishes. His mission was accomplished.

When the elevator doors closed on the twenty eighth floor, they both let out a sigh of relief. Lou took Jude's hand, "I'm so sorry about that. I didn't know that was his intention when he invited you here tonight. You have to believe me."

"I do."

Lou watched the numbers slowly countdown as they descended towards the lobby. Jude squeezed Lou's hand.

"Lou are you happy?"

Lou started crying. "I don't know anymore."

"Do you remember what I said? You need to be happy in three parts of your life. If you're not, it is never too late to change any or all of them. I still have two. I love where I live and what I do. I am not yet with the one I love," Jude said.

"I love what I do, too," replied Lou.

"Well, one out of three is not enough, Lou."

"Jude, you don't know Ben. He's not normally like this. I don't know what has gotten into him," Lou tried to explain. This was a side of Ben that didn't normally surface.

"Lou, I don't know how you can be with someone who doesn't trust you. You should not have to constantly prove your innocence to the one you love," Jude said. They were almost to the lobby. "Remember my note."

Lou turned to face Jude and they kissed. It wasn't the passionate kind of kiss, it was friendly, sweet and healing.

"Good luck," Jude said and exited the elevator as the doors opened. Lou watched the doors close and hit the button, returning her to her life with Ben.

Jude rubbed his hands together to keep warm and jumped into a taxi to take him back to his hotel. What a night! Jude was finally figuring out what made the man tick. He was the kind of man who was straight with everyone and wanted everyone to be straight back. He wanted to trust those around him and didn't like secrets and lies. He loved and wanted to be loved back. If Jude didn't know any better, he could be describing himself.

Jude had to give the guy a break. He had Lou. Who wouldn't fight when he felt the threat of losing her. The taxi dropped him off at his hotel. He had the art show for one more night and then he could go home.

Jude was glad to be back in his room. He took off his coat and shoes and started a hot shower. While the water was warming up, he took off his suit and laid it on the bed. What a night, he repeated in his head. After Jude showered and got ready for bed, he decided to make a couple of phone calls.

"Hi Jude, how are things in the big city? Is the show going good?" Brad asked his little brother.

"Yes. Nearly seventy sold the first night, sixty tonight and then I still have tomorrow," Jude replied.

"Wow, that's fantastic! Great for the foundation, too," Brad said. "So anything else exciting happen in the Big Apple?"

"Lou and Ben came to my show yesterday. I had dinner with them tonight," Jude said.

"Oh man, how did that go?"

"It went how you would expect. An explosion," Jude replied. "I am just ready to come home."

"Well, we have all missed you. Mrs. Jensen called me today to invite us to Thanksgiving dinner. I told her I had to decline because Lisa's family is coming in and she wanted to cook dinner," Brad explained.

"Well that was nice of her to invite you," Jude said.

"Yes it was. She said you are invited, too, of course. And you can bring a guest if you wanted."

"Well, I'll think about the guest part," said Jude.

"Don't think too long. Thanksgiving is next week," Brad reminded him.

"I won't. Thanks, man. I'll see you soon," said Jude.

Jude loved his brother. He may never know if his parents are alive or dead, but he always knew his brother had his back. It was comforting when everything else in his life was chaos. Jude was still too hyped up to sleep. He decided to watch some television and have a drink. He flipped through all the channels twice.

Jude kept playing tonight over in his head. How could he have been so stupid as to accept a dinner invitation from Ben. Whether he was just being friendly or not, he should have known better. He put himself into a dangerous situation and looking back now, it really could have ended badly.

Jude decided to make one more phone call tonight. He checked the time to make sure it wasn't too late.

"Hi, I hope I didn't wake you," Jude said.

"No, I was awake. How is New York?"

"Big and loud. I can't wait to get home," Jude replied.

"When is that going to be?"

"The day after tomorrow. Hey, do you have plans for Thanksgiving? I mean, do you want to come eat at the Jensen's house for dinner?" Jude asked.

"Sure I would love to. Thanks for thinking of me."

"Of course. I'll call you when I get back into town," Jude said.

"I've missed you."

"I missed you, too," replied Jude.

"Well, good night and have a safe flight tomorrow. I can't wait to hear all about your art show. I am so proud of you."

"Okay, and thank you. Good night, Avery."

Chapter 21

"Laura! Have you seen my swim trunks?" Tom yelled downstairs.

In the kitchen, Laura was in full baking mode. She had cans of pumpkin, bags of flour, tiny jars of spices and bowls of every size. It was pie day. Laura's mixer had been going at top speed all morning, so she didn't hear Tom yelling from upstairs.

"For the fifth time," Tom started, seemingly out of breath, "have you seen my swim trunks?" Tom entered the kitchen and soon realized why she had never heard him.

Laura, with flour on her face and apron, her hands sticky from the pumpkin and evaporated milk combination and up to her elbows in peeled apples, looked at Tom with an exasperated expression. "No, Tom, I have not seen your swim trunks. Are you going for a swim? It's a bit chilly this late in November, may I suggest a wetsuit, instead?"

Laura and Tom both started laughing. Laura was in full Thanksgiving dinner mode and Tom was on vacation mode, already packing for their Mexican cruise a few days after Thanksgiving. Tom loved Laura. Lord knows their marriage was not always perfect, but they have been given this second chance by some twist of fate and he wasn't going to blow it this time. Tom walked over to his wife, covered in flour, and gave her a kiss on the lips.

"What was that for?" Laura asked, surprised.

"For being here, that's why," Tom explained.

Laura looked at Tom with a suspicious eye, then smiled. Laura loved Tom. He reached over, picked up a slice of apple that was already coated in cinnamon and sugar, put it in his mouth and walked into the living room to read his paper. Since the accident, it seemed as though everyone was watching her or protecting her. She felt fine. It seemed like Tom was doing things for her that she used to do herself, like driving her to hair appointments or grocery shopping. Tony would come over and wash the car or sweep out the patio when the wind blew too much sand inside. Even Jude would come and trim the bushes in front of the house.

Her memory never fully came back but she would have flashes of recognition or bits and pieces of memories. The man she saw in the hospital, Stanley, never did become clearer to her. No one completely explained to her who he was. Laura never went back to work. She had only worked part time in the real estate office anyway, so it wasn't hard to let it go. She wasn't sure she could do the job very well since her memory loss, so what was the point?

Laura poured her batter into three pie crusts that were already prepared to receive the pumpkin mixture. Suni said she and Hannah would come over and help later, but Laura couldn't wait to get a head start. She had already planned the menu. She was going to make her corn casserole, sweet potato casserole and her famous stuffing. The other items that were always served, such as rolls, waldorf salad, fresh cranberry sauce, homemade gravy, mashed potatoes, and green beans would be made later. She had Tom pick out the biggest turkey he could find, which turned out to be twenty one pounds. She hoped it would be big enough, she had big appetites coming and if her memory served her correctly, there wouldn't be many leftovers. She already had confirmations from Tony and his growing family as well as Jude and a guest. She invited Bradley and his family, but they declined. She planned to have enough food even if they decided to come after all. Who was Laura kidding, she had enough food to feed an army, but she was happy to do it.

Tony, Suni and Hannah came in the front door carrying bags of groceries. "It's snowing!" Announced Hannah, who was jumping with excitement.

"I thought I saw some snowflakes earlier," said Laura.

"The roads aren't too bad, yet," Tony said. "I do not think it's supposed to get any worse today, though. But just in case, I thought I might help Dad put up some of the storm shutters on some of the windows."

"Well, that sounds like a fine idea," said Laura. Then turning her attention to Suni, "How are you feeling? You shouldn't be carrying all of those heavy bags. Here, give them to me," Laura insisted.

"I'm fine. I am only a few months along. I don't need to be treated like an invalid, yet," Suni said. "It looks like you didn't want to wait for your helpers today."

Laura laughed, "You know me, I can not just sit idle. Pull up a chair Hannah, I have a special job just for you." Laura rolled up Hannah's sleeves, washed her hands and put on a child-sized apron that used to be Lou's. "There, all set. Now I need you to mix these apple slices so they get nicely coated with the cinnamon and sugar. Can you do that?" Hannah nodded and got to work.

Progress was being made in the kitchen and the three generations, Laura loved Suni like a daughter, made three pumpkin pies, two apple and one lemon meringue. That was Hannah's favorite to make. Laura wouldn't let Suni stand for too long and pulled out a chair for her. Tony and Suni were both thrilled that Laura and Tom were back together. They relied on them as grandparents a lot when they needed a babysitter. Now that will be even more important when the new baby arrives next summer. Suni still hadn't let it sink in that they will have a baby next summer. She needed to look for her baby things packed away in the attic.

Now that all the pies were baked, the two women sat down to have some tea. Hannah, bored with the idea of sitting around drinking tea, or the hot cocoa that she was offered, decided to find out what her dad and grandpa were up to. She looked everywhere for them, the living room, patio, the beach and then the garage. She finally found them rummaging through tool boxes for some sort of screw or bolt.

"Didn't you have this size in a jar on your work table?" Asked Tony, holding up a screw.

"Well, I did until I combined them with a longer length in a jar in my other tool box," replied Tom.

"Well where are those?"

"Over there."

"Then what are these?"

Hannah laughed as they went back and forth holding up different sized screws. She decided it was more fun hanging out in the garage than the kitchen.

Finding the right sized screw to close the storm shutters was taking the longest. Screwing them in took seconds. But, once all the proper screws were found and the storm shutters were secured, the men were freezing. They couldn't feel their fingers anymore and the snow had continued to fall, slow and steady. Hannah tried to build a snowman, but because there was still only a light dusting on the ground, there wasn't enough. She opted for a snow ball instead and she hit her father in the middle of his back.

"Oh, it's on little girl," Tony joked.

The little girl's laughter that filled the air was contagious. The grown men were crouching behind cars while trying to make and dodge snow balls. Tom loved having Tony and his family so close. He had secretly wished that Lou would have missed this too and stayed, but it just wasn't meant to be. He heard from her on occasion. She was always checking in on him and Laura. Tom wondered if they were the only ones on her mind, but never dared to ask. She seemed happy with Ben and that was good. He was glad they were engaged. Maybe now she could settle down and start a family of her own.

"You three children better get in here and find something warm to drink before you get frost bite," Laura yelled from the kitchen door.

Tony looked at his father and at Hannah, "Race you inside!" More laughter as Hannah ran right between them and into her grandma's arms.

JUDE, ON THE OTHER hand, was struggling with where he fit in right now. Avery was waiting for him at the airport and it was a welcome distraction. Jude didn't know she was coming because she wanted it to be a surprise. She even had roses for him. It was a first for Jude to have a woman bring him flowers.

"What's this for?" Jude asked taking the bouquet of roses from Avery.

"I wanted to show you how much I missed you," Avery answered.

Jude gave Avery a hug and kiss but didn't tell her she met Lou in New York. As far as he knew, the only one who knew was Brad and he wanted to keep it that way. He was not in the mood to try to explain what happened. Jude wasn't even sure himself what happened or why. He just knew that it was nice to see Lou, but it ended very badly. There was no way he could articulate to someone who wasn't there the animosity that radiated off of Ben.

"I want to hear all about your art shows, Jude," Avery said.

"I will, later. Right now I just want to enjoy being home. This trip was hard, emotionally. I was away from home for two months and in the end, I am just glad to finally be back in Erie."

"Well, I ordered dinner to be picked up on the way back to your place. I don't want you to worry about anything tonight. I will take care of you," said Avery.

Jude was happy to hear those words. He really did like Avery, she was always there for him and has been for the last ten years. Of course, they weren't exclusive. Jude knew she dated a lot of guys. It was the companionship that he liked the most. He hated the description of friends with benefits, but that was basically what they were. Jude wasn't proud of it, but he was cautious with his heart. He had girls coming up to him and giving him their numbers all the time. With his little bit of fame in the art world, he could have his pick of any girl. The problem was he didn't want just any girl.

Avery parked in Jude's driveway and they each carried bags inside the house. Brad had been good about checking in on the place while he was away, so it looked just like he had left it. Jude had remodeled the kitchen and bathrooms, put hardwood floors throughout the downstairs and had new carpet put in upstairs. He painted every room and added fresh gravel to the driveway. It was slowly being transformed from a bungalow looking house to a real home.

Jude took his luggage upstairs to unpack a little bit while Avery set up their dinner downstairs. Jude decided to take a quick shower to warm up. Afterwards, he put on sweatpants and a sweater. Jude's curls were still damp when he headed downstairs. The food smelled delicious.

"I got us eggplant Parmesan from Luigi's," Avery said.

"My favorite," Jude answered.

"I know."

"Thank you for doing all of this," he said, gesturing to the food already on plates at the table. "I appreciate it."

They sat down and Avery handed him a bottle of beer. "First a toast. To you!" She said.

They tapped their beers together and took a drink. They ate their dinner, drank more beer and talked about what had been happening the last two months. Avery kept up with all of the gossip around town, so there was plenty of conversation over dinner. Jude wasn't very much interested in gossip, since his name was usually the topic through the years. But the sound of Avery's voice kept his mind from wandering to places he didn't want it to go.

After dinner, she took the dishes to the sink and they washed and dried them together. Jude missed the intimacy of being close to someone. Avery's blond hair was pulled up in a pony tail tonight and after Jude finished drying the last dish, he went over to her and took out the rubber band holding it up. Avery, with her back to Jude, leaned her head slightly to the right. With her pale neck exposed, Jude leaned down and kissed it. He wrapped his arms around her waist and she turned to him. They continued kissing in the kitchen until Jude took her hand and led her upstairs.

Chapter 22

"Mr. and Mrs. Jensen? Mr. and Mrs. Jensen!" The banging continued on the front door. "Please open up, it's the Police."

Laura and Tom heard the banging on the front door. Now the door bell was ringing. They could not make out what the person was saying, but by their tone and insistence, they knew it must be important. Tom, who slept in flannel pants and top, was the first to go downstairs. Laura had to put on her robe first. He answered the front door to see two uniformed police officers standing in the cold.

"Good morning, we don't mean to disturb you, but we are looking for Mr. Tom Jensen and Mrs. Laura Jensen," the first officer said.

"I'm Tom and this is my wife, Laura," Tom answered just as Laura reached his side. "Please come in and tell us what this is about."

"Yes, sir. Thank you." Both officers came into the entry way and took off their hats. "It's about the hit and run that occurred back in August on West 6th Street that caused injuries to your wife."

Tom and Laura looked at each other and Tom put his arm around her shoulders. "Well, what did you find out?" He asked.

"Well, it took a lot of investigating and retrieving surveillance footage from multiple locations in the area. Also, the fact that the driver fled the scene meant that we had to take a chance that a vehicle with significant front end damage would also need to be repaired, so it was a lot of man hours that went into this case." The first police officer paused, seeing the anxious look on the Jensens' faces.

"But we found him!" The second police officer announced.

Tom and Laura's faces brightened. "Oh wonderful!" Tom hugged and kissed his wife. Finally this case will come to an end.

"What happens now?" Laura asked.

"Well, we have officers going to his residence now. If he's not home, we will track him down. He will be booked and placed in jail," the first officer explained.

"He will most likely be released on bond until the trial, but at least we found him and he can be prosecuted," the second officer said.

The two officers, having delivered their message to the Jensens, put their hats back on before turning towards the door. It was still snowing, but not too hard. It was the kind of light snowfall you dreamed about this time of year.

"Thank you officers," Tom called out. "Oh, I almost forgot to ask, can you tell us his name?"

"Leon Dixon," one of the officers called back before getting in the car and driving away.

Tom closed the door and turned to Laura, "Leon." Both of their jaws dropped at the name. It was someone they knew. A friend of Lou's. They needed to tell someone and they couldn't call her. Tom did not want to call Tony, either. He was probably at work anyway. There was only one person he could call.

"Hello?"

"Jude, I'm sorry to wake you. This is Tom Jensen."

"Hi, Tom. You're not waking me. I am up, what's wrong?" Jude's heart was pounding, wondering if something terrible happened to Lou.

"The police were just here," Tom started.

Jude got up out of bed and started pacing the floor. Avery looked at him, concerned.

"Tom, what happened!" Jude was getting worried.

"It was about Laura's accident," Tom continued.

Hearing this, Jude calmed down a bit. "Okay, what about it?"

"They found out who did it, who the driver of the hit and run was," Tom said. "Jude, it was Leon."

Jude sat back down on the bed. Avery sat up and touched his shoulder. Jude was obviously hearing bad news and she would wait until he hung up to ask. "Oh shit!"

"Yes, well, they are out there now trying to arrest him, but it sounded like he wasn't home. Do you know where he might be?" Tom asked. "Leon's a good kid, we know it was an accident, but he's going to need some friends right now, Jude."

"Okay, thank you Tom for letting me know." Jude hung up the phone and looked at Avery. "We have to find Leon." He explained as they got dressed. Jude made one more phone call before getting in his truck.

"Hi, Jude," Tony said.

"Hey, Tony. I don't have much time, so can you relay a message to my brother and maybe your sister?" Jude asked.

"Sure, what's up?"

"They are arresting Leon for your mom's hit and run accident," Jude said. "I think he's at the bar, so I'm going there now to see if they arrested him, yet. If he's not there, I will go to the police station and see if I can't bail him out."

"Oh my gosh! Okay, don't worry I will make the necessary calls to let everyone know. Thanks, Jude." Tony hung up to call Brad first. Then he would call Lou.

Tony wasn't quite sure how to tell Lou the news. He was even having trouble processing the fact that someone they knew, a friend of theirs, was responsible for putting his mother in a coma. Leon was drunk, of course, at the time. He had hoped this would help get Leon sober enough to want to stop drinking. Tony wasn't sure how Lou would take the news. She would be upset, but there wasn't anything she could do, she was in New York City with her fiancé.

"Hi Tony, how are you?" Lou asked.

"Hi Lou, I'm good."

"How are mom and dad?"

"They are doing good, too. Actually, they are kind of why I'm calling," Tony started. "The police came today and said they found out who the driver was that hit mom."

"Oh, Tony, that is great news. I hope they throw the book at him," Lou said.

"Well, I'm not sure you are going to still feel that way after you hear who it is," Tony said. "It was Leon."

There was silence on the line as Lou tried to process the information she had just heard. "Are you sure?"

"Yes. They are arresting him now. He will probably make bail, so you can still talk to him but he was the guy who put mom in a coma."

"I can not believe it, Tony. He did say he didn't remember the accident. He thought he just hit his mailbox. Shit."

"How's Ben?" Tony asked, trying to change the subject.

"He's good. He is up for another award, so there is a big dinner tomorrow night," Lou answered.

"Well, mom's already baked all of the pies for Thanksgiving, so we are sure to gain ten pounds on Thursday," Tony said.

"She always did make delicious pies," Lou responded.

"And dad is asking everyone where his swim trunks are, as if we should know what he did with them since last summer," Tony joked.

The mention of last summer made Lou even sadder than she was. She was starting to regret answering Tony's call. She should have just let it go to voicemail and deal with the news of Leon in her own time. Last summer was another lifetime ago.

"I'm glad they are still going on their cruise. It will be good for them to get away, especially during the winter," Lou said.

Tony noticed a change in Lou's tone and wondered if everything really was fine. He was not sure she would confide in him even if she wasn't happy. Maybe she did with their mother. Tony heard from Lou once in a while, but it was usually quick texts about how glad she was to be home from work. He knew Lou worked too much. He never knew what she did outside of work, like hobbies or things that she did for fun.

"So what are your plans for Thanksgiving?" Tony asked.

"We will probably just go out to eat. I offered to cook, but Ben was not sure what time he would be home from work, so I didn't want to cook for nothing," Lou answered.

"He has to work? That sucks," Tony said.

"Tell me about it."

"Lou, is everything okay? I mean, between you two? Have you set a date yet?"

"Wow, that is a lot of questions," Lou joked. "First of all, yes, everything is fine and no, we have not set a date, yet."

Tony suspected that it wasn't the whole truth, but he wasn't going to push her. Maybe she was blissfully happy and he was misreading the signs.

"I just thought I would ask since I had you on the phone," Tony said.

"Yes, thanks for calling, Tony, and letting me know about Leon," she said.

Tony's phone call left Lou feeling uneasy. Leon was a friend and he almost killed her mother. This was disturbing news. She would tell Ben when she got home tonight. Right now Lou was at work but on break. She was waiting on test results for a little boy who was brought in with an allergic reaction. It was another busy day and now her mind was spinning with this new information. She should have let it go to voicemail.

Ben had been in a sour mood lately. His moods were a roller coaster ride ever since Jude came over for dinner. He had the building's handyman hang all of the paintings throughout the apartment, except the portrait of her, it was still too personal to hang up in their apartment. Lou kept it wrapped up in her closet. Someday she will have the perfect spot to hang it, but for now she kept it all to herself.

Jude's name was never brought up, but she didn't need to remind Ben of his presence. There were the paintings, which Ben admitted were very beautiful and if he saw them anywhere else he very well may have purchased them. There was also the bracelet. Maybe it was her being stubborn or her not caring about Ben's feelings, but Lou continued to wear the beach glass bracelet Jude had given her. It was just a bracelet. Who knows how many things Ben has or wears that are gifts from old girlfriends or lovers? Lou never asked. The one thing Lou never told Ben, something she never wanted him to know, was that she and Jude slept together last summer. It was eating her up inside. She thought it didn't matter, that she could move on and be happy with Ben, but she felt like she needed to tell him. Lou knew he would be angry, but surely he would get over it, right? They were in love and getting married. Maybe if she went ahead and set a date first, he would see she was serious about their relationship and not pining for an ex boyfriend. Would he believe her? Did Lou believe herself?

Lou heard her phone ringing and it brought her back to reality. It was the lab. She needed to get back to work. Lou answered the call as she headed down the hall. Work was a good distraction.

JUDE AND AVERY ARRIVED at Pilgrim's Bar just as the police were taking Leon away in hand cuffs. They were able to talk a few minutes while the police made phone calls and filled out paperwork. Jude would help pay bond, Leon didn't need to worry. He was crying in the back seat of the police car. Leon was hearing his charges for the first time, too. He never remembered the accident, so the fact that he was responsible for putting Mrs. Jensen in the hospital was hard for Leon to believe.

"I'm so sorry! I'm so sorry!" Leon kept yelling from the police car. Even as they pulled out of the parking lot, Jude and Avery could hear his cry.

Jude hugged Avery and they stood there for a moment in the cold. He didn't mind taking on the responsibility for Leon. Leon wasn't from here, he was from the South and never even mentioned his parents. Jude and Avery got back into his shiny new truck and started the engine. Jude had finally caved in and bought a new one after his old one gave out on him for the last time. He followed the police car to the station. This was not a very good start to the holiday season.

Chapter 23

Tom woke up to the smell of turkey. It radiated the whole house. Tom knew without even needing to look over next to him in bed that Laura was downstairs in the kitchen. It was Thanksgiving Day, her favorite holiday. Laura had been prepping for days and it was finally here. Guests would probably not be arriving for at least a couple of hours, so they had the house to themselves to enjoy the peace and quiet.

Tom got dressed and joined his wife in the kitchen. "Good morning," Tom said as he leaned in to kiss Laura.

"Good morning," she answered. She had made cinnamon rolls for breakfast and then poured Tom a cup of coffee. Laura was determined to have a wonderful holiday filled with family and friends, despite the news they received a few days ago about Leon. She had the morning planned and coordinated so everything had a proper time to cook and share the oven. She knew Tony and his family would come early to help, but for now, they sat and enjoyed breakfast.

Tom was reading the paper and Laura starting glancing through the ads. They did not usually do any shopping the day after Thanksgiving, but the kids sometimes did. She would set the ads aside for Tony and Suni. They were going to need things for the baby. They sipped their coffee and turned the pages of the newspaper. Such normal activities on the biggest and loudest holiday of the year. But for now, it was quiet.

Laura set the table for seven, which made it look uneven. Tom and Tony would each be at the ends of the table. That left one side with three and the other with two. For aesthetics, she decided to make it three and three so that it balanced out. The turkey could be set there, she reasoned. The seven guest plates were all decorated with napkins, pine twigs, candy corn and small little turkeys to act as place settings.

While Laura took care of the table, Tom got a fire started in the fireplace. Tony and Jude always helped with chopping wood during the year, so the Jensens had an ample stockpile out back. There was something special about having a fire during the holidays. Tom wished the whole family could be here, for Laura's sake, and his. Lou did not often come home since she left ten years ago, but having her here for three weeks last summer reminded them how nice it was to have her home.

Both finished with their respective chores, so Tom and Laura took their coffee to the enclosed back porch. They liked sitting out here in every season. The sun was rising and not a cloud in the sky. It was going to be a beautiful day. They were leaving for their cruise on Saturday. Laura had been looking forward to this cruise since the moment she awoke from her coma. Tom was more than happy to oblige. They were both excited.

They continued to watch the waves roll onto the beach when they heard the side door open. "Hello?"

"We are out here, Tony," Tom said.

Soon Hannah came running down the hall and out to the porch. She gave each of her grandparents a hug and kiss and then sat in the chair next to her grandmother. Tony turned on the television in the living room and Suni looked through the ads in the kitchen. Laura could see that it was starting to snow harder outside. That was the only drawback of her favorite holiday, it was cold. Too cold to go outside and do anything. The cold was starting to bother her. She didn't mention it to Tom, but she knew he felt it in his knees and back just like she did. Laura heard the timer go off in the kitchen. She rubbed her right knee before standing.

"Well, time to put in the casseroles," Laura said.

"Mom, Suni can do it," Tony offered,

Laura was walking past him in the living room, "Oh I know, but I have to show her my cooking schedule otherwise something will be left out." She continued into the kitchen to finish up the dinner. They usually ate around one, letting the guys watch a game or two and then they would eat leftovers at about five or six. Pies could officially be eaten any time after two. It was a very flexible schedule because the food was never really put away. Whenever a dish was finished it just got washed.

Jude and Avery would probably be here in an hour or so. Jude always came early to help around the house. Sometimes Laura would decide at the last minute that she wanted to put another extension in the table, Jude and Tony would help with that. Or if she wanted the table to angle out from the corner to give one side of the table more room, the boys would move it. Jude and Tony were great friends and wonderful to have around.

Avery was a relatively new addition to the family invitations. Laura figured that since she and Jude were spending so much time together, she may as well get an invitation, too, even if it was just a 'plus one' on the invite. Laura had nothing against Avery, it was just still so hard to see her with Jude. Today she would try harder to get to know Avery. There will be more holidays in the future and Jude was like family.

Tom and Hannah came into the living room to join Tony. The fire really warmed up this room.

"Are there any cartoons on, Daddy?" Hannah asked.

"No, sweetheart, but there is a parade," her grandfather answered instead.

Tony found the parade and they watched as large balloon people floated down the street. "Maybe your Aunt Lou is in the crowd, this is in New York City," Tony said.

"Really?" Hannah asked. "I miss Aunt Lou."

"Me, too." A voice behind them replied.

"Uncle Jude! I didn't know you were here!" Hannah jumped off the couch and ran to Jude with arms wide open.

"We just snuck in the side door," Jude replied and picked her up into his arms. "You know, I found a little bunny outside who said she was looking for you. I told the bunny that I would bring her to you."

"You did?" Asked Hannah.

"Sure did." Jude nodded to Avery who held something behind her back. At Jude's cue, she produced a large pink bunny, just like the one she lost in the lake. Jude took it from Avery and gave it to Hannah. "Here she is, you two are back together again."

Hannah hugged the pink bunny and wanted down. She ran into the kitchen to show her mother and grandma.

Tony was always surprised by Jude's generosity, especially when it was aimed at his family. Jude loved kids, that was evident. Perhaps always trying to make up for the little brother he never got to experience.

"Hey man, thanks for that," Tony said.

"You're welcome," Jude replied. "I have actually had it for awhile, I've just been so busy lately. I am just glad I remembered to bring it today."

"Well, it means a lot that you care so much," Tony said.

"You guys are my family," Jude answered and went to see the ladies in the kitchen.

Everyone got something to drink, mingled around the house and somehow the parade channel got changed to football. The men were watching it in the living room when Laura announced it was time to sit down. Tom was on one end of the table and Tony was on the other end. Everyone else filled in where their place settings told them to sit.

The food had been brought to the table and it looked and smelled delicious. It was so tempting to dig in and start eating but Laura wanted Tom to say Grace first.

"Dear Lord, please bless this food and all who prepared it. Bless our family that is here with us today and those who can't be here or are no longer with us. May all of those who are traveling, make it to their destinations safely. And for those who are going on a cruise, make it home in one piece." Tom paused until their laughter stopped. "Thank you, Lord. Amen." Everyone responded with 'Amen' and started passing the food around.

Dishes were passed from one to the next. There were conversation about the food, about the football game and even shopping tomorrow. There were compliments about each dish and questions about the recipe. Avery seemed to fit in just fine. Hannah had her new pink bunny on her lap that she named Bunny. Laura was so happy to see everyone enjoying Thanksgiving dinner that no one heard the kitchen door open and close. It wasn't until they heard, "Happy Thanksgiving," that everyone turned to look at the visitor.

"LOU!" Her mother yelled. "You made it!" Laura jumped out of her chair and ran to give her daughter a hug and kiss. Laura looked past Lou and out the window. "Where's Ben? Isn't he with you?"

"Nope, just me," Lou answered. She set her luggage in the hallway and took off her coat and boots. "Smells good. I must be just in time." Lou felt awkward walking into this family gathering uninvited. Even though it was her family, she knew she was unexpected. Her eyes searched each face and they were all smiling, except two. Avery just looked disgusted and Jude just didn't look at her.

As more people were making an effort to get up and come to her she told everyone to stay seated. She came around the table and hugged each one as they sat. When she got to Avery, she was civil enough to give a quick hug. When she got to Jude, it was quick but warm. Laura was pulling out a chair that was the eighth place at the table.

"Here we even have a seat for you," Laura said.

"Well isn't that lucky," Lou replied, until she realized it was directly across from Jude. She was also in between Hannah and Laura, so Lou focused her attention to them, "Who is this, it looks like Bunny," Lou asked Hannah.

"It is!" Hannah exclaimed. "Uncle Jude brought her to me. She's been looking for me, he said."

Lou automatically looked at Jude who matched her gaze. Lou smiled and Jude returned the smile, too. Lou was the first to break away. "This looks amazing everyone, thank you for letting me crash the party," she was only half joking. She wasn't sure what anyone was thinking and she had tried to prepare herself the whole flight and drive home. How was she going to explain Ben's absence and why she came home again.

"So Ben isn't with you?" Tony asked.

Here we go. "No." Lou had thought that the less she elaborated the better.

"Is he coming later? Do we need another chair?" Laura asked.

"No."

"How long are you staying?" Asked Hannah.

"I don't know, sweetie."

They were all looking at her now. She knew her answers were not enough, but she was not ready to say anything more. "Can someone please pass the gravy?"

Jude reached beside him and picked up the gravy and handed it over to Lou. As she reached with her left hand, Jude noticed the naked finger. "You're not wearing your ring," he said.

Lou took the gravy and looked right into Jude's eyes. It was a silent plea to not ask any more question. Answers would come in time. "No," Lou answered quietly. She gave a sharp look at everyone around the table. The atmosphere was tense, but no one asked Lou any more question over dinner.

Chapter 24

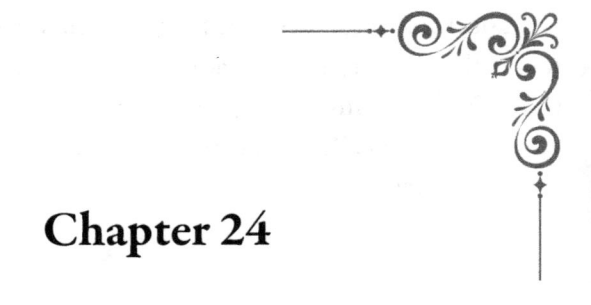

As intense as Thanksgiving dinner was, the time after was even worse for Lou. She helped clear the table and washed and dried the dishes but she knew everyone was waiting to ask more questions. She could feel the stares from across the room and see the whispers that were being exchanged. Lou did not care, as long as she didn't have to talk, she was okay. She didn't know how to explain it. Even in her own rational mind, she couldn't understand what happened between her and Ben. She just knew it was all her fault. Admitting that to herself was one thing, but saying it out loud to her family was another. Lou took a piece of pumpkin pie out to the enclosed porch. She wanted to watch the snow in silence.

Jude approached so quietly that Lou didn't even hear him sit down next to her. "A glass of wine for your thoughts?" Jude asked, handing her a glass of wine.

Lou smiled. "Thanks, but not even a whole bottle could make sense of mine."

"Is there anything I can do?" Jude asked and Lou shook her head. "I won't ask details, I just wanted to know if you are okay."

Lou sighed before answering. "I know I am a strong person, but this is going to take time." She took a sip of wine then added, "I told him about us, last August."

"Oh, shit, Lou! Why did you do that?" Jude looked upset. "He didn't have to know. Of course, he would be upset about that. The guy hated my guts." He ran his hand through his curly hair. Lou had loved running her own hands through it.

"It's okay, Jude, he needed to know. It was a secret that was eating me inside. If he had done something like that, I would want to know," Lou said. "What's up with you and Avery?"

"Avery?" Jude asked. "It' nothing. She means nothing to me."

Just as Jude said that, Avery threw her water at him. "What the hell!" She yelled. "I have stood by your side while she walks all over you. Every time she breaks your heart, I was there for you. We are done. I'll find my own way home." Avery walked out of the room.

"I'm so sorry," Lou said.

Jude had his face in his hands but did not go after her. He hated hurting her like that. Avery was good to him and she didn't deserve that. "I'll call her tomorrow and apologize. She has always been there for me, Lou, when no one else was."

"You mean me," Lou replied.

"Yes, Lou, I mean you!" Jude answered with more force than usual. Jude stood up, kissed Lou on the top of her head and left the porch.

Lou didn't know what to do next. She didn't even know how long she was staying. Her phone rang, it was Ben, again.

"Hello Ben."

"Hi babe, where are you?"

"I'm in Erie."

There was a pause. "When are you coming home?"

"Do you want me to?" Lou asked.

"What kind of question is that? Of course I want you to."

"That's not what you said last night."

"Last night you told me you slept with another man. How do you expect me to react? You are my fiancé, we are getting married and I find out you cheated on me. I think I had a right to be angry."

"You told me to leave, Ben. You told me to get out. What did you expect me to do? I know what I did was wrong and I could not keep it a secret any longer. I love you and respect you, I couldn't keep it from you any more."

"I love you, too. Please come home so we can work through this."

"Not yet, Ben."

Lou just looked at her phone after they hung up. She did need to go back so they could work on it, but she also needed time away to think about things. So did he. They said they loved each other, but she knew he will have a hard time trusting her now and he will be questioning her every move.

Laura was patiently waiting for Lou to be alone so she could sit with her. "Hi honey, can I sit here?"

"Of course, mom."

Laura sat and looked at her daughter. "I know you don't want to talk about it, but did you and Ben break up?" Her mother asked.

"I guess you could say we are on hold. I left the ring in the apartment as a sign to Ben that I needed time to myself. We had a fight. I admitted to being unfaithful and he got mad. He had every right to be angry but I didn't have to stay and react to it. He said some hurtful things because he was hurt, that's normal. We both just need time to think about our relationship."

"Are you happy with Ben, Lou?"

"Yes, he makes me happy and I believe I make him happy but we also make each other angry, jealous and frustrated. We need to decide if the part that makes us happy is enough." Lou realized she had thought quite a lot about their relationship, just never said it out loud before.

"Well, come get some more to eat. It is leftover time now." Laura got up to return to the kitchen.

Lou was sure her mother was also reporting back to the other inquiring minds in there. She didn't care anymore, she was hungry.

Lou went to make a turkey sandwich. Her father came over to make one, too. They went to the dining table to eat.

"Lou, as you know, your mother and I are going on a cruise the day after next," her father said.

"Yes, dad, I am so happy for you," Lou replied.

"We are too, sweetheart. I was hoping that you might stay long enough to watch the house while we were gone. It will only be a week," he said.

"I don't know. I really was just going to stay a couple of days, to give me and Ben a chance to cool off," said Lou.

"I understand. It was just a suggestion. I just worry with it being so cold, pipes could freeze and there wouldn't be anyone here to see in time to shut off the water or something like that. I will have Tony check in from time to time." Her father wanted to make it clear to Lou that she was welcome to stay as long as she wanted.

They both ate their sandwiches and went back for pie. Jude was cutting a slice of the apple pie when Lou reached for the knife.

"I'll get it for you," Jude said. He cut her a piece similar to his.

"You know, I didn't see your truck when I drove in today, did something happen to it?" Lou asked, taking the slice of pie from him.

"Yes you did. See that shiny new red one? That is mine," Jude replied, pointing out through the kitchen window.

"Wow, you finally did it," Lou said appreciatively.

"I have actually made a lot of improvements since you've been here last. You should see the house," he immediately felt embarrassed after suggesting she visit his house remembering what happened the last time they were there.

"Maybe I will some day," she replied. Jude looked up at her when she said this. Did she want a repeat of that night? Being so close to her made his heart beat faster.

Jude took her hand. "I see you are still wearing the bracelet I gave you," he said. She may not be wearing Ben's diamond ring, but she was wearing the beach glass bracelet.

Lou let her hand fall out of Jude's when Tony walked in. "Stop hogging all the pie you guys," Tony joked.

"Don't worry, it looks like mom made plenty, as usual," Lou replied.

After Tony finished his piece of pie, he turned to shake hands with Jude. "Thanks again for the pink bunny, Jude. Hannah is out cold with her arms around that bunny," said Tony.

"Hey man, I love her like she was mine," Jude replied.

Lou was touched to hear that Jude had replaced the bunny that Hannah lost in the lake. It was those small details that set him apart from Ben.

After Tony and his family left, it was just Jude who remained. It was only eight, but her parents were already upstairs getting ready for bed. She supposed when you were up at the crack of dawn to cook a turkey, you want to sleep at eight.

Jude and Lou sat on the couch watching the fire in the fireplace. She had put on another log because she wasn't tired yet. It was comfortable just sitting with Jude in the glow of the fire. Lou turned towards him. "You asked me some hard questions today, now it is my turn."

Jude took a sip of his beer and smiled. "I'm ready," he said with a smirk.

"First, what is really up with you and Avery? You said it was nothing serious, but it didn't look like she felt the same way," Lou asked.

"Wow, starting off with the heavy hitters I see," Jude joked then got serious. "We are not serious. Period. We are friends," he paused, "with benefits. I hate the phrase, but it's true. We are both lonely and need the company sometimes. I know she saw other guys, but for me, I only saw her." He took a chance to look at Lou. Her face was expressionless. "Did that answer your question?"

"Oh yes, quite well thank you," Lou said, glancing back at him. She wasn't expecting him to be so honest.

"I'm sorry if that was more info than you wanted, but I don't want secrets between us, Lou. I mean it, you are too important to me," Jude said.

"Well, that brings me to my second question. Why didn't you tell me you were a world famous artist?" Lou asked.

At this question, Jude literally laughed out loud, nearly spitting his beer out. "Now this one is not all my fault," he protested. "I told you several times that I was a painter. I can't help it if you assume I mean walls and houses. You never asked anything further and I just didn't elaborate."

"But why? That is what I don't get. Jude, I saw your very heart and soul on those canvases and you never wanted to share that with me?"

"I couldn't."

"Why?"

"Because it hurt too much. You are the reason my heart is on those canvases. Ten years ago I started painting for therapy. I would hit the canvas with those brushes because it helped get my anger out. At first, it didn't even look like anything, just brush strokes full of paint. Then I worked through the anger and it turned to heartache. I know I was only a kid of eighteen when you left, but I saw a future together with you. I just channeled all that hurt into my painting," Jude paused. "I couldn't show it to you, it would have been like opening a wound that had been stitched up, healed and scarred. It was better if you didn't know. I was naive to think you would never find out, since everyone else knows, but I just couldn't do it to myself."

Lou took a sip of her wine and yawned. Jude took that as a cue and stood up.

"I had better go. It's been a long day," he said.

Lou walked him to the front door, "It was good to see you today."

"It was good to see you, too," Jude replied.

They gave each other a hug and he left. Lou watched as his new red truck drove out of the driveway and down the street. She was exhausted. Lou carried her luggage upstairs and into her old room. She showered, changed and curled up in bed. It was hard work being an adult. Sometimes it was the comfort of being in her childhood bedroom that brought things back into perspective. She realized she had caused Jude enough pain, she would try to make it work with Ben. She should probably go back home tomorrow. Tonight she dreamed of pink bunnies.

Chapter 25

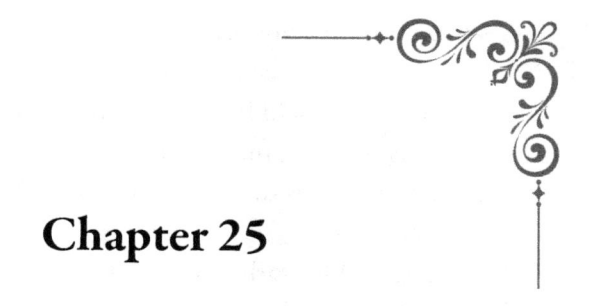

Lou came down to breakfast to see her parents reading the paper. They both looked up when they saw her enter the kitchen. "Good morning, Lou. How did you sleep?" Her father asked.

"I slept good. How about you guys? You turned in early last night," Lou said.

"Oh we slept fine," her mother answered. "But there is something we want to discuss with you. We saw you with Jude last night and decided it wasn't the time or place for it."

Lou brought her coffee to the table and sat with them. "What is it?"

Laura and Tom exchanged looks. "Well, we have already discussed this with Tony, and Jude, and we wanted to tell you but it didn't feel right over the phone, so we kept putting it off."

"Mom, you are worrying me. What is it?" Lou asked again.

"Your father and I are moving to Florida," her mother said.

Lou didn't say anything. Just looked from one parent to the other. "When?" She finally asked.

"When we get back from our cruise, we are going to pack up and go. We have actually been planning this for months. My sister, your Aunt Ann, lives in this nice community for retired folks. There was a place near her for sale and we bought it." Laura took Tom's hand and smiled. "We never wanted to leave the lake, but the winter is just getting too hard for us. The snow and the cold aren't fun at our age anymore."

"What about this house?" Lou asked.

"Well, we haven't decided. We were hoping either you or Tony would want it. Tony said he would think about it, but he was never as fond of it as you," her mother said.

"I'm in no position to own a house here. My life is in New York," Lou protested.

"Is it, dear?" Her father asked. There was a slight pause, "Just think about it. Life is always surprising us. There's no hurry."

Laura sat up straight and changed the subject. "Anyway, we are leaving tomorrow to catch our ship, don't forget. You are free to stay here and look after things while we are gone. But, if you decided to leave before we get back, we will understand."

"Okay, mom," Lou said. She had thought to go back home soon. She would call Ben later and see where his head was at today.

When Lou's phone rang, her first thought was that it was Ben checking up on her but the name of the caller was Rose.

"Lou?" Rose asked.

"Yes, what is it Rose?" Lou could tell by her tone that she was upset about something.

"It's Leon. He was in another accident. Just him. Last night. Hit a pole. He's dead, Lou." Rose was now crying on the other end.

"Rose, wait, are you sure?" Lou asked. Laura and Tom could hear the crying from where they were sitting and they both had expressions of concern.

"Yes, it's Leon. He died."

"Okay, Rose, thanks for telling me." Lou put down the phone. She knew she wasn't going to get any more details from her. Lou laid her phone down on the table and looked at her parents.

"That was Rose. She said Leon was in an accident and died last night," Lou said calmly. "I'm going to have to call someone else to get more details." Lou knew she couldn't call Avery, so she dialed the only other person she could.

"Hi Lou."

"Hello, Jude. Have you heard about Leon?" Lou asked.

"Yes, Rose called but she was too emotional to give much information so I called the police station," Jude said.

"What is he saying?" Laura asked, interrupting.

Lou gave her a gesture that meant 'wait' and continued the call with Jude. "What did the police say," Lou asked him.

"He was drunk. His blood alcohol level was twice the legal level and he hit a light pole. It was instant, Lou. I guess he worked at the bar last night and just had too much, again. You know, I've talked to him many times about gettin help. He was actually sober for a couple of months until he was arrested." Jude paused, "Maybe I shouldn't have bailed him out, then this would not have happened."

"Jude, if you didn't then Rose, Avery or I would have. We are all friends and we each would have done that for him. Don't you dare blame yourself." Lou said.

"I know you're right, but it just sits in my stomach and forms a knot. I don't know how to describe it," Jude replied.

"Leon was lost, Jude. We tried our best, but it wasn't enough for him. I'll miss him, though," said Lou.

"Me, too."

"In spite of everything, he was our friend and now he's gone. We should all meet up at the bar for a toast," suggested Lou.

"Okay, I'll let everyone know."

Lou went on to explain to her parents what they knew so far. They were all conflicted in their emotions. Yes, he was a friend, but he also put Laura in the hospital. He was an alcoholic and was controlled by it. He had tried to fight it but he couldn't. Despite everything, he was still a friend that will be missed.

When Lou walked into the Pilgrim's Bar later that day, she wasn't sure what the atmosphere would be. She knew there would be sadness but also tension because of what happened at her house on

Thanksgiving with Avery. She passed all the pool tables and headed right to the back where they always hung out. Rose and Danny were both there with little Emily, now one and a half. On such short notice, they couldn't find a sitter, so they brought her. Avery was there, glaring at Lou as she walked to their table. Jude came up from behind her carrying a tray of shot glasses and a bottle of whiskey. They smiled awkwardly at each other and she stepped to the side to let him through.

"Thanks for coming, everyone. I know it was short notice but it also felt like it was necessary," Jude said, taking control of the group. "I talked to the officer in charge of Leon's case, they can not get ahold of his parents, no one knows where they are, so I am paying his funeral expenses and it will happen on Wednesday, three days from now. I wanted you all to have enough notice if you wanted to attend."

Avery dramatically got up and hugged Jude. "Oh Jude, thank you for doing that, you are so generous. I can't believe he is gone!" She cried into his shoulder. It was a bit over the top, but they all felt the same sentiment.

"Yes, thank you, Jude," Rose, Danny and Lou all said in unison.

"It was the least I could do," Jude replied.

Lou looked at him and frowned. He was still blaming himself. Would he always be the martyr? Avery released her clutches, but remained standing my his side. Jude filled each shot glass and passed them around.

"To Leon!" Jude shouted.

"To Leon!" Everyone said together.

They toasted a couple of times and then started bringing up their favorite stories of Leon. Lou only had stories from school. "Remember that time Leon got caught cheating on his math test, he got detention for a week." Everyone else had memories of him as an adult, too. The ten years of Lou's absence was becoming obvious.

Avery looked at Lou and said, "I remember when Leon passed his bartenders test and got his license, we all came and celebrated with him. Oh right, except for Lou, she never came back after high school." Avery's smile turned from sweet to a scowl.

"No one is blaming anyone here, it's a wake for goodness sake," Danny said.

"I'm just trying to figure out why Lou is even here." Avery replied. "I mean, when you turn your back on friends, then anything can happen when you're away." She put both arms around Jude's waist but he wasn't going to allow her to speak that way to Lou.

Jude broke free from Avery and was getting angry, "Stop it Avery! Stop attacking Lou. I'm sorry to do this here, but you are acting like a child. We are done. It's that simple. Please leave me alone."

Avery started crying to be even more dramatic, "It's her fault!" She yelled, pointing at Lou. "She has done nothing but try to tear us apart and treat Jude like garbage. She can't stand it when he falls in love with someone else. If she can't have him, no one can, is that it, Lou?" Avery threw her purse at Lou and lunged.

Lou ducked and grabbed Avery by the arms. "Avery, there are babies here, stop!" Lou tried to push Avery away from the table when Jude grabbed her from behind and took her outside.

Whatever he said to her, she did not come back in the bar, instead Jude came back to get her purse. When Jude returned to the table, he apologized and gave everyone the details of the funeral. Rose and Danny left, saying they needed to feed Emily. This left Jude and Lou.

"Are you staying for the funeral?" Jude asked.

"Yes, I will. I was going to call Ben and tell him after this was over," she answered.

"I'm sorry about what Avery said to you. It was rude and untrue," Jude said.

She took a deep breath and exhaled. "Well, some of it was true. I did leave and not come back. I hurt you, I won't forgive myself for the hurt I caused everyone. I had no right to be jealous, but I guess I was a little. I'm not mad at Avery, she is just hurt and lost like the rest of us."

Jude gave her a hug. It was warm and comforting. He had a lot of respect and love for Lou, she was a strong woman and she would get through this. "Let's go get some lunch," Jude said.

"Can I get a rain check?" Lou asked. "I need to call Ben and get it over with. I may not have much of an appetite after that," she joked.

"Okay, fine," Jude replied. "Just remember I am here if you need me."

"I know."

Lou drove home to make the call to Ben. He wasn't going to be happy to hear she was not coming home, yet. Hopefully, she could make him understand why. It's not like she planned a car accident, death and a funeral just to stay home longer.

"Hello babe, how are you doing?" Ben asked.

"I'm good."

"When are you coming home? I miss you."

"Well, I was planning to come tomorrow, actually, but something terrible has come up. I need to postpone," Louise said.

Ben paused before responding, obviously disappointed by her answer. "What happened?" He asked.

"Well, you remember my friend, Leon, the bartender who happened to be the one who hit my mother?"

"Yes."

"Well, he was in another car accident only this time he was alone and it was fatal. His funeral is on Wednesday. I'm planning to stay until then," Louise said.

"Oh my gosh, Louise, I'm so sorry. Should I come?"

"No, Ben, I'll be okay. My family and friends are here, I'll be fine. I'll come home after it is all over," she said.

"I love you, babe," Ben said.

"Love you, too."

Lou needed to clear her mind. There were too many conflicting thoughts in her head. She should be mad at Avery, but she's not. She should be mad at Ben and at Leon, but she's not. She should be mad at Jude, but she never could.

Lou put on her boots, winter coat, hat and gloves and went out the back patio to walk on the beach. She always dreamed of walking on this beach whenever she wasn't home. The lake was different in winter. It was white and starting to freeze over. It snowed last night, but it wasn't snowing now. The sun was shining and the sky was blue. The lake was also a conflict in her head. It was the cause of one of the greatest tragedies in her life, yet it was also the one thing that brought her the most peace. Why was her forgiveness so easily bestowed on others but yet denied to herself? Didn't she deserve it, too? Lou let the lake calm her thoughts.

Chapter 26

The house felt empty. With her parents on their cruise and the funeral still a day away, Lou had too much idle time. Her mother had suggested that, since she was staying, she could help pack up the last minute things she didn't get to before they left. She wrote down on a piece of paper everything she still needed to be packed up for their move to Florida. It was mostly some dishes, kitchen items and glasses that she wanted to take to Florida for their new house. There were also some things from the closets and garage, but that was mostly it.

She decided to call Tony to come and help carry things down from upstairs and sort through it. "Sure," he said, "I'll be right over."

They decided to start upstairs and work their way down. Their parents were going from a large, four bedroom home to a two bedroom condo, so they really didn't need to take very much. Lou and Tony worked side by side all day. Taking breaks and raiding the fridge. "Are you taking the house?" Lou asked him.

Tony was shaking his head. "I don't think so, too many memories."

"But isn't that a good thing?" She asked.

"Maybe for you, but Suni and I have a family, a growing family, and we are making our own memories in our own home." Tony explained. "What about you? Don't you want it?"

"I would love it but I'm not in a position to move to Erie," Lou said. "I have my job in New York, and Ben."

There was silence when Lou mentioned Ben. She knew he didn't make the best impression when he was here last time and the fact that Lou was standing in their parent's kitchen was further evidence that things were not going well.

"Well, I think we did everything on mom's list," Tony said, changing the subject.

"Yes, if there is anything we forgot, someone can send it to her," she replied. "Thanks for giving up your Tuesday for me, I appreciate it."

"Anything for you, little sister," he said.

Before he left, they hugged. She really could count on Tony for anything. Lou sat down in the living room and turned on the television. She curled up with a glass of wine and flipped through the channels. It reminded her of her old apartment. The one where she lived alone and could feel secure. This house had the same feeling. Her muscles ached from the strain of packing and moving boxes around. She was cozy on the couch and she fell asleep.

Lou woke up as the bright sunshine came through her bedroom window. She had woken up shortly before midnight and took herself to bed. She slept good, but it was a strange feeling being in this house alone. Even last summer, when her mother was in the hospital, her father was in the next room and it was comforting. She pulled back the curtain and admired the view, snow flurries. Perhaps that is fitting for a funeral.

She got dressed in black slacks, gray wool sweater and leather boots. The services would be inside the chapel. No cemetery service today, not until the spring thaw when they could bury the casket. Downstairs, Lou made coffee and put some bread in the toaster. She still had a couple of hours before she had to leave, so she went into the living room to eat and watch the news.

Lou went into the kitchen to refill he coffee when there was a knock on the front door.

"Your paper was laying out front, so I thought I would bring it in for you," said Ben.

Lou couldn't believe her eyes, she was at a loss for words.

"Are you going to invite me in, or not?" He asked, snowflakes accumulating on his hair and shoulders.

Lou stepped aside, "Of course, come in Ben."

Ben stomped his feet to get the snow off and set down his carry on bag. "I know this is a surprise, but you mentioned the day and time of the funeral and I wanted to be here for you," he explained,

"Thank you," Lou said. "This is a complete surprise."

"I know I should have called, but I wasn't even sure I could get on the flight because so many were getting cancelled due to weather. And when I did, I figured whether it was a good thing or bad thing, I am here."

"Yes you are," she said.

Ben came close to her and gave her a hug and a kiss. He took his coat off, hung it on the coat rack and followed her into the kitchen. "Are you hungry?" Lou asked.

"Just coffee if you have any," he answered.

Lou poured a cup of coffee for Ben and they sat at the table. She opened the newspaper as he sipped his coffee. It was all so surreal. It was just like sitting in their apartment in New York, only they weren't. He was here in her parents house wanting to go to the funeral of her dead friend.

"We will leave in thirty minutes if you want to change or freshen up," Lou said.

"I just need to use the restroom."

"Okay, you know where it is," she said.

She cleaned up their dishes and thought about calling Tony or Jude to warn them that Ben was here, but what was the point. He was here. They would have to deal with it just like she was dealing with it. It will be a shock for everyone to see Ben beside her, but they would be leaving soon anyway. Lou was sure he probably had return tickets for them for tomorrow.

When Ben returned to the kitchen, Lou said, "Well, we had better get going." There was no more delaying the inevitable. They took Ben's rental and drove to the chapel. Pulling into the parking lot, Lou recognized all the cars and trucks, especially Jude's new red one. They walked into the small chapel, Lou entered first followed by Ben. There was a slight chatter when Ben appeared and Lou's eyes did a sweep of the room. Rose and Danny were there, without Emily. Tony and Suni were there, Brad and Lisa and finally her eyes met Jude's. Avery was noticeably absent. Jude seemed to stand up a little taller and pushed his shoulders back when she and Ben came and took the pew behind him. There was a picture of Leon next to the casket. He was smiling. Rose was already dabbing at her eyes with a tissue and it hadn't even started yet.

The service was short but sincere. The people that spoke really knew him. Lou wished she knew him more than simply a classmate from school. He lived a wild life, according to their friends, a life she would have liked to have been a part. Everyone agreed to meet back at the Pilgrim's Bar for a drink. Lou remembered what happened last time they were there, but without Avery, it probably would not end the same way. Lou could only hope.

Everyone went straight to the back table at the bar. Jude got shot glasses and a bottle of whiskey from the bar and brought it to the table. "Okay everyone, a toast to our good friend, Leon!" Jude announced. They all raised their glass and said in unison, "To Leon!"

As Lou drank her shot, her hat fell to the floor. Jude bent down to get it, but Ben was faster. "I got it, Jude," Ben said.

Jude backed up and put his hands up as if surrendering. "No problem, man. Didn't know you were coming," Jude said.

"I was surprising my fiancé," he replied.

When Jude heard the word fiancé, he looked at Lou, who was only now becoming aware of the exchange going on behind her.

"That hasn't been decided, yet," she said to Jude.

"Louise, I wasn't aware that status had changed," Ben said to her.

"Ben I don't want to discuss this here," she said. "Everyone, let's go back to my place!" Lou announced to the group of friends.

Brad and Lisa, as well as Rose and Danny, regretfully declined. That left Tony, Suni and Jude. They headed out toward the exit as Jude grabbed the bottle and slapped a one hundred dollar bill on the bar. He nodded to the bartender who nodded back.

At the house, Tony ordered some pizzas and Lou lit a fire in the fireplace. Jude set the whiskey bottle on the kitchen counter and looked for glasses. Lou and Tony had packed a bunch of glasses yesterday, so Jude produced a selection of juice glasses. They each took another shot and then spread out around the house.

Lou and Ben were sitting on the enclosed back porch. "You know, my father offered me this house. They are moving to Florida," Lou said.

"I didn't know that. What did you say?" Asked Ben.

"I didn't answer," Lou replied. She started laughing at the irony. "I guess I do that a lot. I run away from big decisions. I didn't answer you at first, I have not set a date and now I can't even answer my father."

"Why would you want to stay here?" Ben asked. "Your life is in New York."

"Ben, I have always been drawn to that lake, but something happened on that lake that I have never told you." Lou looked at Ben. "I never spoke about it to anyone other than those who were there." She looked back out to the frozen lake. "I was seven and my brother, Tony was ten. Tony and I went out on the lake with the three Weber brothers, Brad who was twelve, Jude, seven and Jackson who was five. It was late, probably close to eleven at night. Brad had told us little kids that there were fish that glowed in the dark. These glowing fish never came to the shore, we needed to take the boat and go out into the middle of the lake to see them. We believed him."

Lou continued, "I don't know if Brad had ever taken the boat out before, it was night and he was only twelve, but he was the oldest and we trusted him. We were all hanging over the sides of this little motor boat looking for these mysterious glowing fish. We stayed out there a long time before Brad started laughing, it was a joke of course, but he wouldn't give up. Brad stood up on this little boat and acted like he saw them. He said they were still twenty feet away and started the motor. What Brad didn't realize was that little Jack was so excited to see the fish he was leaning over the most. When Brad sped up the boat, little Jack fell out. The rest of us were already screaming and laughing, making all kinds of noise because we thought we were finally going to see the glowing fish, so no one heard Jude yelling that Jackson was gone. When Jude pulled on Brad and finally got his attention, we had traveled so far from the spot he went in."

Lou paused, remembering that moment. She choked up as she continued, "We couldn't find the exact location. Brad circled and circled but it was so dark and we weren't sure if we were in the right spot. Jack was only five." Lou stopped to blow her nose. She heard someone else blowing his nose and turned to see Jude. She didn't know how long he was standing there. He entered the room and sat opposite her. She continued the story for Ben. "Anyway, my brother and I were grounded the rest of the summer, no swimming or going out on any boat. I think secretly they were glad it wasn't one of their kids." It was hard for Lou to admit in front of Jude, but she continued. Ben needed to know. Jude reached a tentative hand on her knee as permission from him to keep going.

"The Weber family suffered the most," she said. Ben looked up at Jude who was looking at Lou. Ben noticed the hand on her knee but decided to say nothing for now. "Their parents grounded them and worse. They were blamed for Jackson's death and they carried that into their adult lives. Their parents became ghosts and eventually separated and left the boys alone when Jude turned eighteen. The same summer I broke up with Jude and went to college in New York. You see, we all carry this guilt but we are still drawn to the lake."

"Why didn't you ever tell me this before?" Ben asked.

"Because I thought it was all in the past."

Chapter 27

Crying, Lou walked into the kitchen. She poured herself a glass of wine and realized everyone else had gone home. It was just her, Jude and Ben. It was cathartic to tell the story, but it also brought all those feelings to the surface. She wasn't sure how to deal with these emotions and what Ben would think of her now. She leaned on the counter and started eating a slice of cold pizza.

Jude and Ben remained seated in the enclosed porch. It was almost sunset, which at this time of the year, was early. Jude could tell Ben was moved by the story he had just heard. How could you not be? Jude's little brother is gone all because of them. His whole family was torn apart. Jude knew Lou still carried guilt about that night, but hearing it told in such chilling detail after more than twenty years made his heart ache. He knew that guilt, remembered it, until he learned to forgive himself.

"I'm sorry, I didn't know," said Ben.

"She is not happy, you know," Jude said.

"I know," Ben admitted. There was a long pause as the two men eyed each other. "You think you can make her happy?" Ben asked.

"I think I know better what she wants, yes," Jude replied.

"So this is the part where you tell me you are better for her. That moving back to a small town is what she really wants to do, right?" Ben implied.

"I'm not here to tell you anything, Ben. You are asking the wrong person those questions," Jude said. He then stood up and went into the kitchen. He saw Lou sitting at the kitchen island and went to her side. He brushed the hair out of her face and placed it behind her ear. "Are you okay?" He asked.

"I will be. I'm strong, remember?" Lou asked jokingly.

"I just need to know that if I go home and leave you alone with him that you will be okay," Jude said.

Jude didn't hear Ben approach, "Wow, man! You have some nerve asking my fiancé if she is going to be safe with me," Ben said.

"It's a legitimate question considering how upset you have been with her lately," Jude said, moving closer to Ben.

"Well, it seems to me that all of our troubles revolve around you," Ben said, poking Jude in the chest.

"Keep your hands off of me, Ben."

"Don't think I haven't seen it. The missed calls, the bracelet she never takes off, the hand on her knee, the paintings of her that fill an art gallery for God's sake! She still loves you and I can't stop it, I can't even compete. A neurosurgeon from New York City can not compete with an artist in a pick up truck. That's irony for you!"

"Ben, it wasn't like that," Lou said.

"Don't deny it now, Louise. It's a side of you I never knew," Ben accused.

"You never asked," said Lou.

"No, you never let me in because he was already there!" Ben jumped up and with two hands grabbed the front of Jude's shirt.

Jude punched Ben in the jaw and Ben punched back. They exchanged punches until Lou threw herself in between them. Ben had inadvertently hit her shoulder and she fell to the floor.

"Stop it! Both of you!" Lou yelled.

Ben held his hand to his chest, obviously hurt, too. "Get the hell out of here!" He yelled at Jude.

First, Jude knelt down next to Lou, "Are you alright?"

"I'm okay, just leave us alone right now," she said to Jude.

"Fine, I'm leaving," he said to Lou. "But if he gives you any more trouble, call me or 911." This time Jude was looking at Ben.

Ben helped Louise up and they both sat in chairs around the dining table. "I'm so sorry Louise, I never meant to hurt you," Ben said. Those words had so many meanings.

"Ben, I think you should leave. This is not going to work out," she said.

They both sat at the table, not knowing what else to say. Lou got up to get ice for both of their injuries. Ice will help the outside, but she didn't know what would heal the inside. Ben was on his phone when she returned with the ice.

"There's a flight out tonight, I'll go to the airport now," Ben said.

"I think that is best," Lou agreed.

"I do love you, Louise," he said.

"And I wish that was enough," she replied.

Lou watched as Ben grabbed his bag with his good hand and walked out the door. She was left in an empty house again. It felt different than last night. Tonight all of the ghosts were out of the closets. It was not scary, just sad. Tonight she would dream of glowing fish.

THE DAY HAD FINALLY come when Tom and Laura arrived home from their Mexican cruise. Lou was excited to hear all about their vacation. They showed pictures, told stories and gave out souvenirs. Her parents had a wonderful time and were now ready to make the move to Florida. It was going to be a whole new way of life, having warmth and sunshine all winter long.

Laura was only a little surprised to see that Lou was still staying at the house. She was surprised to hear that Ben had come and gone in the time that they were away. Lou tried to explain to her mother how Ben and Jude acted around each other, but all her mother did was nod her head.

"Well you know it's because Ben's jealous that you and Jude are still in love with each other," her mother said matter of factly. Lou just stared at her mother, "Oh don't try to deny it, it has been written all over your face since you first came home in August. I was in a coma and only saw your face for a couple of days and I still saw it. Imagine what Ben sees everyday, especially when you and Jude are in the same room with each other. It is practically written in neon lights."

Her mother had never expressed this to her before. In fact, no one had ever said that to her, not even herself. Was it true? Was she still so much in love with Jude that it was sabotaging her relationship with Ben?

"Lou, I'm sorry to say it to you so bluntly, but I think you really don't see it," she said. "Your father and I discuss it all the time. We gave you credit for trying so hard with Ben, but the simple fact that you have never set a date is a clear sign that you know Ben is not the one."

"Stop, mom. Just stop," Lou implored. "Enough, please." Lou went up to her room and curled up on the bed. She was suddenly exhausted. It was too much to think about. The things her mother were saying reminded her of what Jude always said. People needed to be happy in three areas of their life. Jude always said he had two and she always assumed he was happy where he lived and with Avery. But after seeing his art in the gallery, Lou knew he loved what he did. So that must mean he wasn't happy with the person in his life. She needed to talk to Jude, but not yet.

The next couple of days went by fast. The house was full of activity as the arrival of the moving truck was approaching. Tomorrow Tom and Laura would be headed towards their new house and new life in Florida with Aunt Ann. The beds they were taking were disassembled, the pictures they wanted were taken off of the walls, and the rugs were rolled up. There was still plenty of furniture left for anyone who chose to live here. Lou was starting to believe it was a possibility for her.

The last few days were actually unseasonably warm. There wasn't any snow on the ground and no snow was forecast for the next few days. Lou wanted to plan one final bonfire tonight before their parents left tomorrow. She called Tony who said he would take care of it. Lou suddenly felt excited. It was something happy to look forward to instead of dreading the day her parents left for good. Lou had to admit, it was not fair for her to be sad, she hasn't lived near her parents for over ten years, they deserved to be happy no matter where that took them. Now she just needed to heed her own advice.

Tom came to sit down next to Lou in the living room. "Lou, I want you to know that the house is yours. I went today to the lawyer and had everything put in your name," she was about to say something, but he stopped her. "Let me finish. I know you are at a crossroads in your life right now, so I want you to know that you don't have to go back to New York if you don't want to. I am sure you can be a pediatrician around here if you wanted to. We just want you to be happy and live the life you deserve."

Lou put her arms around her father, tears coming down her face, "Thank you, dad," she said. "This means a lot to me."

"And if you decide not to stay here, then that is your decision, too. Sell it or give it to Tony, it will be your decision," her father said.

It was a lot to take in. Lou decided to bundle up and take a walk on the beach. It was the best way she knew how to clear her head and think things through. She could see parts of the lake that weren't completely frozen. She looked down at the sand and saw some beach glass. She bent down to pick it up then saw some more. She had an idea and collected all that she could find. Lou walked up and down the beach until she was satisfied.

Lou stayed out on the beach and stared out at the water. The patches of water that were still showing were calm. Soon it would be frozen solid and full of people ice fishing in their little wooden houses. She remembered doing it a few times growing up. Trying to stay warm in a wooden box with a hole drilled in the ice all the while trying to catch fish with a fishing pole. It was no wonder little kids got bored with it after awhile. Well, at least she did.

She had stayed outside long enough, it will be better tonight with a huge bonfire to keep warm. But for now, Lou went back inside to make some hot cocoa. Her parents were happy to have an occasion to see everyone one last time. She took her hot cocoa to the dining table, pulled out all of her beach glass and got to work.

Chapter 28

The bonfire brought everyone to the house. Rose, Danny and Emily came. Tony, Suni and Hannah came. Brad, Lisa and Brian came. Jude came. Lou had even told Avery she was welcome to come if she wanted to, she could even bring a guest. It was a house full of family and friends. The perfect send off for Tom and Laura Jensen.

The guys had collected plenty of wood and they were ready to light it. Everyone was standing out on the beach as the sun was starting to set. Tony stood with the ceremonial torch, but first he had something to say.

"Today we say goodbye to our parents, Thomas and Laura Jensen, as they set off on their next adventure battling alligators and geckos in Florida," Tony joked. "But seriously, we all love you and wish you well. Don't worry about the lake house, you have handed the keys over to the capable hands of Louise Jensen who will carry on the traditions of bonfires and sunset watching." There were a few laughs in the crowd, but Lou saw Jude look at her when Tony mentioned her having the keys. "Let us now light this fire in honor of Thomas and Laura and hope that we don't burn the house down!" There were cheers and applause as he lit the bonfire with his torch.

The blaze was beautiful and mesmerizing. Tony had set up speakers to play Christmas music and Lou had put up a few string lights around the patio for ambiance. Tom and Laura would not be back for Christmas, so they were celebrating now while they were here. Lou spotted Avery in the distance with her arms around a tall, handsome dark skinned man. Of course she would bring a plus one. Lou was glad she came.

Lou was sitting on a log watching the bonfire when Jude approached. "Is this seat taken?" He asked. Lou shook her head. "You know, there were some things mentioned in Tony's speech that I didn't know about. Something about your owning the house now? Does this mean you are staying?" He took a sip of his beer and waited for a response. He had tried to keep his voice calm.

"I'm keeping my options open," Lou said.

Jude smiled and looked at her, "I'm glad."

"Are you happy?" She asked. Usually it was him asking her that question. This time she needed to know his response.

"I have two out of three," he said and took another sip of beer.

Lou looked at him and took a sip of her wine, then went back to watching the fire. "I don't know what I have anymore," she said. "I thought I had it all, three out of three. Turns out I'm lucky if I have one. I love what I do. That's all I know for sure anymore."

"Well, I will always love you," Jude said.

"Jude, you always say that but what does that even mean. You say it, you write it on scraps of paper and hand it to me in front of Ben, what does that mean to you?" She demanded.

"It means I love you, Lou." Jude was watching her expression. There was a slight smile when he said it, but no other reaction. Then Lou reached in her coat pocket.

"I made this for you today," she pulled out a bracelet made from the beach glass she collected on the beach that day. She took Jude's hand and turned it palm side up and placed the bracelet in it.

He turned it over in his hand and looked at her. His expression told her more than any words could. The wind was blowing his blond curls in his eyes, but Lou could still see straight into his soul through those blue eyes. They were filled with love. "Will you help me put it on?" Jude asked.

Lou had taken her time making this bracelet so that it would withstand being worn every day. She undid the clasp and put it around his wrist and secured the clasp again. She was so close she could hear his breathing, fast and shallow. They were both nervous.

Jude couldn't believe she had made the bracelet for him. He was touched by the gesture but his heartbeat raced when her delicate hands touched the inside of his wrist. They were the hands of a doctor, precise and accurate. It took no time at all for her to put the bracelet on and secure the tiny clasp. When she withdrew her hands he touched the beautiful shiny beach glass. It meant so much to him that she made it. The one he gave her was store bought, but he noticed she still wore it, even tonight. "Thank you," Jude said.

"You are welcome," Lou replied. "Now we match." She pulled back her sleeve and showed Jude the bracelet he gave her that she never took off.

Jude put an arm around her and kissed her cheek. There was more that he wanted to do, but not here. They needed to talk, but not here. It wasn't the time or place for a serious talk about them. Today it was about her family. They were moving away and it would be a sad time for them.

"I want you to know that I'm here for you, if you or Tony need anything. It won't be easy with your folks gone but at least they are only a phone call away," Jude said.

Jude, who had to endure his own folks abandoning him at eighteen, was always thinking of others. Lou, who was not normally a needy or clingy person, suddenly needed to be near this man. She took his hands and held them. They sat there holding hands and watching the bonfire. Finally Lou couldn't hold it in any longer. She reached up and placed a hand on either side of his face and kissed him. It was passionate and without care as to who might see.

Jude responded by bringing his hands to the sides of her head. He kissed her back without any restraint. It was something they both had wanted to do but never had the nerve to do it.

Their kiss did not go unnoticed, in fact, everyone did and they all approved. Even Avery couldn't be mad at something she had felt all along, that they still loved each other, it was as plain as the kiss at the bonfire. When Lou and Jude finally pulled away, they stayed touching foreheads. They knew things would never be the same again and that was okay with them.

Brad came over to Lou and asked if he could talk with her. Not sure what it was about, she agreed. She stood up and walked a little ways with Brad before he turned towards her.

"I want to apologize to you," Brad said.

"For what?"

"For being a jerk when I saw you last summer. I think about it a lot, especially watching Brian and remembering the cast on his arm. I was hard on you about Jude and I'm sorry," Brad said. "I see you guys together and I know he still loves you, but more importantly, I think you still love him. Well, that's all I wanted to say, I'm sorry."

Lou gave Brad a hug. "Thank you for that," she said.

Later, Jude asked what that was all about. "The beautiful thing about people is that they can change, and so can I," said Lou rather cryptically. She went over to Avery and gave her a hug. "Thank you for coming, I'm so happy you did."

Avery, a little surprised, introduced her date, Bruno. There weren't any problems that evening. Everyone had fun. Maybe it was the Christmas atmosphere that helped keep everyone in a good mood. Lou didn't care, it was the best send off for her parents she could have imagined.

The next morning, Lou was still replaying the kiss with Jude. It was all she could think about. It was moving day for her parents, though, so she needed to get up. She ran downstairs and saw that the moving truck was already here. She went to find her parents to see what they needed her to do.

"Nothing sweetheart, it's all taken care of," her mother said. Lou watched as furniture, boxes and luggage were being carried onto the truck. It was like memories were being removed from the house, never to be seen again. She was starting to feel sad and she did not want her parents to see it.

"I hope you liked your party last night," Lou asked her father. He was sitting at the dining table, just like any other morning.

"Yes, it was perfect," he said. "I think you had a nice time, too." He smiled at his daughter and sipped his coffee.

Lou just smiled back. She didn't know how to explain it or articulate what she was feeling. She would just have to see where it went. For now she was content to not say much at all. Her feelings for Jude were suppressed for so long, she wanted to be sure that what she was feeling was real and not just a retaliation against Ben. That reminded her, Ben had called her a few times yesterday and the day before. She decided to get it over with.

"Hi babe," Ben said.

"Hello Ben."

"I just wondered how you were doing?"

"Really? After you and Jude get into a boxing match in my kitchen because you accused us of having a secret affair behind your back," Lou said.

"Well, you did," he said.

"You know what, Ben? We are done. Let me say it officially to you, we are finished. Keep the ring, but please send my things to my house in Erie. I'm not coming back to New York."

"It was a joke, babe. Come home and let's talk about it," Ben said.

"I'm done talking, Ben, and I'm tired of your jokes. It's over."

"I still love you, Louise. I'm sorry, it was a bad joke," he said. "I'm tired of fighting." There was a long hesitation as he waited for her to respond. When she did not, Ben simply said, "I'll have your things sent over."

Lou didn't know if she ever truly loved him. She should have known the moment she hesitated the first time he proposed. Did he ever really love her? Would she have just been a trophy wife for him? It didn't matter anymore. She closed that chapter and felt a weight lifted.

Laura busied herself by cleaning. She had the kitchen spotless, the floor mopped and garage swept. She told Lou that anything left in the attic was hers. She went through and took what she wanted, the rest was hers or donation. Most of it was holiday decorations that she wouldn't have room for in their new, smaller place.

Tom was ready to go. As much as he loved their house on the lake, it was time for a simpler life. It was time to pass it on. He was anxious to play golf and go swimming in the middle of winter. He sat out in the enclosed porch one last time. Lou came to join him.

"Enjoy the house, Lou. It is a special place," Tom said.

"I will," Lou answered. "Thank you, dad."

"You're welcome. I'm just sorry things didn't work out for you in the big city."

"Maybe things happened just as they were supposed to," Lou said.

AS LOU WAVED GOOD BYE to her parents, she felt lighter and freer than she had ever felt before. She finally felt like she was able to do whatever she wanted. If she wanted to open her own practice in Erie, she could. Being able to start over was something not everyone got a chance to experience.

Lou decided to start living her new life. She started with a phone call to Jude.

"Hello, Lou."

"Hi, Jude," she said. "Are you doing anything tomorrow?"

"No, not really. Why?" He asked.

"I am in need of a Christmas tree and you have a shiny new truck."

Jude laughed, "I do."

"Well, maybe you can help me find, transport and decorate a Christmas tree tomorrow," Lou said.

"I think that can be arranged."

"Great, come anytime. I suddenly have an open schedule," she said.

"You know what? I do, too," he replied.

"We might be able to find something to do together if we try hard enough," Lou teased.

"I'm pretty sure we can," he said. "How are you doing? Did your parents leave already?"

"Yes, about an hour ago," Lou answered. "I'm doing okay. I have a hot date tomorrow."

Jude laughed again. "Anyone I know?"

"He is tall, with blond curly hair and he has a nice smile," Lou said.

"Is that all?" Jude asked.

"No, he has my heart."

Chapter 29

Lou was going through boxes of Christmas decorations when Jude knocked on the door. "Oh good, you're here," she said. "I need help with some of the heavier ones in the attic."

"No problem," Jude took off his coat and went up the stairs to the attic. He carried box after box until all the ones marked Christmas were down. They separated them according to whether they were ornaments, decoration, lights or stockings. When Lou had done all the preparations she could without an actual tree, she stopped.

"Are you ready to help me find a Christmas tree?" Lou asked.

"Always," Jude answered.

They climbed into his truck and drove to the nearest tree farm. Lou was busy checking out the interior since this was the first time she rode in his new truck.

Jude was having fun watching her touching buttons and turning knobs. He laughed as she unexpectedly made her seat recline. "Before you break my new truck, can you please tell me where we are going?"

Lou smiled. "Sorry, keep going straight, you can't miss it," she said. "I remember coming here as a kid, I hope it's still there."

"I am sure it is," Jude said. Not wanting to ruin their outing, but he had to ask a question. "Have you talked to Ben?"

"Yes, last night."

"How did it go?" He asked.

"How do you think? He wanted me back but kept bringing up your name."

"I'm sorry, really I am," said Jude.

Lou knew he was sincere. She nodded her head but didn't want to go into any more details with Jude. "Suffice it to say, it is over. He will send me my things and that is that."

"What will you do for work?" Jude asked.

"For now, I'm not worrying about it. I had thought about opening my own private practice as a pediatrician. It would be easy enough. I just need to find out what the state of Pennsylvania needs me to do and then find a place. Other than that, I have no plans."

"That sounds like a real start, though. You put some thought into it. If there's anything I can help you with, just let me know," he offered. "I have a show coming up in a couple of months, maybe you want to come with me?"

"That sounds like fun. Maybe," Lou answered.

They pulled into the tree farm and they started searching for the perfect tree. At first, they were being silly, finding the ugliest, scrawniest and smallest trees they could fine and laughed up and down the isles. Finally, when they were actually getting cold, Jude took her hand and they walked together. It didn't take long after that to find the one they were looking for. The workers cut it down and helped tie it up in the back of his truck.

The whole way home, Lou starting singing Christmas carols. Jude joined in from time to time, but usually he let her sing solo. She was definitely getting into the holiday spirit. They passed by houses that were decorated with blow-up lawn animals, others had a thousand strings of lights. Lou wanted hers to have some lights outside and inside, but the focal point was going to be the tree.

Lou offered to help carry it inside, but Jude said he could handle it. He did, until he had to make a ninety degree turn from the dining room to the living room. She wanted it right against the glass looking out to the beach. She didn't care about people seeing the tree from the front, she wanted to see it from the back of the house. The branches were just long enough, the height was perfect and the smell filled the entire house. She was happy with her purchase. Now it was time for the lights.

The box that contained the lights was a mess. Whoever put these away must have been mad or drunk because Lou and Jude had to stretch each string of lights all over the floor just to untangle them. They would laugh when they thought they had it untangled just to get it tangled some more. Jude had gotten one string completely untangled, put it on the tree just to find out it didn't work. Even with the frustrations, they were having fun together.

When Lou determined that the tree had just enough working lights, she moved on to the ornament boxes. She saw that her mother had gone through them, so some were missing. Still, there were plenty to fill her tree. Jude was in charge of decorating the top of the tree and Lou, the bottom. They kept bumping into each other as they reached for more ornaments. With the lights and ornaments on the tree, they stopped to find something to eat. Lou pulled out the leftover chicken marsala and heated it up. As she went to get dishes down from the cupboard, he was reaching over to get glasses. They passed by each other face to face and stopped. Lou put down the plates, Jude put down the glasses and they kissed.

It was not planned, it just happened. They were having a great morning and it felt so natural. Jude reached up to her face and Lou reached up at his neck and chest. The kiss was slow and soft and was the product of their playful flirting all morning. The microwave beeped and, reluctantly, they went back to their respective chores. This open affection was new to them. There wasn't anyone watching or any significant others who must be kept in the dark. Just Lou and Jude.

They took their lunch to the dining table and ate. Lou explained how she wanted the house to look on the inside and outside. She hadn't been able to do this in so long, she really wanted to go all out for Christmas this year. This was a year of new beginnings for both of them. When they finished eating, Lou put the dishes in the sink and decided she needed Christmas music. She went to the record player and found some Nat King Cole. It was sentimental and romantic and she started swaying to Nat's singing. Jude came up behind her and took her hand. They slow danced until the song ended.

Jude found the box with the tree skirt and stockings. Lou wasn't sure what to do about everyone's stocking. She really only needed hers but she wanted one for Jude. "We need to get you a stocking," she said.

"I have mine at home somewhere. I haven't dug it out in years," Jude replied.

"Well that is your homework, find your stocking so I can put it next to mine," Lou said.

Jude found some artwork in the box, the kind that kids make at school and bring home to their parents. There were several made by Lou and Tony in the box. She held them up and examined each one.

"What's wrong?" Jude asked as she started tearing up. "Do you miss your parents already?"

"No, it's not that. I see my friends and family having kids and I want one, too. I never really felt a biological clock like other women, but lately, since being home, I do," Lou said.

"So you want just one?" Jude joked.

"Well, one or two or three. It doesn't matter," she said.

Lou looked around and decided that they had made a lot of progress, but also a lot of mess. There was still more to do, they hadn't even done anything outside, yet. It was getting late and she was ready to call it a night. Her emotional outburst most likely meant she was exhausted.

"Lou, I had fun today, thanks for inviting me along," Jude said.

"Well, you had the fancy new truck," Lou reminded.

Jude laughed, "Right. So, I would love to stay and help you some more, but I promised Brad I would help him move some equipment in his garage tonight. Can we finish tomorrow?"

"I was going to suggest the same thing. I'm tired," she said.

"Okay, great. I'll see you tomorrow."

They kissed goodbye and goodnight. Lou watched him back out of the driveway and down the street. She liked that she didn't feel any pressure from Jude. He had waited a long time, she wasn't going anywhere. Not anymore. Lou came back to the living room and starting going through more boxes. She was surprised to find an ornament with a picture of her and Jude. Her mother must have made it when they were dating in high school. She didn't remember the ornament, but she recognized the photo. It was junior prom. She stared at that photo for what seemed like hours and decided it needed a place of honor. She stood up and placed it on the mantel.

Lou turned to admire their hard work today by turning on the tree. She walked towards the enclosed porch and saw the light reflected in all the windows. Something outside, low to the ground caught her eye. At first she was afraid that it was something inside the house, but no, it was outside. The closer she got the easier she saw the two little blue eyes, pink nose and pointy ears of a small white kitten. She opened the back door of the porch and went out to rescue the small intruder from the cold. She looked around the whole area to see if there was more than one. No, just one.

The little kitten's meow was so loud, she figured she had probably been trying to get her attention for awhile. She brought the little kitten into the kitchen and poured some milk into a bowl. She drank it all up. Lou rummaged through the fridge for anything resembling food appropriate for a kitten and found some turkey lunch meat and shred it into pieces. She loved it. When she determined that the kitten was properly fed, she cut a box down to look like a litter box and shred up a bunch of old newspapers. This seemed to please the kitten who knew exactly what to do in the litter box.

"You need a name," Lou determined. "Well, you scared me like a little ghost outside my window so 'Casper' you are!"

Casper curled up on the warm blanket beside Lou as she continued to go through boxes. Every time she found something to look at, she would pet little Casper. Otherwise, she was digging in box after box until she believed she had looked at each one. She cleaned up her mess as best she could without disturbing Casper too much. Lou had a cat when she was growing up, but not in her adult life. She knew how to take care of one, but hadn't had the need to own one until one showed up on a dark winter's night looking for her.

"Wait until you meet Jude," Lou said to Casper. "You are going to love him, too."

Lou locked up the house and shut off all the lights. She carried Casper upstairs to her room. As Lou showered and dressed for bed, little Casper curled up beside her pillow as if waiting for her to come to bed. Maybe she should have had a cat as an adult, it might have helped to have someone to talk things over with. Someone who didn't judge or be jealous of who she talked to. Lou was careful climbing into bed tonight so that she didn't disturb her kitten. She could hear Casper purring loudly next to her ear. Tonight, Lou fell asleep dreaming of little ghosts.

Chapter 30

Waking up to the quiet purrs of Casper was a pleasant reminder of what a great day Lou had yesterday. It was fun, productive and emotional. She liked reconnecting with Jude again. They could laugh and spend time together without worrying about what any one else thought. He had promised to come over again today to finish putting up her Christmas decorations. Wait until he sees the new addition to her family!

Casper drank her milk as Lou sipped her coffee. The kitten was a welcome distraction for her now that she was starting over alone. It felt good. She took out her laptop and researched getting her Pennsylvania doctor's license. If she could take the licensing exam this month, she would be one step closer to opening her own practice here in Erie for the new year. Lou was excited that a plan that she had been thinking about for months, might actually happen. This encouraging outlook helped her believe that anything was possible. She was getting her independence back.

Lou pulled a steak out of the freezer for dinner and then hesitated. She wondered if Jude would want to stay for dinner and decided to take another one out just in case. She looked at her watch wondering where Jude was. She decided to get started without him and went into the living room to tackle some more Christmas lights for the outside of the house when she heard a knock on the side door.

"I'm sorry I didn't call, but I was already in the neighborhood," Jude started.

Lou gave him a hug and a kiss, "Well, next time you had better call, because you never know, I might be entertaining guests and might not want to be interrupted," she teased.

Jude's confused expression changed when Lou picked up a scrawny white kitten from the floor where she was eating. She held little Casper to her nose and then turned the kitten in his direction. "Meet Casper," Lou said.

Jude reached out to take the little kitten in his hands. "Hello Casper. I'm Jude, it is very nice to meet you," he replied, formally. "Where did you get her?"

"Actually, she found me. Last night she was peeking through my window and I brought her inside."

Jude carried Casper into the living room followed by Lou. "Well, where do we start today?" He asked her.

"I was thinking we should do the outside lights."

Jude put the kitten down on the couch as they started untangling string lights again. Casper thought this was the best game ever. The kitten jumped around from string to string as Jude and Lou got one untangled and then another. When Lou announced they had enough lights, they went out front to decorate the entrance. Jude wrapped lights around the railings, Lou placed them on the bushes. After becoming sufficiently cold, they came back in for warmth.

"Do you want some coffee?" She asked.

"Sure, if you have some," he replied.

Lou poured him a cup of coffee and left him alone in the kitchen while she went to retrieve something from the living room. She came back holding the small ornament that she had put up on the mantle last night. Jude, who was leaning against the kitchen counter reached for it when Lou offered. It took him only a second to recognize the two teenagers in the photo. He smiled and then looked at Lou.

"A lifetime ago," Jude said.

"I still remember that night, we were almost seventeen," she replied.

"I do, too. I told you I loved you that night," Jude said.

They both stood there, leaning on the kitchen counter looking at the little ornament that held so many memories for the two of them. They were both lost in thought when little Casper came into the kitchen meowing. Lou laughed.

"I guess she got lonely," she said.

"Well, let's go keep her company while we finish the decorating. Tell me what you want done and then we'll clean up all the boxes. It will look like a proper Norman Rockwell painting," said Jude.

"I don't want a Rockwell. I want a Weber," Lou said. "To be more specific, I want a J. Henry Weber original."

Jude looked up. "Actually, I have been spending some time in my studio lately. I'm working on some new collections," he said, staring at her. "I've been inspired."

"I would love to see them sometime," Lou said.

"I would love to show them to you," Jude replied.

Lou and Jude finished the decorations and cleaned up everything in time for dinner. She went to the record player and chose a Bing Crosby Christmas album and played it. Again, Lou stood in front of the record player, swaying to the dream of having a white Christmas. Jude came up behind her and held her.

"I love this song," she said softly.

"And I love you," Jude replied.

Lou turned around and stopped dancing. "Do you want to stay for dinner?" She asked.

"Yes," Jude replied. "Do you want help?"

"Sure."

Jude grilled the steaks as Lou prepared the salad. They each worked on their individual tasks in the kitchen with comfortable silence. Sometimes she would hum to the music and he would look over and join in. It was nice for Lou to just be herself and let loose with someone who understood her. Someone who understood the amount of work that went into being able to be this happy. Lou knew this was the case for Jude, too. Maybe she never gave Ben enough credit or trusted him enough to let him into the deepest and darkest parts of her. She will never know the real answer to that.

Lou and Jude ate their dinner and drank wine at the dining table. He had insisted on lighting the candle that was in the center of the table. This time they were not silent. Jude talked about his new paintings, the colors he was using and the size of his canvases. Lou mentioned getting her Pennsylvania doctor's license and her plan to open her own practice. They each spoke of their future dreams and ambitions.

"I want a family, too" Jude said. "I see Brad with Lisa and Brian. I think they want more kids, I don't know, but that's what I want."

"I know," Lou replied. "Like with Tony, he has Suni, Hannah and another one on the way. Maybe there's still time to have it all."

"You never wanted that with Ben?" He asked. Not entirely sure he wanted to hear the answer, but was curious enough to ask.

"I thought I did. But it took me a couple of years to learn that he wanted a lifestyle of ambition and beautiful things, not the mess and chaos of a family," she said. "Maybe I waited too long to figure that out with him. It may be too late for me."

"I don't think so," Jude said quietly.

Jude helped Lou clean up. He appreciated her honest answers to his questions. He didn't like bringing up Ben, but each time she talked about him, he could tell she was getting over him. The last thing Jude wanted was to rush things with Lou. She had been through enough and didn't want to scare her away, again.

Lou walked into the living room and adjusted a table that was in the corner. She had set a ceramic snowman on it and tried to angle it a different way. As she did this, she saw an old photo album on the shelf below that she hadn't noticed before. Lou blew the dust off the top and brought it to the couch. Jude had just finished adding a log to the fire and had picked up Casper. They joined her on the couch.

"What's that?" Jude asked.

"I'm not sure," she answered. "It's an old photo album but I don't remember it."

The cover cracked when she opened it. Lou held the photo album between her and Jude so they could both see the grainy images from twenty five years ago. They were shoulder to shoulder and practically touching heads as they leaned in to read her mother's handwritten captions under each photo. It started with 'Louise and Anthony, ages 3 and 6' then there were images on the beach 'Louise and Anthony, ages 4 and 7'. She turned the pages slowly, giving both of them time to admire the photo and remember the moment.

"I remember some of these, especially the ones on our beach," Lou said.

When they were near the end, only a few pages left, a photo brought Jude to tears. 'Weber boys, Jackson, Jude and Bradley, ages 5, 7 and 12'. It was the summer Jack died. He wiped his tears on the sleeve of his shirt.

"I'm sorry," Jude said.

"It's okay," Lou said, putting an arm around his shoulders. Even Casper stretched and stood up sensing something was different.

"It's just that I haven't seen a picture of Jackson since he died," Jude wiped his eyes again.

"What do you mean? You don't have any pictures of Jack?" Lou asked, shocked.

"No," Jude replied. "Mom destroyed them all, along with the rest of the photo albums. She either burned them or ripped them up, I don't remember. She reasoned that since we were not a family anymore then we don't need to be reminded of the past."

"Oh Jude, I'm so sorry," she said. "I didn't know."

"It's okay, no one knew. It's not the kind of thing you talk about," he said. "You just don't go into school the next day and say 'My mother went crazy and burned all of our pictures' or 'I can't talk about Jackson anymore because he died'. I was just a kid, I had to live with my own guilt about his death, then the guilt of my family falling apart."

"You went through a lot at seven years old, Jude. You didn't even tell me everything while we were dating. You hide your pain well," Lou said.

"It comes out in my art. I am grateful to have painting as therapy."

Lou remembered the angry brush strokes from his paintings. The anger from their break up that he channeled into his art. Jude had a life of sadness sprinkled with dots of happiness. She wanted Jude's future to be filled with happiness.

"Well, I am here now. I will protect you," Lou said. "And so will Casper."

They both laughed as Casper continued to sleep and purr in Jude's lap. "Yes, she is pretty vicious, just like her mother," Jude said.

Lou nudged Jude in the ribs and then kissed him. They closed the photo album and set it on the floor. Lou leaned into Jude's shoulder as he put his arm around her. She stayed with her head on his shoulder and listened to the music. He kissed the top of head and squeezed her. He had just been through a roller coaster of emotions and landed on his feet. He wasn't seven anymore. He was able to see that none of his family's problems were his fault.

"This is nice," Lou said.

"Yes it is."

They stayed this way until the record stopped. Then, Lou removed herself from Jude's arms and turned it off. She looked at her watch and yawned. "It's ten o'clock already."

"Yea, I'd better get going. I have work to do tomorrow, if that's okay?" Jude asked.

"It's fine. I am no longer in need of your assistance," Lou replied.

Jude laughed. "Good, because I might have to go out of town for a few days, too. I'll give you a call when I am back."

"Ok, that sounds good. It will give me time to work on my to do list, as well," she said.

Lou walked him to the door. They had a bond that no one could deny. It may have skipped a decade, but it was still there.

"Good night, Jude," Lou said, "Thank you for all of your help."

"You're welcome," Jude answered. "You know you can call me anytime. Good night."

They kissed with longing and passion, but also with sadness. Lou waved as he drove away. She loved him, that was also undeniable. She carried Casper upstairs to bed. Tonight she dreamed of the beach.

Chapter 31

"I'm running late. I'm so sorry, Lou, I'll make it up to you," Jude promised. "Something came up and it's completely unavoidable."

"But it's Christmas Eve!" Lou protested.

"I know, I know," Jude said. "I'm very sorry. I will be there as soon as I can!"

"Everyone is already here," Lou said.

"Just start without me. I'll be there soon."

Lou hung up her phone and turned to her guests. "Well, Jude is running late, so let's eat while everything is hot," she announced.

Hannah and Brian ran to the kitchen first. The appetites of the children could not wait any longer. Lou had prepared a bunch of appetizers and hors d'oeuvres. She always liked serving finger foods at parties in New York, so she decided to try that here. She had finger sandwiches, crackers with a variety of spreads, mini meatballs in a sweet sauce and chicken tenders. There was also a vegetable tray, a cheese tray and a fruit salad. The adults followed the children into the kitchen to eat.

Suni mentioned to Lou that she and Tony wanted to go on a getaway before the baby was born. She wondered if Lou would be willing to watch Hannah. "Of course," Lou said. She loved spending time with her niece. They chatted a bit more before they both made a plate and sat down.

Lou wanted the atmosphere to be casual, so she had Christmas music playing in the kitchen, there was a Christmas movie marathon playing on the television, and a fire in the fireplace. The tree was lit, as well as the lights outside and there were presents under the tree. Lou had showed the old photo album to Brad and he and Lisa were looking at it now. She could see Brad wiping his eyes with his sleeve and left them alone in this private moment. At one point he overheard Brad telling Brian, "That's your Uncle Jackson." She didn't stay for the rest of the conversation. That was up to Brad to explain as much as he was comfortable with.

Everyone ran into the living room when they heard a scream. It was Hannah. She was running down the stairs, chasing Casper, when she fell and started crying. Everyone ran over to her, but she cried when her arm was touched.

"Can you wiggle your fingers, Hannah?" Lou asked. She could. "I don't think it's broken," as Lou felt the bones of her left arm. "I think she just dislocated her elbow."

"Should I call for an ambulance?" Suni asked.

"No, it will be okay, honey," replied Tony.

In a room filled with health care workers, they were also glad that there was a doctor in the house. Tony came over to assist Lou. She explained how he was to hold her upper arm in one position so that she could rotate the lower arm in another position and pop it back into place. It worked. Lou wrapped it up and Suni gave her some children's pain medicine and told her to sit and play with Casper, no more running. Tony, Suni and Hannah found a seat in the living room. Casper loved all of the attention. She had gotten a little bigger since Lou found her and knew exactly where to hide when she wanted to. In fact, Casper went running when someone started banging on the side door.

"Ho ho ho!" Someone was yelling. "Ho ho ho!"

Hannah and Brian's heads turned towards the commotion as a man in a red suit was coming through the door. He had a white beard, red hat and a bag filled with presents in his hands. "Santa!" Yelled Hannah. Her hurt arm nearly forgotten.

Santa made his way into the living room and set down his big bag in the middle of the floor. Lou pulled up a chair for him and he looked around the room.

"I thought I saw Brian earlier, where did he go?" Asked Santa.

Brian came out from behind his father, "I'm over here," he said tentatively.

"Well this present has your name on it. Come on over and get it, Brian," Santa said.

Brian, still unsure how Santa knew his name, came to take the gift. He ripped off the paper as everyone looked on. "Wow!" Exclaimed Brian as he unwrapped a Star Wars Lego set that he had wanted, or at least Brad said he was asking for.

"Hannah, you are next," said Santa.

Hannah came up and accepted the gift. She sat next to her mother and opened it. Inside was a paint set complete with canvases. "Thank you, Santa," Hannah said, obviously pleased with her present.

Santa went around the room presenting gifts to all the adults, too. Brad got a new Steelers shirt, Lisa received the novel she wanted to read. Tony opened a new drill and Suni got a diaper bag. Everyone wanted to see each others gifts and take pictures with Santa. The men got up to get a beer and Santa followed them to the kitchen. Brad patted Jude on the shoulder, "Good job, Santa."

Jude went into the garage to change out of the red suit. He folded it up and put it in his truck. He grabbed something from the front seat and ran back in the house. Everyone was enjoying the evening and the food, no one noticed that Lou never received a gift. She did think it was odd, but didn't think any more about it.

"Uncle Jude, you just missed Santa!" Hannah announced.

"Is that who I just passed coming in here?" Jude asked. "There were reindeer on the front yard, but your Aunt Lou has a habit of collecting stray animals, so I thought that was why they were there."

Hannah giggled all the way back to her mother. Even Casper, sensing the threat of a big red suit was gone, came back out to lay on the floor. Jude followed Lou into the living room.

"Everyone, if I could have your attention please," started Jude. Everyone stopped what they were doing and looked at him. "Santa stopped me on my way in and apologized. It seems there was one present left in the bag that he forgot to give out. This one has the name Louise on it."

Everyone in the room was silent as they watched Jude pull a little black velvet box from his pocket and get down on one knee. Lou stood there, stunned. She brought her hands to her face and started crying.

"Lou, we have known each other all of our lives. There was a time when I thought I would never see you again but here we are. We have another chance and I won't let you get away again. I want us to spend the rest of our lives together. Will you marry me?"

Lou, unable to speak at first, simply nodded her head. Then, "yes, YES!" She yelled.

Jude stood up and put the diamond ring on her finger. Everyone in the room cheered. Jude and Lou kissed and he picked her up so her feet didn't touch the ground. More pictures were taken and congratulations were said. This was, indeed, a Christmas to celebrate.

It was the best news these two families had heard in awhile. They supported Lou and Ben's engagement because they believed it was what she wanted, even though it didn't feel right to them. This was different, this felt right. Their relationship may have taken a decade long detour, but they still managed to get back on track and finally get engaged.

No matter what bad feelings Brad may still hold deep down against Lou, they were all washed away the moment Jude chose her to be his wife. He was happy for his little brother and proud of him. Life had really started to turn around for Jude. Tony was glad this day finally came, too. He secretly hoped this would be the outcome the moment Lou walked into his house back in August. Even when they were so worried about their mother, Tony could see sparks fly between her and Jude whether they did or not. He wanted to call their parents to let them in on the news, but he knew this was not his news to tell.

When Jude and Lou were finally alone later that evening, she was letting it all sink in. She just agreed to marry Jude. They would be husband and wife. The boy she grew up with, dated in high school and then broke his heart now wanted to be her husband. Was it all a dream? Would she wake up tomorrow and the ring would mysteriously vanish?

Jude had also brought in a bottle of champagne from his truck. He grabbed two glasses and joined her in the living room. She sat on the floor leaning her back on the couch. She watched the fire dance in the fireplace and absently pet Casper on her lap. There was a plate beside her with crackers, cheese, salami and grapes. The sounds of another Christmas record was playing in the background. Jude sat down on the floor next to her.

"I would like to make a toast," Jude said as he prepared to pop the cork on the bottle of champagne. He managed to do it without spilling any on the floor. "To us."

"To us," Lou repeated as they sipped their drinks. They sipped and ate as Lou fed grapes and cheese to Jude. They laughed as she tried to fit more and more onto a cracker before it wouldn't fit into Jude's mouth.

"Are you trying to kill me?" Jude joked.

"No, I'm just trying to feed you," Lou replied.

"Well, I can think of something else I'd like better," he said, pulling her closer.

First Jude kissed Lou on the neck. He pulled her hair back and then went to her ear. With his other hand, he turned her face to his. They kissed softly and with care. Lou kissed his cheek and then his forehead, moving aside a few locks of blond hair. It was slow and sensuous. It progressed to more passionate kisses, kisses that let each other aware of their own needs. Their hands searched each other's bodies for more places to explore.

Since August, they had been consciously avoiding any contact that would lead them to crossing the line again. It was deliberate and difficult. It was a mistake then, they both knew it, but they did not regret it. But, Jude would never again put her in that kind of situation. Even when they decorated her house for Christmas, he was tempted and so was she, but he was careful to not let anything develop beyond kissing. He respected her too much. He needed to make sure she felt the same way about him as he did about her.

Tonight was different. Now Jude and Lou made a promise to each other in front of their family. They would spend the rest of their lives together.

"Do you want to call anyone, like your parents?" Jude asked, kissing her neck.

"Not now," Lou replied. "Tonight is just for us."

Jude moved the plates and cups out of the way as they laid down on the rug. In the warmth of the fire, they each took off their clothes. There was no judgement or embarrassment, just love. They made love in front of the fire that night. They emptied the champagne and nibbled on more food. No longer having to hold back or show restraint, they enjoyed each other until they fell asleep. It was a peace that neither one had experienced before. They slept in each other's arms all night with Casper right next to them.

Chapter 32

"Merry Christmas," Jude said.

"Merry Christmas, fiancé," she added.

Jude grabbed her and kissed her. They rolled on the floor until he was on top of her. "I have one more surprise." He grabbed a blanket off the couch and wrapped it around him. Jude went into the kitchen and reached behind the table. He came back carrying a large square package wrapped in brown paper.

Lou was so surprised that he had another gift. She thought the ring was enough. However, looking at the size and shape of this, she knew instantly it was one of Jude's paintings. "Is this a Weber original?" She teased.

"Yes," Jude replied. "I felt inspired these last few weeks."

Lou, anxious to see what it was, grabbed another blanket off the couch and sat down. She carefully unwrapped the brown paper and marveled at the image. No, Jude hadn't painted this kind of subject matter before. It was a man and a woman, holding hands and walking on the beach. The woman's long brown hair was blowing in breeze, just like her long dress. The man's head was turned towards the woman and they were walking side by side. The water from the lake was coming up to their feet and they were both carrying their shoes. It was precious and intimate.

"It's us," Jude said.

"I know." Lou cried happy tears as she set the painting down and picked out a gift from under the tree. She handed the box to him. "For you."

"For me?" Jude asked. "You didn't have to get me anything, Lou. I'm so happy with you." He pulled the red ribbon and unwrapped the green paper. When he lifted the lid and peeled back the tissue paper protecting the gift, he teared up.

"Do you like it?" Lou asked.

Jude held the silver picture frame and looked down at the three Weber boys. "How did you do this?"

"I had the picture enlarged and retouched. I didn't want you to go another day without you seeing your little brother," Lou explained.

Jude stared at the eight by ten of him and his brothers standing together on the beach. A memory and a brother he no longer had was now in front of him. His finger touched each face. He looked at Lou. "Thank you for this. I feel like you brought my brother back into my life."

Jude hugged and kissed her. He was touched by the thoughtfulness of the gift. It was an emotional morning for both of them. They decided to get dressed and make breakfast. Having the mundane task of cooking eggs and making toast brought them back down to their everyday life.

"Do you want to move in here?" Lou asked.

"I guess I could. I want to keep my studio, though," Jude replied.

"Of course, I don't want you to change anything just to be with me. Once I get my practice up and running, I'll finally have something to do everyday," said Lou.

They carried their breakfast to the dining table, sitting across from each other. Jude had some difficult questions to ask. He wasn't worried so much about Lou's answers, rather he was worried she wouldn't be truthful.

"Will you be satisfied living in Erie instead of New York City? I can't help but think about when you left after high school. You wanted more," Jude said.

Lou had already considered this herself. "I already experienced New York and I know my home is here. When I left at eighteen it was because I was scared. We were getting so serious and that night we slept together after senior prom, it scared me even more. It wasn't your fault, it was me. I needed you so much back then. I relied on you for my happiness. I knew I needed to find myself first, so I left."

"And became a doctor," Jude said. "I was so proud of you when I heard. I would ask Tony for any little update he could provide. Just like I am so proud of you now. I just hope I'm enough."

"You will always be enough. I'm not that scared eighteen year old anymore. I know what I want. I am happy in all three areas," Lou said. "Are you happy?"

"I had only been happy in two out of three for as long as I can remember. Today I can finally say I have three out of three," answered Jude.

Lou kissed him. They were both finally happy in all aspects of their lives. She looked at Jude and she felt love. She was where she was meant to be. Her home was on the lake. Her home was with Jude.

After breakfast, Lou decided to call her parents with the good news. She didn't know if they would truly be surprised. Even her parents knew Jude was the one she should be with, not Ben.

"Hello, Mom?"

"Hi, Lou? How are things going up there?"

"Things are going really well. Jude proposed," Lou announced.

"Oh that is wonderful news! Finally!" Laura started laughing on the other end and Lou could hear her tell Tom the news. "We are so happy for you both."

"Thank you," Lou said. "I've never felt this happy with a decision in a long time."

Lou's parents talked about Florida and her Aunt Ann. She promised to let them know when the wedding will be. It was a very comfortable conversation, but Lou was still a little sad they were so far away. Especially now that she had decided to move back home.

Jude walked in the room and saw that she had become a bit sad. "Is everything okay with your parents?"

"Oh yes, they are great," Lou replied. "I just wish they were still here in Erie, that's all."

Jude came over and hugged her. He knew the feeling of missing one's parents. He still thought about his mom every once in a while. Jude let her be sad. She wasn't crying, but sometimes a hug is more therapeutic.

"Let's set a date!" Lou announced.

Jude pulled away and looked at her. "Sure, if that's what you want."

She walked to the kitchen island and sat down. "This summer. June 22nd."

"Sounds good to me. Can we plan it in six months?" He came and sat beside her.

Lou took Jude's hands. "Jude, it's me. I do not want a fancy wedding. I want it here, on our beach with our family and friends by our side."

Jude smiled, "If that's what you want, then just tell me what I need to do to make it happen."

Lou laughed at his enthusiasm. They would be married. Here on the lake. Her future with Jude was coming into view like something from a painting.

Chapter 33

Spring had arrived in Erie. The lake was beginning to thaw, temperatures were warming and Lou kept busy with her plans. Sometimes she thought she was crazy trying to open up her private practice as a pediatrician while planning her own wedding. Both tasks required so much of her time. Lou wanted her new office to be close to home. Her realtor kept trying to show her places near the hospitals, or near the mall, or even in the suburbs. Lou kept saying 'no', confident that the right office in the perfect location would open up.

It did. She found an old dentist office on Westlake Road that could easily be remodeled to a pediatrician's office. It already had multiple patient rooms, a waiting room and ample parking. The best part was that she was less than ten minutes from home. It would not take long to be ready for her own little patients. Lou knew this is what she was meant to be doing. Having patients that she could get to know and see grow up, that's what excited her.

Jude was pretty much moved into Lou's house. He decided to keep his studio at his old place. There was plenty of room on her property to make another studio for Jude on the lake, but he liked the separation. Having a studio away from home gave him a different perspective. He found his art had grown in depth since proposing to Lou. It no longer focused on her, she was his. Having happiness in three out of three aspects of his life finally allowed him to bring his focus elsewhere. It was no longer only lakes and Lou.

Jude was painting trees, forests, boats and anything else he wanted. It was freeing to be so happy. He could come home to see her at the end of the day and not have to rely on producing a perfect replica on canvas. Jude felt lighter and brighter, if that was possible. Everything was possible with Lou.

For now, he rented his house to a friend. He knew this was a short term answer, but for now it worked out well. Even Brad noticed the change in Jude. He was relieved it was working out and that Lou was making plans to actually stay and not just say the words. Her actions were speaking volumes to Brad and that made him happy, too.

Jude walked in the kitchen door and saw Lou sitting at the dining table. She had her laptop out and she was focused on more spreadsheets. Jude worried that she was taking on too much at once, but she always seemed to handle every wrench thrown her way. At first, the contractor said they needed a new roof and then her new equipment had a delay in shipping. Lou handled it all with ease. She was a professional. She was also planning a wedding, which left her emotional.

When Jude came over to her at the table, Lou was looking at her wedding timeline and stressing out over the caterer and the invitations.

"I don't think they will be done in time," she said.

"What won't?" Jude asked.

"Everything!"

Lou slammed her laptop shut and laid her head on her crossed arms. Jude came over and rubbed her shoulders. He didn't really know the details of the wedding, he just knew that he and Tony were making a pergola type trellis for Lou to decorate, but other than that, Lou and Suni were planning most of the details.

"Is there anything I can do? Can I pick something up or call someone?" Jude asked.

Lou stood up and hugged him. She even let a small laugh escape. "No, I will handle it," Lou answered. "But I do have some good news. The office space is almost done. I have some interviews tomorrow for nurses and my office staff, but I'm almost ready to start advertising. Little Angels Pediatrics with Dr. Louise Jensen."

"I love it, Lou. But, you won't be Jensen much longer," Jude said.

"I know, but it will open before the wedding, so I have to be Dr. Louise Jensen until then."

Over the next couple of weeks, things moved even faster for Lou. She hired her employees for the office, she had her picture in the paper announcing the grand opening of Little Angels Pediatrics and she was having her ribbon cutting today. Everyone was there, Tony and his family, Brad and his family, Rose and her family, even Avery came to see her friend plant roots. It was emotional for Lou, she looked out at her family and friends and finally felt at home. It was a dream she didn't dare to dream in New York, but here anything was possible, especially with Jude by her side. Jude was by her side. He stood by her when she cut the ribbon and kissed her.

He was so proud of her hard work. Lou loved what she did and was good at it. She had a way of talking to children that calmed them down and made them trust her. Jude was sure that her practice would grow fast with a solid foundation. As soon as the office phone was connected, they were receiving appointments. Lou gave her staff a few days to get ready, then patients were walking in the door. It was exhausting at first. She had to learn to pace herself. She wanted to see everyone and still give everyone plenty of time with her in the room. It was a fine balance she had to learn.

In the beginning, at the end of each day, Lou would come home and relax with a glass of wine. Since spring still had cool temperatures in the evening, Jude would have a fire going and would rub Lou's feet. Casper would curl up on Lou. It was a comfortable routine they were enjoying. Advertising and word of mouth spread, making her schedule full every day. She was happy. The only thing that would make her happier was to be Mrs. Jude Weber.

"I hate to leave you when you are so busy," Jude said.

Lou opened her eyes. "Don't worry about me, I have Casper to keep me company. Besides, you will only be gone a couple of weeks."

"Yes, I wish it wasn't so long, or that you could come with me, but I will be home before you know it," Jude replied.

"I'm so proud of you, Jude. Your new collection is fabulous and Chicago is lucky to have first peek at your new work. I just wish I could be there to see their faces when they see the new look. J. Henry Weber is no longer focused on water and a girl named Louise, he actually paints other things now!" Lou teased.

Jude tickled her feet and Lou pulled them back. Casper did not like all of the commotion and jumped down. They both laughed and then looked into each other's eyes. "Seriously, I'm so proud," Lou said softly.

Jude leaned down and kissed her. It was soft at first but became more demanding. Lou responded by sitting up and putting her arms around his neck. Jude pulled away, "I'm going to miss this."

"Me, too," Lou replied. She looked at the beach glass bracelet on his wrist. The bracelet she made for him that was similar to the one he gave her. They never took them off. It was a connection for them when they were apart from each other.

Jude carried her upstairs. They had claimed the master bedroom and had redecorated the other bedrooms. Lou no longer had a childhood room filled with memories and knick knacks. It was a guest room. Their room was the master bedroom. They purchased a king sized bed and Lou made sure everything was a shade of blue. From the walls to the rugs, everything was blue. Jude loved the new look. He was always surprised to learn more about Lou everyday. She had an eye for design, he knew that from the apartment she shared with her ex in New York. But it seemed to feel different here, it felt like home.

Jude would be gone for two weeks in Chicago which gave Lou time to take on another project. Now that her practice has taken off and no longer needed her attention while at home, she could think of other things. Wedding planning was still on going, but until the invitations came, she had time to plan a baby shower. Suni was due in a couple of months and since it has been six years since she had a baby in the house, Suni needed some baby things. She called Lisa to see if she wanted to help plan the shower and she was thrilled to be included.

Lisa said she would take care of the cake and door prizes. Lou wanted to find a caterer and decided to call Rose to see who she used for Emily's party. Rose was so happy to help that she wanted to be involved in the planning, too. This was great news. Lou delegated jobs for each of them and planned to have the shower at her house in two weeks. She called Tony to explain the plan and he was so grateful for her thoughtfulness.

"Lou, she is going to love it! Thank you," said Tony.

"I'm so happy to do it. She deserves to be pampered," Lou said. "Besides, it's not just me doing it. Just bring her to my house a week from Saturday. She might want to dress up, so suggest that you are taking her out for lunch."

Lou even called her mother in Florida to invite her to the shower. Her mother was so excited that her Aunt Ann was coming with her. "Nothing better than another baby in the family!" Lou's mother said. She knew there was a hint or a jibe in there somewhere aimed at her, but one thing at a time.

Then next day Tony called Lou. "Suni had a doctor appointment today, she found out the gender," Tony said. "It's going to be a girl! Lou, we are having another girl," he said.

Lou could tell he was so happy. Hannah would have a baby sister. "Congratulations, Tony! And thanks for the information. I'll let Lisa know we have a color scheme to work with, pink!"

Lou had a smile long after she hung up the phone. She went outside and sat on a log facing the lake. The sun was getting ready to set. Soon the days would be longer, but tonight, the sun was showing its reds and oranges. She would never get tired of this view. Now that Jude's large paintings that she purchased from his New York show were hanging in her house, she could look at that view from every room. Her portrait, number two fifty, was hanging in their bedroom. Lou was no longer shy or embarrassed to hang it. She loved that the artist and his muse could look at it everyday and enjoy it.

"Hello Lou,"

"Hi Jude," she said. "I'm sitting outside watching the sunset and I was thinking of you."

"I was thinking of you, too. How's the baby shower planning coming along?"

"Oh, Jude, it's a girl. Everything will be pink. You will get home just in time. I asked Brad to pick you up and bring you home," Lou said.

"Sounds good. I can't wait to see you."

"How's Chicago? How is the show going?"

"It's beyond our expectations. The new collection is nearly sold out. I guess they like the new J. Henry Weber."

"Well, I know I do."

Lou couldn't wait for him to get home. It seemed like forever since they agreed to spend their lives together, they didn't want to spend time apart. She had been mad at herself for losing ten years, but she was a different Lou then. She needed to forgive herself and look forward. They had their whole future ahead of them. They had found each other, again.

Chapter 34

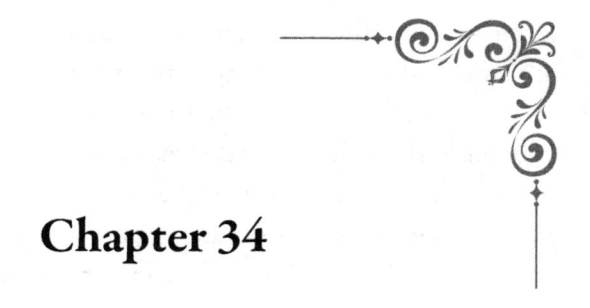

Pink balloons were everywhere. They were flying from the mailbox, on the railing, inside the house and on the beach. May was even a little bit warmer, so Lou wasn't sure if people would want to sit outside or not. There were huge signs on the front yard announcing 'baby shower' and the cake was a tower of pink frosting. Chairs were arranged, gifts were set on the table and Lisa and Rose were coming in the door with more bags.

"Where are we doing the games?" Lisa asked.

"Where do you want the food set up?" Rose asked.

With directions given and games set up, the ladies looked around at their finished product. They were pleased with what they had accomplished in such a short time. Danny would be bringing Emily and Brad will be bringing Brian after he picked Jude up from the airport. Her mother and aunt Ann were in the kitchen getting plates, cups and utensils ready on the island. They stayed in the guest rooms. Lou's mother said she never stayed in the other rooms of her house before so it really felt like a hotel or a bed and breakfast. Lou laughed and said she would slide the bill under her door in the morning. They all laughed. It was good having her mother there, even if only for a few days.

Luckily, everyone arrived before Tony and the guest of honor. Lou had included Hannah in on the secret and Tony kept reminding her not to tell her mother. As far as he knew, she did not tell her secret to Suni. They all waited and watched as they pulled into the driveway and made their way to the door.

"Surprise!" Everyone yelled as Suni came through the front door. Obviously the balloons and signs gave it away, but it was still fun to yell. Suni was emotional as she looked around the house and saw all the planning and effort her friends went through for her. Lisa showed her where to sit and the games began. It was fun as everyone played along with the chocolate in the diaper game or the alphabet game. The guys were invited to play, too.

After the games, everyone went into the kitchen for food and drinks. Everyone had a great time. Laura enjoyed introducing Ann to all of their family and friends. Together they purchased the stroller for Suni, it was the biggest item on her wish list. Suni was so thankful for all of her gifts. She was emotional and gave everyone a hug. She said she wasn't as scared about having another baby now that she felt more prepared. Lou was glad to hear that.

Tony walked over to Lou as guests were starting to leave. "Thank you for this. You made Suni very happy which makes me happy." Tony gave her a hug and a kiss on her cheek.

"You're welcome, big brother. You are family. I can't wait to be Aunt Lou again."

The house was back to normal. Everyone helped cleaning up and Lou was exhausted. Laura and Ann sat in the living room and watched the news. Casper curled up with them. Lou and Jude went to sit outside on the beach. It was the first time they have been alone together in over two weeks. They held hands and Lou laid her head on Jude's shoulder. They didn't need to say anything. They sat and watched the sunset until it became too chilly to stay outside.

The next day at work, Lou met a new patient. Kevin Wilcox was a single dad. He and his son, Billy, just moved back into town and were staying with his dad, Frank, until he found a place of his own. He picked up a construction job and was out of the house most of the time. She could see that Kevin was a nice looking man and cared about his son. When Lou walked into the exam room, Kevin was wearing old jeans and a t-shirt and covered in dirt.

"Hello, doctor, I'm sorry for my appearance, but I just got off from work. I'm doing construction down on 12th Street," Kevin started. "Well, when I got home, Billy was complaining of pain on his right side and I thought I'd bring him in."

"Well, I'm glad you did, Mr. Wilcox. Hi Billy, how are you today?" Lou asked.

"I'm okay," Billy answered.

"How old are you?"

"Seven."

Lou did all the preliminary tests of looking in his eyes, ears and mouth. She made him lay down and she pressed on certain areas of his belly and sides. Billy winced when she touched his right side. Lou lifted his shirt and saw a large bruise on Billy's right side.

Lou looked at Kevin, "How did this bruise happen?"

"I, I don't know. Like I said, I just got home from work and he said he had pain, so we jumped in my truck and came before you closed."

"So you never saw this bruise before?" She asked Kevin.

"No."

"Billy, do you remember how you got hurt?" Lou asked.

Billy looked from his dad to the Lou, "I think I just fell."

Lou went to her laptop that she carried with her that kept all her records and typed into Billy's record.

"I can order an X-ray for Billy at the hospital to be sure there are no internal injuries." Lou said.

"I don't think that'll be necessary. As long as there aren't any broken bones, he should be fine," Kevin said, standing up.

"I would feel better having an X-ray taken, Mr. Wilcox."

Kevin was already helping Billy off the table. "No, we will be fine. Thank you for your time." Kevin took Billy's hand and walked out of the room and into the lobby.

Lou typed more into Billy's report about refusing an X-ray and went on to her next patient. Later that night, Billy would be in her thoughts. She even mentioned to Jude the fact that a child came in with mysterious bruising, careful not to give away any private information. Jude agreed it was unusual, but kids get hurt all the time, especially boys climbing trees and stupid stuff like that. He was sure he went to the doctor several times with bumps and bruises when he was a kid.

After that incident, Lou decided to not bring work home with her anymore. She would not think about anything after hours if possible. She was thankful for the distraction when her wedding invitations arrived. She did not have a lot of people to invite, but she did want to send an invitation to her friend Valerie in New York. She added a plus one to Valerie's invitation, thinking of that gentleman she took to Jude's art show. Lou thought they were pretty serious, but whoever she brought, she knew they would be attractive.

Lou knew that not everyone was going to be able to attend, but that was okay. She even asked Brad for their grandmother's address in Ohio. She didn't know if their mother was still staying with her but it wouldn't hurt to send them all an invitation. Would it? It was a long shot, but she sent it out anyway. Lou was happy that wedding plans were coming along. She had tried on dresses a few times and had narrowed it down to two. She would try one more shop before making a decision. She was going Saturday with Suni to try on dresses at the last shop.

"If I don't find anything here that I like, I'm going back to Diane's Dresses and getting the one I liked there," Lou said as she picked the ones out she wanted to try on.

"I have a good feeling about this place," Suni replied.

Lou was starting to get discouraged until she tried on her fourth dress. She held it up and looked at the small straps, the slight gathering around the waist and the beading detail on the bodice. As she slipped it on and zipped it up, she felt different. She turned to look in the mirror and immediately started tearing up. What what wrong with her? It was only a dress. But this dress felt different.

Lou gathered the bottom of the dress and walked out into the front room where Suni was sitting on a red couch. As soon as Suni saw her she brought her hands to her mouth.

"Oh Lou!"

Lou stood on the low pedestal and let the dress fall. She looked at herself in the mirror and turned to see the back. She turned in both directions and started crying. Was this the one? Lou asked herself that question over and over in her head. It was not tight on her body, but not like a princess dress, either. It was fitted on top with small beads round the bodice. It gathered at the waist and with a slight fullness, went all the way to the floor. It was perfect.

The sales woman came over to Lou. "What do you think of this one?" She asked.

"I love it," Lou said.

The sales woman brought over a veil and put it on Lou's head. The complete bride, it was too much for her. "How much is it?" Lou asked.

The woman came over and looked at the price tag. "Well, since this is last year's Lake Series, it is on sale."

Lou looked at Suni who was still emotional. Partly it was just pregnancy hormones, but also because, like Lou, she knew this was the one. "I'll take it!"

The rest of Lou's wedding planning was coming together just as smoothly. She was glad because her office was getting busier. They seemed to have a full schedule each day, which was great. Her accountant was also pleased and suggested that within a year, she may be able to hire a partner. Lou was truly thankful for the community's welcoming embrace.

Jude and Lou's wedding was now less than two weeks away. Time was going fast because they were all staying busy. Valerie replied that she was coming and bringing a date. Her parents and Aunt Ann would be here a week before the wedding. They booked their honeymoon for Paris. Jude had been there for an art show, but didn't really get a chance to sightsee too much, so he would be seeing it all for the first time with her.

Since Lou was the only doctor at Little Angels Pediatrics, they would have to close down when they went on their honeymoon. The staff made their own vacation plans, so everyone was looking forward to their time off. Lou was humming to herself until she saw the name of her next patient.

"Hello, again, Billy. What brings you in today?" She asked Billy while looking at Kevin.

"My back and leg," Billy answered.

Lou looked over at Kevin again, who just sat silent on the chair. She told Billy to lay down and she lifted up his shirt. There were more bruises on his back and the back of his legs.

This time Lou directed the questioning to Billy's father, "Perhaps you can explain how these bruises got on Billy?"

"Honestly, doc, I don't know, I just came home from work and he said it hurt," Kevin replied. Lou typed into her laptop.

"Mr. Wilcox, unless you can provide me with a better explanation as to the origin of these bruises on your son, I will be forced to report this to the authorities," she said.

Kevin stood up, "I didn't do this!" Kevin was getting angry and Lou saw that this was a dangerous situation. Lou made her way to the door and called for one of the nurses to come. "Mr. Wilcox, I have recorded two instances of unexplained bruising on your son. I am mandated to report any suspected child abuse. If it isn't, then that will all be explained to the authorities, but as a doctor, I must report it."

Kevin's eyes darted from Lou to the nurse. "I would never hurt my son. I didn't do this, I've been at work all day. How dare you accuse me of child abuse. You'll be hearing from me!" Kevin took his son and left the building. She nodded that the nurse could go and Lou called the police. If there was anything to substantiate her claim, the police would find it. If not, it was better to report it and be wrong then not report it and be right.

Chapter 35

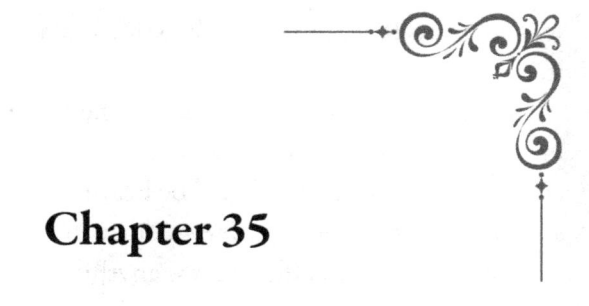

Lou felt uneasy after the second altercation with Mr. Wilcox. She wanted to follow up with the police and find out what happened, but not tonight. Her parents came in later that night for the wedding next week. Lou had the guest rooms ready for her parents and for her Aunt Ann. Jude was such a big help while she was at work. He went grocery shopping and did the laundry. He even got wood for a bonfire later.

Lou's parents settled in quickly and she showed her mother her wedding dress. Laura loved it. She would finally see her daughter walk down the aisle. It was something she almost gave up on until last Christmas. Laura was happy to finally be officially welcoming Jude into their family. She secretly dreamed that Lou and Jude would find their way back to each other.

When Valerie arrived in Erie, she called Lou. They had booked a hotel nearby and she wanted to get together the next day. Lou sent her the address and said to come by the house around five tomorrow. They would have dinner with her family. Val sounded hesitant, but accepted the invite. She thought it would be nice to see Val again. She liked that a piece of her life from New York would be here to witness her new life. She never invited Ben, of course, but she was sure he knew about it. Maybe he would call and congratulate her.

Lou arrived home just minutes before Valerie arrived. Lou had just enough time to change clothes before running back downstairs. She almost collapsed right in her kitchen when she saw Valerie and

Ben standing in her house. Jude caught Lou on the elbow before she fell. Everyone was in shock and the room was silent until Val came over to give her a hug.

"Congratulations, Louise. We're so happy for you," Val said.

"What are you doing here!" Lou asked Ben.

"Um, we are together now," answered Val.

Lou just stared at Ben and Ben stared at Jude. It was a standoff that made the tension in the room so palpable, Lou's parents excused themselves to the living room. The four of them just stood there watching each other. Ben spoke first.

"It's good to see you, again." Ben looked from Lou to Jude, so she wasn't entirely sure who he meant.

"Good to see you, too," Jude replied. "Glad you were able to make it to our wedding." Jude put his arm around Lou's waist and kissed her. "I'll go check on the steaks."

Lou watched Jude exit the room. She turned back to Val, "You could have said something."

"I told her not to say anything," Ben said. "I was afraid you wouldn't let her come if you knew we were together."

Lou did not want to admit she might have considered it, but she was glad to have her friend here. If that meant putting up with Ben for a few days, then so be it. Lou offered drinks and led them to the dining room. Jude reappeared with the steaks and Laura brought the other dishes in from the kitchen. They all sat around the table and tried to keep the conversation light. Only Lou's Aunt Ann wasn't aware of the animosity between the two men and the history between her and Ben. Surprisingly, dinner went well, thanks to her parents for talking about Florida and their new house.

Lou felt Ben's eyes on her and asked Jude not to leave her alone with him. He did the best he could until she went into the kitchen for more wine and saw Ben refilling his glass, too.

"It really is good to see you, Louise."

"Ben, I'm sorry how things turned out between us. I put you through a lot and I'm sorry," Lou said.

"I'm sorry, too. I see how you and Jude are and I should have seen it earlier. I wish you only the best," said Ben.

"Thank you."

"I hear you have your own private practice. That's great, I'd love to see it."

"Well, maybe tomorrow. I'm leaving work early in order to pick up some things for the wedding, but I can meet you back here at the house around six. Then we can all go over and see it," Lou said,

"That sounds great."

The rest of the evening went better than Lou could imagine. Ben and Jude even spoke to each other civilly for a few moments. We took our drinks out to the beach and Val loved it. The sunset was coming later and later as we were now in the middle of June.

"I understand the paintings now," Val said.

They all enjoyed the evening on the beach. Maybe Lou and Jude would do the bonfire tomorrow when they came over again. Ben and Val said good night and went back to their hotel. Her parents and aunt went upstairs to bed. It was getting late.

"Don't forget, I'm leaving work early to pick up that blue fabric for the chairs, tables and walkway. I'm leaving around three and will be home around six. Ben and Val are meeting us here to come back and see the office together. Maybe we can go out to eat afterwards."

Jude nodded his head. "Anything for you, Lou."

The next day, Lou went to work excited for the coming days. She was getting married on Saturday, three days from now. She greeted her nurses and staff with her usually cheer, but today was even more cheerful. She had a schedule full of patients and stayed busy. Lou kept watching the clock and was glad when it finally said two thirty. Almost time to close. She was in an exam room when she heard a commotion in the front lobby. She put her stethoscope away and told the mother and daughter to wait here a moment.

Lou walked to the front and was shocked and terrified to see Kevin Wilcox holding a gun aimed at her nurse. She immediately put her hands up and yelled down the hall to another nurse to get everyone out the back door. Lou walked closer to Kevin so that he was distracted from the nurses getting everyone out the back safely.

"You!" Kevin said, now aiming the gun at Lou. "You called the police."

"Yes, Mr. Wilcox, I had to, remember?"

"I didn't do anything wrong! I would never hit my boy."

"Mr. Wilcox, that's what the police will look into. They will find out what really happened. Just relax and be patient."

"But you think it was me! It wasn't me!"

"Mr. Wilcox, this is not helping. Why don't you put the gun away and we will talk about it?" Lou said.

"You don't believe me! I know you don't! You wouldn't have called the police on me and make me go down to the station. It was not me!"

"Mr. Wilcox, if it wasn't you, then who? Did Billy just fall?"

Kevin sat in the waiting room chairs, gun pointed at Lou. He didn't seem to mind that everyone else in the building had gotten out the back door. The nurse had also called the police and Lou wondered how they would handle this situation. Hopefully they wouldn't come to the front, maybe they would sneak in the back door. She had a view of the front parking lot and did not see any police. She could also see that the clock said four.

No one would be missing her yet, except the fabric store. She was supposed to pick her fabric up an hour ago. Kevin just kept sitting on the chair saying the same thing over and over, it wasn't him. Lou thought she saw movement outside and to the right. There was a cluster of trees and the police might be hiding there, wanting a good shot of the gunman. She needed to get Kevin to stand up and move. Better yet, go outside.

At home, Ben and Val arrived early. They said they drove around the city and had extra time. Maybe they could just meet Lou at her office? Jude wasn't sure the time frame that Lou had planned for everything, but he did remember she was picking up fabric at three. It was now four, so he looked up the number and called to see if she had been there, yet. The lady that answered the phone said no, she hadn't been there.

Jude thought maybe he misunderstood and decided to call Lou. Voicemail. Then he tried the main line at the office. No answer. Ben suggested that they go get the fabric for her and on the way they could see if she was still working. Jude offered to drive, so Ben and Val got into his truck. He did not want to admit that he was worried about her.

"Mr. Wilcox, I don't think it was you who made those bruises. Let me call the police back and tell them." Lou offered. She just wanted to calm him down.

"Do you think I'm crazy and a child abuser? Why would I let you call the police again?"

"Who else is with Billy, Mr. Wilcox. Does he go to school everyday?" Lou asked.

"Of course he goes to school. I'm not a monster."

"I don't think you are, Mr. Wilcox. Who watches Billy until you come home?"

"My father, Billy's granddad."

Lou paused her questioning. She thought there was more movement out front but didn't want to draw attention to it in case the police had a plan to come in. She turned back to Kevin and thought for a moment.

"Does Billy's granddad ever get mad at Billy?"

This time, it was Kevin who paused. "Sure, he's a seven year old boy who gets into everything around the house." Kevin kept the gun pointed at Lou and she kept her hands up in the air.

Jude was coming up on Lou's office soon. "Her office is there, on the left." Just as Jude pointed and slowed down, he noticed her car still parked on the side of the building and police cars around the back. Jude made a sharp left and pulled into the parking lot beside Lou's car. He jumped out and ran to the first police officer he found.

"What's going on?" Jude asked.

Ben and Val were coming up behind Jude. They all were looking at the police presence and Lou's single car parked in the lot.

"We got a call that there is a gunman inside with a hostage."

Jude's knees started to buckle and asked for more details.

"We think the hostage is a doctor and the gunman is a patient's father. We have officers coming around front waiting for a shot and officers going in the back door."

"I believe that's my fiancé inside, the hostage," Jude said. Ben looked down. Val patted Jude's arm. "What can I do?"

"Just leave it to the police. They think they can take him out."

Lou was watching Kevin. "Mr. Wilcox, do you think your father would ever get mad enough to hurt Billy?" Lou knew she was taking a chance. Asking a man with a gun if his father is abusing his son.

Kevin stood up and looked at Lou. "I, I don't know."

Just as Kevin stood up, a bullet came through the front window and shattered glass all over Kevin and Lou. Neither person was shot, but it made them both duck and take cover. Police entered the building from the front and back doors and quickly disarmed and handcuffed the gunman. As they were taking Kevin to the the police car, he kept yelling 'I didn't do it'.

Lou, shaken from the quickness of the police, finally stood up and walked over to one of the officers.

"Officer, I think there's been a big misunderstanding. A couple of days ago I reported child abuse against a minor, Billy Wilcox. I mentioned the father as the abuser. Now I believe it is his grandfather who is the abuser."

"Okay, Dr. Jensen, we will go talk with the grandfather. We will also need your statement about what happened here today."

Just then, Jude came running through the glass and hugged Lou. He hugged her so hard it lifted her feet off of the floor. "Thank God you are okay!" Jude kissed her and hugged her again.

"What are you doing here?" Lou saw Ben and Val come in behind Jude.

"I was worried and you never picked up the fabric. Thank goodness Ben suggested we come see if you're still working," Jude turned to Ben.

Ben came and hugged Lou. It was not passion or to make Jude jealous. Ben was glad she was safe. It was the hug of a friend.

"Thank you," Lou said to Ben and Jude. "I am lucky to have friends like you in my life."

Ben looked around the pediatric office. "Now about that tour?"

They all looked around and laughed. The adrenaline that carried Lou through that ordeal was wearing off and she was starting to understand the seriousness of the situation. She started to cry.

Chapter 36

Jude wanted to get Lou away from the office. He drove to the fabric store and picked up her order, then took everyone home. Jude gave Ben the number to order pizza and then took Lou upstairs. He helped her get in the bathtub and then went to talk to her parents. He explained what happened and suggested she stay home until the wedding. Tom said he would call her insurance company and have someone get there as soon as possible.

Jude went back to Lou. She was soaking in the bubble bath with her eyes closed. "How are you feeling?" Jude asked.

Lou opened her eyes and smiled. "Better now."

"If you want to postpone the wedding we can."

"No! We are getting married Saturday," Lou said. "I want to be your wife. A mad gunman cannot stop that."

"I know. I just wondered if you wanted more time to process what just happened to you. This kind of trauma might take a while to get over." Jude said.

"Jude, I'm okay," Lou said. "I know he had a gun and it was scary, but I kept Kevin talking and we both actually made a breakthrough. It was a mistake, Jude. Kevin just went to work and came home at night. Billy was with his grandfather all afternoon. It was the grandfather that was abusing him. Even Kevin didn't make the connection."

"Wow, that's great," Jude said.

"I know. We figured it out. We might not have if he never came in today."

"No, I mean, it is incredible how calm you are under pressure. I love you so much and can't wait for you to be my wife." Lou stood up and he hugged her. They kissed and Jude handed her the towel. "Ben is ordering pizza. If you want to stay up here, I understand."

"No, I have a pizza party to go to," Lou said.

"WHERE'S THE HAIRSPRAY?"

"I can't find my tie."

"The photographer is here."

"Is it raining?"

The Jensen house on the lake was in chaos. The women were still doing hair and make up and the men were figuring out how to tie a bow tie. The sun was shining. It was Saturday. The day Jude and Lou have been waiting for. Tony, having escaped the madness going on inside the house, was walking on the beach. It was the perfect day for a wedding.

Jude and Tony had worked on the small pergola. The four pieces of wood at the corners were eight feet tall. The top had four cross beams with space in between. The women had it draped in blue fabric, tulle and flowers. It was positioned so that you looked through it towards the lake. Tony admired the finished product. The blue fabric was blowing in the breeze. The rows of chairs facing the water were also decorated with blue fabric. There were flowers at the front and at the end of each row of chairs.

Ben and Val arrived early. They brought gifts and wine. The caterer came in after them and Ben showed the caterer where to set up. Beautifully dressed people were starting to trickle down from up stairs. First was Laura, Tom and then Ann. They wanted to give the others more room up there. Where pink balloons were a month ago, now blue balloons were flying. They were outside, inside and on the beach. The bonfire wood was stacked and ready to be lit.

Brad, Lisa and Brian were next to arrive. They also brought gifts. They went straight out to the beach and walked around. This was a big day for his little brother. He thought of Jackson on days like this. Momentous days that Jack will never have but his presence is still felt. Brad saw Rose, Danny and Emily arrive. They came to the beach to let Emily run around. Now nearly two, she had much more energy. When Avery arrived, her and her date went right to Rose and Danny.

Tony looked around and thought that most everyone had already arrived. He saw Jude coming downstairs and figured it was only Suni, Hannah and Lou left upstairs. Tony shook Jude's hand and slapped him on the back.

"We never did a bachelor party," Tony said to Jude.

"I feel like I had eleven years of bachelor parties. I'm ready for that to end."

There was a knock on the door, the deejay. Tony quickly showed him where to set up out back. Another knock made Jude question who else it could be. Everyone else was already here. Jude went to open the door. He was ready to tell these women that they must have the wrong house before he hesitated. There were two older women on his front porch all dressed up, dressed as if they were going to a wedding. One was older than the other. Jude studied the younger woman's face and nearly felt his knees buckle. He held on to the door frame for support.

"Jude," the woman said.

"Mom?" Jude asked.

"Yes, I received an invitation to your wedding. I almost didn't come," Betty said and turned around to go back down the stairs. "Maybe I shouldn't have come. I will go back now."

Jude ran over to the woman, "No, mom, stay for my wedding. You, too, grandmother." Jude spoke to the older woman and held out his hand to her. She took it and came inside with Jude. No one was really paying attention to Jude coming in with two elderly women except Brad. Brad stopped in his tracks. He had been coming into the kitchen for a glass of water.

"Mom?" Brad asked.

Betty nodded her head. "Bradley, you've gotten so big." Brad and Jude took turns hugging the women. They led them out to the other guests and introduced them around. No one asked any questions or made any comments about the two women who left the Weber boys alone over ten years ago. This was not the day for that. It was his wedding day. Jude walked the two women, his mother and grandmother, to the front row of chairs. He was crying and didn't even know it. They were happy tears, he was sure of it.

Jude didn't realize everyone else had taken their seats. Even Suni and Hannah were here which meant Lou was ready. Jude stood with Brad, his best man, at the top of the aisle with the minister. The deejay started the music and Jude tried to focus on the other end of the aisle. His eyes kept filling with tears and Brad handed him a napkin. Jude looked at him and he shrugged, it was the only thing he had on him. Jude smiled at the memory.

Hannah was slowly walking down the aisle, throwing flower petals on the blue fabric that ran from one end of the aisle to the other. Suni was next, her maid of honor. Suni smiled and winked at Jude when she came to stand at the front. Now the music changed. The wedding march. Jude looked out at the water and took a deep breath. When he turned to look to the back of the aisle he saw Tom and Lou. Lou had her arm through Tom's. She was beautiful. Lou's veil was blowing slightly in the wind. He could see her face, but barely. Her dress was simple and white. There were some beads at the top, but it was perfectly Lou. She held a bouquet of blue and white flowers tied with a blue ribbon. Her hair was pulled up and she was the most beautiful woman he had ever seen. Jude's teenage dreams were never as wonderful as this moment.

Lou was nervous as she stood next to her father. "Don't let me fall," Lou said.

"Never."

Lou heard the wedding march and felt faint. Her father took her hand and placed it around his arm. They started up the aisle. Tom was watching the guests, the blue runner they were walking on and every once in awhile peeked over at Lou. She only stared straight ahead. She was not looking at the water, the people or the minister, only Jude. Lou could only see Jude in front of her. He was handsome in his tuxedo and blue tie. She knew in that moment that she never needed to be afraid of anything else in her life. She was walking towards her future. To Jude.

Tom lifted Lou's veil and kissed his daughter. He shook Jude's hand and went to sit down. Lou was now his. Jude was now hers. They said their vows, exchanged rings and kissed in front of all their friends and family. This was a sign that they were one and nothing or no one else mattered. Ben was now merely a face in the crowd. So was Avery. Lou did notice a couple women that she didn't know in the front row.

As they walked back down the aisle as husband and wife, they kissed again. Everyone stood up and came to offer congratulations. Since the wedding and reception were basically one location, they started the party right away.

When Jude and Lou had a private moment, he said, "I want you to meet someone." Jude led her to the two older women. "Lou, this is my mother and my grandmother."

Lou tried not to let the shock show on her face. Of course she remembered his mom from when they were kids, but she was here. "You got my invitation. I'm so happy you came," Lou said.

The four of them sat on the porch. "How are you?" Jude asked his mother.

"I'm doing good. It's your grandmother who is in failing health. She's 91 and doesn't have much time left. I was going to leave her home, but this might be the last time she saw the boys." Betty said.

Jude watched his mother as she started to weep. He took her hand.

"I'm so sorry, Jude. I left because I didn't know what else to do. I've wanted to call or come back so many times over the years but I was afraid."

Jude looked at Lou as if to ask how she made this happen. She just smiled. "Where are you staying now?" Lou asked Betty.

"Well, the house is actually owned by her neighbor," Betty said, pointing to her mother. "He wants to sell it and I think he's just waiting for her to die and then kick me out."

Brad had come and sat down with them when he heard that. "Maybe I can call them and explain the situation," Brad offered.

"No, I have a better idea," Jude looked at his mother. "How would you like to move back here, to Erie. I have a house and no one is in it right now."

Betty looked from Brad to Jude and then stood up in front of Lou. Betty put her hands on Lou's cheeks, "You are a Godsend. Without your invitation to your wedding with Jude, I would never have come and reconnected with them. Thank you. You always were good for him."

Jude hugged Lou. "I love you Louise Weber."

"I love you, too."

Jude looked at his mother and said, "I will call and have your things sent to your new house. I'll take you there tonight to get settled. If you need anything, you can call Brad. I'm leaving for my honeymoon in the morning."

COMING HOME

Lou and Jude enjoyed the rest of the evening with friends and family surrounding them. Tony lit the bonfire and Brad opened champagne. They sat on a log facing the lake. The sun was setting and it was their favorite time of the day. Jude still in his tuxedo, minus a tie, some buttons and the jacket, was holding Lou's hand. She was still wearing her wedding dress, minus the veil, flowers and her shoes.

They were at the lake house. They were finally together and home.

Acknowledgements

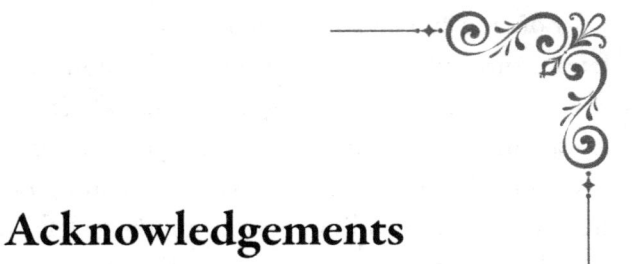

To my husband, Yoshi, for giving me the time and space to write. To my daughter, Alisa, for reading my first draft and loving it.

To my son, Leo, for his constant encouragement.

To my friends and my sister for always being willing to read my first drafts and saying that they were perfect, even when I knew they weren't. Your encouragement has brought me to where I am now.

To Maggie Stiefvater for creating a writing seminar that provided life changing inspiration.

To my parents, who are no longer with us, for their constant love and support.

About the Author

Amy Iketani lives in Stockbridge, Georgia, with her husband and pet cat. Originally from Erie, Pennsylvania, Amy met her husband while working for Club Med and has lived in Florida, Japan and Hawaii. Amy enjoys crocheting, reading, spending time with her two grown children, Alisa and Leo, and traveling with her husband, Yoshi, of thirty two years.

Follow Amy on Instagram @amyiketaniwrites

Printed in the USA
CPSIA information can be obtained
at www.ICGtesting.com
LVHW071024250923
759235LV00006B/53

9 798223 230717